mr perfect

"Yeah but. . ." I hadn't even considered what she was suggesting. As far as I'd been concerned, my preoccupation with Max could only possibly be one-sided. It had never occurred to me that the attraction might be mutual, and I certainly hadn't been thinking how I might develop it further. Not until that moment; until Ruby had sown the seed. "Do you think I should?"

"Do I think you could, do I think you should," Ruby said, raising her eyes heavenwards. "Never mind what I think. What do *you* think?"

"I think," I said, slowly, "that I can't get him out of my mind. That nobody's ever affected me like this before. That's what I think."

"Then there's your answer." Ruby chuckled. "Want to know what I think? He's not going to know what's hit him!"

Other titles by Catherine Robinson:

Tin Grin
Celia

www.catherinerobinsonbooks.co.uk

Scholastic Children's Books,
Commonwealth House, 1-19 New Oxford Street,
London, WC1A 1NU, UK
A division of Scholastic Ltd
London ~ New York ~ Toronto ~ Sydney ~ Auckland
Mexico City ~ New Delhi ~ Hong Kong

First published in the UK by Scholastic Ltd, 2003

ISBN 0 439 98296 0

Printed and bound in Great Britain by Cox & Wyman Ltd, Reading, Berkshire

1 2 3 4 5 6 7 8 9 10

chapter one

OK, I admit it. Perhaps I was wrong all along.
Maybe I should have listened, and ended it
before it all properly began. But that's with the
benefit of hindsight. Wonderful thing,
hindsight, isn't it?

At the time, though, I thought it was all too
cool for words. Well, who wouldn't? I was so
caught up with the glamour of the situation, the
deliciously illicit appeal of forbidden fruit, that
I couldn't see the reality – that it was like being
on an out-of-control fairground ride, careering
wildly along and threatening the stability of my
entire family.

I put it all down to moving house. Well,
maybe not all of it – there were other elements
involved – but to my mind the entire thing, the
whole crazy, exciting, exhilarating, mad
experience, began on that cold grey morning in
February when we packed up our former lives
and moved out of the little three-bedroomed
semi that had been home for as long as I could
remember. I say little semi, but I suppose it
wasn't *that* small, not compared to where Dad

grew up, which was Oop North and only one step removed from the old cardboard-box-in-t'middle-of-t'road joke, if you're to believe his fond reminiscences. But little it undoubtedly was in comparison with the solid red-brick Victorian former rectory we were moving into.

The Old Rectory, it was called. Imaginative or what. My brother Hugh, who reckons he's pretty funny (even if nobody else does), said we should rename it Dunsaving, given the size of the new mortgage; but the parents just smiled indulgently and said things about it being a bargain because of needing some work doing on it, and that you can't take it with you when you go so why not. This uncharacteristic parental laid-backness in the face of major financial expenditure was fairly surprising in itself, but then again the two of them had been in a practically non-stop good mood since Dad had come home just before Christmas with the news that he had been promoted at work. Hence more money, you see, and hence, in its turn, The Move.

I suppose purists might say that, in that case, it was Dad's promotion that kicked it all off, but I'm sticking to my original hypothesis. If we hadn't moved to The Old Rectory, Hugh wouldn't have invited Danny Oldfield round to check out his groovy new top-floor pad, and if

Danny hadn't come round there almost certainly wouldn't have been any of the resulting developments between him and me, nor all the attendant fall-out and knock-on effects.

But perhaps more importantly, if we hadn't moved, Mum and Dad wouldn't have had their house-warming party, which is really where it all kicked off. Because it was at the house-warming party that Max and I met again for the first time since I was a kid of about Hattie's age, eleven or twelve years old, and far too young to take any notice of him.

Hattie moaned like hell about moving. Which was typical. Hattie complains about everything – school, her so-called friends, Hugh and me. The weather. Her favourite phrase is "It's not fair", and she habitually acts as if the entire world should organize itself purely for her convenience. In other words, she's your quintessential little sister. The parents usually treat her by veering wildly between brisk chivvying along (Mum) and indulgent spoiling (Dad), but on this occasion they both tried patiently to talk her round, which did my head in, frankly. Anybody would have thought they were proposing sending her to a Romanian orphanage, not moving to a whacking great semi-palace with massive rooms and a garden the size of Regent's Park. (OK, I exaggerate, but you doubtless get my point.)

"But what about all my friends?" she whined, for the zillionth time. "When am I going to get to see them?"

"Oh, dur, at school?" I suggested, under my breath, but Hattie ignored me. It suited her much better to pretend her whole life was in a state of unbearable flux; acknowledging that she'd still be going to the same school as before would have spoiled the illusion.

"It's miles away from where they all live."

"Not that far, love," said Dad, reassuringly. "Only five miles or so."

"Oh, great! *Only* five miles!" Hattie clearly was not at all reassured. "I'm never going to see them again, face it!"

Dad tried again. "They can come and stay over. We'll have the space now. You can start having those pyjama parties you're so keen on."

"Yeah, right. Like they're going to get in their cars and *drive* over! And anyway, they're called overnighters. Pyjama parties are for kids."

"But Harriet," I put in, in my best tones of sweet reason, "you are a kid, remember?"

She turned on me then, her jaw square, like a mutinous toddler. "And you can butt out, too!"

Cue Mum. "Come on now, you two. Flora,

4

stop winding your sister up." *But it's so easy,* I felt like saying, *and such fun!* I kept my mouth shut, though. I know when to avoid hassle, even if Hattie doesn't.

"I'll drive them over," Dad went on, going over to her and putting an affectionate arm around her shoulders. "And drive them home again, in the morning. I'll even cook breakfast for you all. How's that?"

He was doing his best, fair play to him. He must have been reading one of those How To Help Your Kids Through Times Of Change books. But Hattie wasn't having any of it.

"I hate cooked breakfasts," she hissed furiously, shrugging his arm off. "I've been your daughter for twelve years, and you don't even know that about me! You and Mum are trying to ruin my life, and it's JUST SO UNFAIR!"

And she flounced theatrically from the room, slamming the door behind her for maximum effect. God only knows what she's going to be like when she's a teenager.

Things did improve once we'd actually moved in, though, despite Hugh instantly commandeering the big attic room at the top of the house, which nearly set Hattie off on another tantrum. But Mum just said "He's the oldest", in a voice that broached no argument, and that was that – sorted. After a bit Hattie started seeing the benefits and stopped whingeing about the move, which was a miracle in itself, although needless to say it didn't last long. As for me, I loved it. I loved all the space, and the privacy, the fact that we could go and hang the washing out the back or put the bin out without Mr Nosy next door wanting to know what we'd all been up to over the weekend. I enjoyed being able to go home after school without tripping over Mum's private piano pupils, who she grapples with after teaching music all day in a posh private school just down the road from the one the three of us attend (which is neither private nor posh). There had been no escaping the pupils in the old house – we only had the one big downstairs room – but in The Old Rectory the piano was tucked away in a little room behind the kitchen, what had been called the breakfast room but was now referred to, rather grandly, as the Music Room.

But the thing I loved most of all about the new house was having a bedroom all to myself. Sharing with your twelve-year-old sister is pants enough in itself, but when you take into account just who that sister is you start approaching nightmare territory. The problem with Hattie (correction: one of the problems with Hattie) is that she has no conception of privacy. She'd throw a mental if I ever touched anything of hers, but she seems to consider my things fair game. So it was something of a novelty to be able to leave my make-up and CDs and stuff lying around in my room, safe in the knowledge that when I returned they would still be where I left them. I didn't even have to keep my diary under lock and key any more, although as things turned out it might have been better all round if I had.

A couple of weeks after we moved in, Ruby and Nat came back with me on the school bus to give my room their seal of approval.

"I've got loads more space than in the old one," I told them, as we got off the bus and walked up the lane and past the church that had given The Old Rectory its name. "Dad said we could hire a sander so we can strip the floorboards, and I'm going to feng shui it."

The three of us have known each other for ever, since we started primary school together, so I was quite confident they'd be suitably impressed with what they saw. Even I wasn't prepared, however, for just how impressed. As we turned into the driveway there, skewed rakishly sideways on the untidy gravel, stood an old Mini, its racing green paintwork streaked grubbily with winter mud and salt from the lanes. In the back window a red and white sign proclaimed "Rugby Players Do It With Hookers."

Nat's face lit up. "Hey," she said, her voice bubbling with excitement. "I know that car!"

"Yeah," Ruby agreed. "It's Danny Oldfield's. You never told us he was going to be here too!"

She didn't even wait for my reply. You couldn't see them for dust, my two best mates, as they galloped up the stone steps and through the front door like a couple of lovestruck groupies after an autograph.

Perhaps I ought to say a word here about Danny Oldfield. Or two words. Sex Bomb just about sums it up. Six foot two, eyes of blue kind of thing. What the women's mags call chiselled features. Muscles to die for. Not really my type, if I'm to be completely honest, but I could see he had his attractions. Ruby and Nat obviously thought so – you could practically see the trail of drool they'd left on the tiles in the hallway.

Danny and Hugh were in the kitchen. The sound of tortured piano arpeggios drifted in through the closed door: Mum was obviously home, too. My brother was lounging against the counter with his legs crossed and a mug of coffee in his hand, and Danny had his head in the fridge. All that could be seen of him was his admittedly rather tasty jeans-clad bum.

"And we were really whanging it along the lane," he was saying. Sensing an audience, he withdrew his head and shut the fridge door with his elbow, a chunk of clingfilmed cheddar in one hand and two cold sausages on a saucer in the other. He and Hugh had never been especially matey in the past, but since Hugh had started editing the school magazine at the beginning of Year 13 and Danny began helping him out after the Christmas holidays, they'd been hanging around together more and more. Their new-found friendship had, I secretly suspected, quite a bit to do with the fact that Danny had his own wheels and my bro didn't – but that's probably just me being cynical.

Hugh saluted us with his coffee mug, slopping some of it on to the floor. "Wotcha, girls."

Danny's mouth curved into a slow smile as he regarded each of us in turn. "Well, hello," he said, at last, giving the last syllable at least four "O"s and sounding like one of those old British actors who always played the part of the sleazy ladies' man. He was looking directly at me as he said it, and it's a curious thing but I had the oddest sensation in the pit of my stomach, like a hamster running round on one of those little wheel things. Strange but true.

"'Lo," I said, and smiled back.

"Hi," Nat panted. I swear it – she was actually panting. "What are you doing here?"

Ruby just scowled – she has attitude, does Rube – but I could tell the two of them were well

9

impressed that Mr Love Magnet was standing in my – *my!* – kitchen. I suppose that's what made me say what I did next.

"Oh, he's Hugh's new BF, aren't you Danny? They're always hanging out together these days," I said, airily, to the room in general. In actual fact, it was the first time he'd been to the new house, but Danny didn't let on. He put the cheese and sausages down on the kitchen table and looked intently into my eyes.

"What makes you think I'm here because of Hugh?"

Off went the hamster again. *My God!* I thought. *Sex Bomb is flirting with me!*

"Well, I just thought," I floundered, irritatingly flustered all of a sudden, "you know, as we've been seeing so much of you. . ." I trailed off, and gave what I hoped was a face-saving *femme fatale*-esque shrug.

"Play your cards right, babe," Danny growled, "and you could be seeing a lot more of me." And still holding my eye, he picked up one of the sausages and bit into it in a manner that can only be described as suggestive. I felt my face begin to turn an unflattering shade of pink. Luckily for me, Hugh interceded at that point.

"Oi, you," he said to Danny, mildly. "Stop chatting up my baby sister."

10

"Less of the baby, matey," Ruby objected. "We could show both of you a thing or two."

Danny grinned wolfishly. "I'll bet."

He put out an idle hand – the one not holding the sausage – and gave Nat's bottom a squeeze. Nat squealed like a stuck pig, and at that moment the arpeggios stopped abruptly and the door to the Music Room swung open.

"Hey, guys," said Mum (for it was she). "D'you think you could keep it down to a dull roar? B flat major's getting awfully tangled up in there."

Danny instantly stood to attention and went into "Yes Ma'am" mode. "Yes, Mrs Wilcox. Sorry, Mrs Wilcox."

"Three bags full, Mrs Wilcox," I muttered, pulling a face. "B flat's about right. How can you stand it?"

Mum frowned at me and lowered her voice, drawing the door closed behind her. "Don't be unkind, darling. Philip does his best."

She went back in, and Philip's hapless arpeggios were replaced with some Bach being murdered *fortissimo*. I took advantage of the interruption to prise Ruby and Nat out of the kitchen, and the three of us clattered up the as-yet uncarpeted stairs, Nat squeaking all the while about Danny.

"He is so fit! God, Flora, you are so lucky!"

"Why's that?"

"Well, he's majorly pally with your brother, isn't he? So how often does he come round?"

"Forget it," Ruby declared.

"Forget what?"

"It's Flora he fancies, not you."

Nat and I both protested vigorously.

"No he doesn't!"

"It was my bum he pinched, not Flora's," Nat pointed out.

"So? One bum pinch does not a romance make," said Ruby. "I saw the way he was looking at her, even if you didn't."

"Yeah? And what way was that, then?" Nat demanded, a touch peevishly.

"You know. Like, take me baby, I'm all yours."

"Oh, he so was not!" I objected.

But Ruby wouldn't be swayed, and an hour or so later, after they had both gone, I went back downstairs. Hugh was sitting at the kitchen table, watching *Neighbours* and making inroads into a plate of beans on toast.

"Little friends gone home?" he asked, shovelling in another mouthful.

"I was about to ask you the same thing." I looked around the kitchen, elaborately. "Where is he, then? Oh, I know – hiding in the fridge, finishing off all the leftovers."

"Ha ha." He got up, the legs of his chair

scraping along the floor, and stacked his dirty plate in the dishwasher. "We're growing lads. We need our grub."

"Evidently." I opened the fridge door. "And everybody else's as well, by the look of things. There's nothing left in here, it's like a plague of locusts has been visiting."

Hugh just shrugged, and picked up his school bag. "Oh well. Best get on with the homework, I suppose." But at the door he stopped, and turned round again. "Oh, by the way. I almost forgot. You've got an invite. To Danny's eighteenth."

"Oh yeah?" Despite myself, I felt a little thrill of – what? Excitement? Anticipation? Foresight? "When is it?"

"Saturday week. The third. And your two mates, too – he says he needs more girls to make up the numbers."

He gave me a grin that implied we both knew that couldn't possibly be the case, and that Danny's motive for asking us all must therefore be of the ulterior kind.

I had decidedly mixed feelings about the invitation. On the one hand, Danny Oldfield wasn't my favourite person at that precise moment, his presence in the house having rather stolen my new bedroom's thunder. Ruby and Nat's response hadn't been unenthusiastic, exactly, just uninterested – they'd plonked themselves down on the bed, and it was quite obvious that all they really wanted to do was minutely dissect Danny and his various doings.

But on the other hand, I couldn't deny that his attentions had left me feeling oddly revved-up – that, plus Ruby's assertion that he fancied me. Even though I knew it was hardly likely to be the case: why on earth should he fancy me, plain boring me, when he had all the sixth-form glamour girls to choose from? Going to his party might be interesting, though – a chance to see whose instincts were correct, mine or Ruby's.

"Right," I said briskly, slamming two slices of bread into the toaster and reaching for the butter. "Tell Danny I'll mention it to them. We'll see if we've got a window."

chapter two

First score for instincts: Ruby one, Flora nil. At school the next day, Danny hardly left me alone. It was dead weird, but not in an unpleasant way – I just didn't know how to respond. I could have coped with him coming right up and asking me out, but he didn't. I just kept catching him eyeing me up in the sixth-form centre, or in the school cafeteria, with a secretive little smile on his face, as if he knew something I didn't. Described like that it all sounds a bit sinister, but it wasn't. It was actually quite flattering. I kept glancing at my reflection in the mirror above the handbasins in the loo, wondering if he saw something different when he looked at me than the slightly flushed but otherwise decidedly normal image that gazed back at me. Which only goes to prove, I suppose, that old adage about pride coming before a fall.

Needless to say, Ruby and Nat weren't what you might call oblivious to all this. Oh no. Their radars are too well tuned in to any trace of movement on the boy/girl interaction front.

"See," Ruby said decisively at lunchtime. "He's

been looking at you continuously for a good ten minutes. If he doesn't fancy you, I'm a cream puff."

"Doesn't prove a thing."

"Yeah, it does. He's even let his chips go cold, look. If he'd rather eyeball you than eat his lunch, it must be *lurve*."

Even Nat had to agree he was paying me more attention than was either usual or decent. Which was quite surprising, really, considering she fancied the pants off him herself – I would have expected her to swear blind that he was actually watching her and I just happened to be standing next to her, thus deflecting the warm and tender beam of his gaze, kind of thing.

But the fact was, it wasn't her. It was me. There was no doubting it. I was beginning to enjoy myself – I'd never been on the receiving end of this sort of attention from anyone with real phwoar appeal before, and Danny Oldfield is definitely the biz. I mean, we're talking Premier League Love God here. By the end of the day I was even beginning to fancy him back, despite him not really being my type – all the attention was just *sooo* thrilling.

In my defence, though, I have to say that I wasn't entirely taken in by it. I'm not that shallow. At that stage, a small but sensible voice deep inside me did wonder just what he was playing at. But as the days went by, Danny stepped up the charm offensive and my little inner voice became smaller and considerably less sensible, and was then eventually buried without trace beneath – well, what? My ego? Come to think of it, it probably was. But all I can say is, it would have taken a much stronger person than me to resist the onslaught.

It was like being besieged. He started standing next to me in the lunch queue and fondling strands of my hair. He left notes in my locker – nothing heavy, just "Hi babe", kind of thing, but even so. Notes. From Danny Oldfield – it was like getting text messages from Brad Pitt.

About four days into the campaign he gave me a lift home from school in his funky little Mini. Not only that, but he left Hugh behind. Hugh was well hacked off about it when he got home.

"You want to be careful of Danny," he grumbled. Given that he had just had to make his own way back on the deeply uncool school bus, I didn't exactly take his comment seriously. My mistake, as it turned out.

"Oh yeah?" I challenged him. "Why's that, then? Afraid he's going to dump me, like he seems to have dumped you?"

He didn't answer that one, just stood and looked at me for a couple of moments.

17

"You've really fallen for it, haven't you?" He shook his head, patronizingly.

"I haven't fallen for anything," I declared. "Hasn't it occurred to you that he might just like me?"

Hugh shrugged. "Maybe. Maybe not. All I'm saying is, I've seen it all before. It's the way Danny operates – he hits on girls like it's love at first sight, then he drops them from a great height."

"And why would he do that?"

He shrugged again. "Beats me. Sadist, maybe. Perhaps he used to pick the wings off flies when he was a kid. How do I know?"

"I thought you were supposed to be his mate? Doesn't he share these things with you?" I laughed, confident in my belief that, however Danny might have treated girls in the past, I definitely was not just the latest victim. "Perhaps you're just jealous."

"Yeah, right," Hugh scoffed. "Why would I be jealous?"

Because he can have his pick, and you're left with his cast-offs. I thought it, but didn't say it. I didn't want to go down that road, not when Hugh had only split up with his girlfriend Clare a couple of weeks previously – Clare, who had taken up with Hugh after being unceremoniously dumped by Danny. I didn't think it fair to mention it, not just to make a point.

"You know what he's like," I said instead. "He likes having a – what's the word? An *entourage*. You know it, I know it. But we're just friends. It's fun. It doesn't necessarily mean anything."

He wasn't convinced, I could tell. "So where is he, then? If you're 'friends'? Why isn't he still here, pigging out on the contents of our fridge, as usual?"

"He couldn't stay, he had to go home and finish some coursework."

Hugh gave a little laugh, down his nose. "Coursework my arse! Unless Suzy Davies is a little-known part of the A-level Physics syllabus."

"Are you saying he's with Suzy Davies?"

"Spot on. Another new member of his *entourage*. Or harem, as it's also known," he muttered darkly, and ran a hand through his hair. "Look, Flo. I don't want to spoil your fun. I just don't want to see him mess with your head the way he messed with Clare's, that's all."

Hattie burst breathlessly into the kitchen, hair flying and school tie askew.

"Amy said she saw you getting into Danny Oldfield's car at school!" she gasped. "Is it true? Are you going out with him?"

I gave her my best indulgent smile. "Of course

I'm not. He just gave me a lift home, that's all."

"Bet you want to cop off with him, though. He's a babe – Amy said she wouldn't kick him out of bed on a cold night."

"Like Amy would have the chance," I said, with contempt. "Look, he just gave me a lift, OK? I don't know what the big deal is."

Hugh gave me a look as he went out of the kitchen, a look that quite clearly said we both knew what the big deal was. But I didn't take any notice. I knew what the score was with Danny, and I had no intention of letting him just toy with me. Even so, I couldn't help myself becoming increasingly excited at the prospect of his party and wondering if, to quote my sister's elegant phrase, I was indeed going to cop off with him.

Danny wasn't the only one having a party that night. Mum and Dad announced they were having a house-warming do the same evening.

"But why then?" I complained.

"Because we want to have it before the new carpets are delivered," she explained. "Get all the wine-spilling and dog-end dropping over and done with on the floorboards."

"But I won't be able to come," I wailed. "Neither will Hugh. It's Danny Oldfield's eighteenth."

"Sorry, love," Mum said, cheerfully. "But we

didn't realize you two would want to hang out with us old fogies."

"It's our home too," I grumbled, but deep down I knew she was right. It would only have ended up with me and Ruby and Nat sitting in my room with a couple of bottles of Red Square and a packet of Twiglets, trying not to listen to the parents and their elderly friends getting steadily pissed and shaking their funky stuff to groovy sounds like Status Quo and the Bee Gees. I kid you not. Dad actually has all their albums – on vinyl. Sad or what.

The day before the party, Danny stepped things up a notch. He was waiting outside the English room when we came out after the lesson.

"Hi," he said, nonchalantly, and my heart thudded against my ribs. I couldn't help it. I'd gone from indifference to full-on worship in under a fortnight. It was as if he'd bewitched me.

Nat beamed at him, and pushed her long pale hair back behind her ears in that way she has. I wondered how he could resist her – all his previous girlfriends had been blondes, and Nat is drop-dead gorgeous to boot.

He turned his thousand kilowatt smile on her.

"Like the earrings," he remarked, and she practically passed out with bliss. I felt a brief pang of something that felt uncomfortably like jealousy, until he took a step forward and slung a casual arm around my shoulders. *Oh yes!* I thought, my stomach doing a wild fandango. *Yesyesyes!*

"You coming tomorrow night, then?" He didn't need to say where.

"You bet," I assured him. "I've been looking forward to it."

"Me too," he said gruffly, lowering his head until his forehead almost touched mine. Beads of nervous perspiration broke out along my upper lip, and I prayed he wouldn't notice it. I didn't know much about him, but I'd lay money on him not liking his women sweaty.

"I'm coming too," Nat squeaked. I could see her bobbing up and down beyond the bulk of Danny's shoulders, like a kid in class eager to be chosen to answer the question.

"Cool," said Danny, without taking his eyes off me. "See you both then, then. About eightish, yeah?"

And off he strolled in his arrogant loping way, leaving me and Nat practically clutching each other for support.

"You lucky cow," Nat observed, without rancour. "Just wait till I tell Ruby."

Ruby doesn't do English, so she hadn't witnessed this little development. I didn't want to admit to feeling so electrified by Danny's touch, though, not even to Nat. Not even, if truth be told, to myself. I wanted to play it cool, appear unaffected and unruffled.

"What's to tell?" I raised a dignified eyebrow, but Nat wasn't fooled.

"Come on, Flora! He was practically snogging you right there in the corridor! This party's going to be interesting – we'll get to see if he's just been stringing you along, or whether he is actually going to jump you."

"Oh, nice," I said drily. "Very nice. Why don't you and Rube open a book on it – you know, start taking bets?"

"We already have," Nat answered, with her sweetest smile, and for a moment I almost believed her.

Deciding what to wear to the party was a nightmare. I couldn't make up my mind whether to go for the Hello Boys clubbing-type combo of micro mini and bra top, or the Don't Mess With Me look of combat pants, hooded sweatshirt and DMs. Or one of the million miles of choices in between. In the end I settled on jeans, flip-flops and a black Posh Spice handkerchief top – not too boho, not too revealing, but with a nice flash of fake-tanned back.

Hugh didn't say a word about how I looked as we climbed into the taxi, which is always a good sign as my brother tends to operate on a needs-to-know basis when it comes to my choice of dress on the rare occasions when we go out together. I didn't even get the usual you're-not-going-out-looking-like-that-are-you spiel from Dad, though that could have been because he was in the bathroom performing his own tarting-up operations when we left, adjusting his John Travolta medallions no doubt, and splashing on his Brut. Or whatever. The problem with my parents is they don't realize that being into the Seventies is only hip if you don't remember them the first time round.

We could hear the music as we turned into Danny's road. It spilled out on to the pavement, along with the light that blazed from every window. As Hugh and I walked up the path to the open front door, a girl with beaded dreadlocks stumbled out and was vastly sick into the circular flowerbed that was set into the middle of the front lawn.

"Obviously a good party," said Hugh. It wasn't even nine o'clock.

Inside, the festivities were in full swing. The music was wall-to-wall, the rooms full of heaving bodies, the booze flowing like – well, like booze at an eighteenth birthday party. Danny was nowhere to be seen. Hugh disappeared to find his mates, and I went into

24

the kitchen in search of a drink, feeling a trifle let-down. God knows why. It wasn't as if I'd been expecting Danny to be waiting on the doorstep to greet me with brass band and balloons and streamers. A hello would have been nice, though.

Nat and Ruby were already there, in the kitchen, Nat deep in characteristic eyelash-fluttering conversation with a tall skinny lad who, unless my nostrils deceived me, was smoking a joint, Ruby leaning moodily against the sink and taking desultory swigs from a bottle of lager. She brightened up when she saw me.

"Oh good," she said. "The entertainment has arrived."

I put my contribution to the party – six cans of Woodpecker – down on to the kitchen table. "Well, sorry to disappoint you," I said, "but I left my juggling balls at home."

"Very funny. You know what I mean."

"So where is the birthday boy, then?"

Nat broke off from chatting up Spliff Man. "Last seen out the back," she said.

"Out the back?"

"Yeah," Ruby put in. "In the garden. Giving mouth to mouth resuscitation to Suzy Davies," she added grimly, "in case you want to go and whack her one. Or him, come to that."

Spliff Man gave a nasty little snigger, and slunk out into the hallway.

"So what? It's a free country," I said boldly, but the let-down feeling sunk even lower.

Nat came over to me and put a concerned hand on my arm. "Are you OK?"

I resisted the temptation to shake off her hand, burst into tears, and rush out in a tantrum. "Of course I'm OK. Why shouldn't I be?"

"Look," said Ruby, reasonably, "Danny's a lad, and he's seriously good-looking. And he knows it. Therefore he's a bastard. Fact of life. Now why don't the three of us go on in there," she indicated the sitting room with her head, "and grab a piece of the action?"

Under the circumstances, it seemed like the best plan. After all, I'd only just arrived – plenty of time to size up the opposition and decide whether to go in fighting or retire gracefully. Danny had been giving me the come-on for days, and I wanted to give him the chance to put his money where his mouth was. So to speak.

"I'm just popping to the loo first," I told them. "I'll be down in a sec."

As I picked my way up the stairs, past the snogging couples, I noticed that half of one of the couples was the infamous Suzy Davies. I also noticed, with a distinct lifting of my spirits, that the other half was most definitely not Danny. *Cool it*, I told myself, firmly. *You haven't come to this party just to get off with Danny Oldfield. He's probably been acting in exactly the same way to loads of girls, just to keep his options open.*

When I came out of the bathroom I could hear the loud electronic thuds and whizzes of a computer game being played in the room next door, interspersed with raucous cheers and wolf-whistles from the lads. (Of course lads – what girl in her right mind plays on these things?)

"Go on Dan, give her one!"

"Whoa, yeah! Right between the eyes!"

"Way to go, my son!"

It seemed that the birthday boy was ducking his party so that he could play Tomb Raider, or something equally grown-up. How sweet, thought I, hovering outside the door. I debated whether to be Mrs Forward and barge in, demanding a dance and dragging him downstairs.

"So you really reckon she's up for it?" I heard someone say, and from the tone of his voice I somehow didn't think he was talking about Lara Croft. I strained forward, eager to hear who they were discussing. Well, a girl's got to keep up with the goss, hasn't she?

"Adam Barnes said she wouldn't leave him alone. He said he was knackered with it all."

More ribald laughter. I wondered who Adam Barnes had been slagging off this time. I'd gone out with him myself, briefly, about six months ago, but got fed up with him keeping his brains in his trousers. I took a deep breath, pushed the door open and went in.

"Hi guys," I said.

Danny leapt up as if he'd been shot.

"Oh, er, hi," he said, and it's a funny thing but I could have sworn he'd gone bright red. Surely not – only me and Japanese geisha girls blush. It must have been a trick of the light. "So what brings you here, then?"

Not one of the greatest chat-up lines, it must be said.

"Er, you invited me?" I said. "To your party? Which is going on downstairs without you? I just thought. . ." Mrs Forward deserted me suddenly, and I ran out of words.

"Yeah, right. Of course. I'm just coming," Danny said, which naturally set The Lads off again like baboons up a tree. He slid an arm around my waist and gave them the finger as we left the room and went downstairs.

What can I say about the rest of the evening? That it lived up to all my expectations? Well, yeah – except that I hadn't really dared to expect anything. Hope, yes, but not expect. I've been disappointed too many times in the past for that.

Anyway, suffice it to say that Danny paid me a very satisfying amount of attention, Suzy Davies went home with her tail between her legs, and Ruby and Nat cleaned up on their bet. At least, they would have done if it had been a real one, rather than a wind-up.

It was around midnight, and we were at the slow-dancing stage, glued together mouth to mouth, when Hugh suddenly materialized in front of me.

"Sorry to interrupt," he said, "but I'm going to push off now. I've just rung for a cab. Are you coming, Flo, or are you going to make your own way back?"

"Stay," Danny whispered in my ear, and tightened his grip on me.

Tempting though it was, I couldn't help thinking about the English and History homework I was supposed to be handing in on Monday morning. Call me boring, but I'm a girl who needs her sleep – I can never get work done after a mega-late night.

I disentangled myself. "I'd better go," I said, reluctantly. "I've got to get up tomorrow, I've got stuff to do."

Danny held me at arm's length, and looked me up and down. "D'you always go running when your big brother whistles? *Flo*," he added.

A tiny little worm of unease moved inside me.

Oh no! I thought. *Please don't spoil the evening!*

"No," I said, forcing myself to sound calm and reasonable. "But like I say, I ought to be getting back. And I'd rather go with Hugh than by myself. It's a long way."

Then he smiled, dazzlingly, and my disquiet vanished. "OK, sugar. I'll get your coat."

"Didn't bring one."

"Jesus." He looked at me again, his eyes lingering appraisingly on my chest. "You must have frozen. Did I tell you I like your top?"

"Do you?"

"Yeah. It's very –" He groped for the right word. "Very you."

"Thanks." *Danny Oldfield likes my top!*

"Hey, listen. I'll give you a call, yeah? Perhaps we can catch a movie, or something?"

"Oh, right. When?" *Shit! What did I say that for? Now he'll think I'm desperate!*

"Soon." He caressed my bare shoulder, gently, and my heart started thumping like a piledriver. "Very soon. You take care now, Flo-Flo."

Flo-Flo! If anyone else had called me that I'd have ripped their face off, but coming from Danny it sounded sweet and tender. Affectionate. I was touched – maybe it was going to be his pet name for me, what he'd put in my birthday and valentine cards. What he'd whisper down the phone to me when he rang, after we'd spent all day together; *"Hi, darling Flo-Flo. It's me."*

Oh boy. Was I in for a nasty surprise.

In the excitement, I'd completely forgotten about the parents' house-warming party, which rather surprisingly was still in full swing when Hugh and I arrived home. In the wildness stakes it wasn't quite in the same league as Danny's, but even so there were still plenty of people in various stages of pissed-ness, gyrating self-consciously around the still-unpacked tea chests in that way people of that generation have. They were all singing along and doing the actions, led by Dad, to an excruciatingly loud old number about being at the YMCA. Why is watching your parents dancing so embarrassing? It rates right up there with tucking your skirt in your knickers after going to the loo. Naff wasn't the word. I slunk into the kitchen to see if there was anything left to eat.

Mum was in the kitchen, talking to a man and a woman.

"Hi, love." She waved her glass at me. "Did you have a good time?"

"Fab, thanks." I picked up a slice of quiche. All of a sudden, I was starving. Lust always makes me hungry.

Hattie came in, one of her little friends in tow.

"So did you, then?" she asked me. "Amy and me have been wondering all evening."

"Did I what?" I mumbled, through a mouthful of crumbs.

"Get off with Danny Oldfield, of course!"

Amy was looking at me with big round eyes, like I was some kind of celebrity. *God!* If she was impressed with just the possibility, how much more sensational would the reality of Flora And Danny As An Item be! I couldn't resist the temptation to show off – yeah, I know, pathetic, but you've got to understand just how big a coup it was. Danny Oldfield only hangs out with A-list babes: so, by definition, I was now one of those babes. It felt pretty good.

"As a matter of fact," I said, popping a mini scotch egg into my mouth, "I did. We were together all evening. And he's going to ring me," I added, casually.

The girls stared at me, awestruck. "For a date?" Hattie whispered.

I nodded. "Uh-huh."

"Wow!"

There was a moment of silence, and I basked in the unaccustomed respect until I realized, to my slight embarrassment, that the silence was total. Mum and the couple she had been talking to had stopped their conversation and were all regarding me with amused expressions.

Mum turned to them, smiling. "This is my elder daughter, just back from a party."

"A very successful one, by the sound of it," the man said, with a grin. He was very dark, tall and slim, dressed in a black suit that looked to my unpractised eye like Armani, and a black T-shirt. "I know who this is. It's Florence, isn't it? I haven't seen you since you were small."

"Oh, darling, don't embarrass her!" The woman by his side was frighteningly elegant, her white-blond hair cropped short as a boy's to show off her perfect bone structure, her heels and fingernails long and pointed. She looked at me with an all-girls-together little smile. "Isn't it just so tedious when grown-ups tell you how much you've grown?"

Grown-ups? Oh, puh-lease! "Yeah, right."

The woman gave a brittle little laugh, and turned back to the man. "I'm sure Florence doesn't want to be bored by us, darling. Come on – let's go and have a bop."

She took him by the hand and led him into the sitting room, where the YMCA song had been replaced by Abba. As he drew level with me he crossed his eyes slightly at me, behind the woman's back, and gave me a small, almost imperceptible but definitely sympathetic wink.

And that was how Max came back into my life.

chapter three

The next morning, the sun was shining and the sky was blue. Well, it would be, wouldn't it? Danny Oldfield had danced with me all evening and I was in lurve. The weather, on the other hand, was rank – blowing a gale and chucking it down with rain. And the kitchen was a tip, littered with empty glasses and brimming ashtrays, the floor strewn with spilt crisps and trodden-in bits of pizza and other unidentifiable rubbish. I didn't care, though – I had my thoughts of Danny to keep me warm as I fiddled with a bowl of Frosties and gazed, unseeing, out of the kitchen window.

Dad, still in his pyjamas, plodded heavily into the kitchen, crisps crunching under his bare feet. He winced as he opened the fridge door.

"Who's throwing stones at that window?" He took out a carton of orange juice and looked at it uncomprehendingly, then put it back, picked up the milk and glugged it straight from the carton.

I turned, and pulled a face. "Urrgghh! That's disgusting, even Hugh puts it in a glass first!

And nobody's throwing stones, it's only the rain."

"Sounds like stones to me. Handfuls of gravel. S'going right through me."

"Yeah, well, you shouldn't have got wasted last night," I replied cheerfully. "Self-inflicted wound, if you ask me. I've got no sympathy."

"This is the voice of your conscience," he muttered. He trudged over to the sink, rested his hands on the edge, and peered into it as if seeking the meaning of life.

"What's the matter now? You're not going to throw up, are you?" I asked him, alarmed.

"No, I'm not going to throw up. I've just got a bit of a headache, that's all. Your mother sent me down to get something and I'm trying to remember what it was. Oh aye, tea, that's right."

I took pity on him. "Why don't you go back to bed? I'll make it and bring it up for you. So to speak." I can never resist the vomit jokes, but on this occasion it just rolled off him. So to speak.

"Would you, pet? Ah, you are a little treasure." He staggered off, eyes bloodshot and hair like an unmade bed, nursing his hangover. He probably hadn't even drunk that much; he just can't hold his drink, gets silly on a half of brown ale and then suffers all the next day.

I filled the kettle and switched it on; got mugs down, then changed my mind and took out cups and saucers from the dresser, Mum's fancy Wedgwood tea-set that had been a wedding present from an aunt. I laid a tray properly, thinking I'd treat them, in an absurdly good mood, wafting round the kitchen humming dreamily. I suddenly realized I was humming the *Wedding March*, and stopped, abruptly. What *was* I doing! I told myself it was because I'd been thinking about the tea-set, Mum and Dad's wedding present, and had nothing, absolutely zilch, to do with my previous thoughts about Danny.

Just at that moment my mobile bleeped at me from the kitchen table. Somebody had sent me a text message. At nine o'clock on a Sunday morning! Surely none of my friends would even be conscious at that time, let alone awake enough to compose a text. I picked it up, certain it was a wrong number, and then nearly dropped it again when I saw who it was from. Danny. Well, it said D at the bottom, and I didn't know anyone else called D. Apart from Dad, and I somehow didn't think it was from him.

HIYA GORGE, WASSSUUUP? U WERE GR8 LST NITE, WANNA HOOK UP L8ER? D X

Not just D, but D kiss. Awake, un-hungover (presumably), telling me I'd been gr8 – and asking for a date! Just how much better was the day going to get? There was only one thing for it – I had to ring Ruby and Nat, and pronto. Sunday morning or no Sunday morning.

An emergency meeting was convened for eleven at Rube's; I didn't feel I could impose my post-party hovel of a home on my friends, let alone the parents' headaches and resultant bad moods. When I got back, however, the kitchen had been blitzed – the surfaces cleared, the floor clean – and Mum was loading glasses into the dishwasher with Classic FM on the radio and a smile on her face. She turned as I walked in the back door.

"Morning, love."

"Afternoon," I retorted. "So who had a good time last night, then?"

"It was good, wasn't it?" She picked up half a tumbler of colourless liquid with two sodden cigarette butts floating disgustingly on top, threw its contents down the sink, and added the glass to the dishwasher.

"Shame about the mess, though." I couldn't resist rubbing it in. She's always going on about us lot causing messes; it was quite pleasant to be able to turn the tables for a change.

She just smiled again, serenely. "Oh well, not to worry. The perils of parties."

"So where is everybody?"

"Hugh's gone for a run, not sure about Hattie.

On the computer, I think. Dad's gone back to bed, says he feels fluey."

I snorted, unsympathetically. "Yeah, right. Only flu that's ever been caught from the bottom of a glass." My eye was caught by a bunch of flowers on the table. Or rather, a bouquet – half a florist's shop, wrapped in thick expensive cream tissue paper with scalloped edges, and hand-tied with a long piece of sage green string. Class. My stomach did a somersault as the wild thought came into my brain they might be from Danny – bonkers, how could he afford that kind of thing? Then I caught sight of the card tucked inside them – *Dearest Julia and Roger*, was all I could see, written in black ink in an elaborate swirly hand – and my insides re-established themselves.

"They're nice; where did they come from?"

"A courier brought them, just before you got back."

A courier, eh. Interflora clearly wasn't good enough. Not just class, then; serious class.

"No, I meant who are they from." I leant forward, and plucked the card from the flowers. "Max and Venetia – who're they?"

"Max Cooper. He was at the party last night." She touched an enormous ivory lily with a forefinger, reverently, as if it might break. "Beautiful, aren't they? He always was a thoughtful boy."

"Boy?" I racked my brains, trying to think of any lads at the parents' bash last night who would have the dosh to afford that kind of thank-you gesture.

"Figure of speech. I still think of him as a boy – he used to work with Dad at the paper; it was his first job. He's come a long way since those days, by all accounts; he's something fantastically exciting in television now." She took a vase down from a cupboard and filled it with water from the tap. "He's just moved back to the area – such a coincidence, Dad and I bumped into him in Sainsbury's the other day so of course we had to invite him to the party."

"So what does he do on the telly, then? Is he an actor?" I felt a flicker of curiosity despite not usually taking much interest in the parents' friends, who for the most part are distinctly unglamorous fellow teachers or newspaper workers.

"No, he's on the other side of the camera. A producer, or was it a director? Can't recall." She started to take the flowers from their wrapping and put them in the vase. "You met him, remember; we were in here talking when you got back from your do."

I had a fleeting memory of the man in the black suit, his conspiratorial wink behind his blonde companion's back.

"Oh yeah, I remember. His girlfriend was the one who was talking about *grown-ups*." I put on a silly voice, imitating her. *Venetia*. She would be, wouldn't she. "Nice taste in flowers, anyway."

"Oh no," said Mum confidently, pushing another bloom into the vase and looking at it appraisingly, "that'll be Max. It's the sort of thing he does, as I said; anybody else would ring to say thanks, or send one of those awful text things, but he sends flowers. He's a sweetie."

She buried her nose in the lilies and sniffed appreciatively, lost no doubt in thoughts of the sainted Max, but her mention of texts reminded me of more important things.

"Is it OK if I go out tonight?" I said, casually, getting my mobile out of my pocket.

Mum frowned slightly. "Don't forget it's school tomorrow."

"Yeah, I know. I won't be late. It's just. . ." I trailed off, looking at the phone in my hand.

"It's just you've been asked on a hot date by this hot guy, and you don't want to turn him down?" Mum hazarded.

"How did you know?" It's spooky, the way she always seems to guess these things.

"Because, my darling girl, I've been there myself. Believe it or not."

Somehow, I couldn't imagine my parents ever

having been on hot dates. "You mean you used to think Dad was a hot guy?"

"What makes you think I'm talking about Dad?" She smiled mischievously, tweaked a leaf or two and picked up the vase. "Just make sure you remember it's Monday tomorrow."

I promised I would, but school was the last thing on my mind. It was too full of thoughts of Danny. Or rather, Danny and me, as a couple. Together. The fact was, I'd already told him I'd go out with him that evening. It was almost unbelievable, but he'd sent me two more texts when I was round at Rube's, of the same sentiments as before. When my mobile bleeped yet again Nat had grabbed it from my hand and stared at it in wonder.

"Oh my God! It's another one from him! I don't believe this, Flora, you lucky thing – aren't you going to answer him?"

"Treat 'em mean, keep 'em keen," Ruby growled, which up until then had been more or less my philosophy. This time, however, things were different. This time, it was Danny Oldfield who I had dangling, waiting for my response, and not the usual class of dork who pays me attention. Something told me there probably wouldn't be another message from him.

I kept my reply short and to the point. THANX 4 YRS. GISSA CALL?

Within seconds, my mobile rang. Nat squealed with excitement, and Ruby raised her eyes to the ceiling and tutted in an it'll-end-in-tears kind of way, but I ignored both of them.

"Hello?"

"Yo babe!"

Bad start. I can't stand it when people say "yo". In the interests of romance, though, I decided to overlook it.

"Hi Danny. How're you?"

"Sweet. So where shall we go, then?"

"Errmm. . ." I couldn't think what to say. I wasn't prepared for such a direct approach; I'd assumed we'd indulge in the normal small talk, discussing last night's party, who'd done what with whom, blah blah blah, before he possibly – just *possibly*, you understand – sounded me out about a date later in the week. Not "where shall we go", just like that. "Errmm," I said again, feeling a complete drongo.

Luckily, Danny didn't appear to notice I was lost for words. "How about if I come round yours about seven," he suggested brightly, while out of the corner of my eye I noticed Ruby shaking her head violently and making throat-cutting gestures with her hand. I hadn't a clue what she meant, and besides, she was distracting me. I turned my back on her and put a finger in the ear my phone wasn't pressed against.

"Yeah, sure. That'd be cool. What shall we do, then?"

Danny laughed. "Well, that depends on you, sugar!"

"A movie, then? Or a pizza?"

"OK. Whatever. I'll see you about seven, yeah?" And he hung up.

"Well?" Nat demanded breathlessly, her eyes round and eager. "What did he say?"

"We're going out. On a date. About seven," I added, needlessly. I felt pretty breathless, too. I was going out with Danny Oldfield – we were going to be a couple. I thought about all the other girls who'd give their eye-teeth to be in my shoes (if you get my drift). It was a real coup, no question.

I have to say at this point, if I'm to be honest, that the biggest thrill was the prestige of him asking me out. I didn't think about how much I liked him, or how nice it would be to spend some time alone together – just the glory of being seen in his company. *Danny and Flora. Flora and Danny.* It had a nice ring about it, I thought.

"Well, whaddya know," Ruby was saying, drily.

I turned to her. "What? And what was this –" I copied her gestures, drawing a hand across my throat and shaking my head – "all about?"

"I think you should've let him stew a bit longer, that's all."

I snorted with disbelief. "Yeah, right. Like you'd have turned him down. I don't think so."

"I'm not saying I'd have turned him down. Not as such. I just wouldn't have said yes so quickly. 'That'd be cool, where shall we go?'" she repeated, in an over-eager little voice, batting her eyelashes girlishly.

Nat jumped to my defence. "Oh, she didn't sound like that!" she protested, but I put up a silencing hand.

"It's OK, Nat. I can take it. I know she's just jealous."

"No I'm not," Ruby said, with a scowl. "Don't look at me like that, you two."

"You are jealous," Nat told her. She glanced at me with triumph. "You said so, just before Flora got here. You said, how did Flora pull that one off. You said—"

"OK, OK," Ruby interrupted, hastily. "Maybe I am jealous, just a bit. I already said I wouldn't turn him down, didn't I? I'm just concerned."

"*Concerned?*" My voice rose theatrically. "And why are you concerned, pray? Don't tell me he's a white slave trader, and asking me out is a front for his evil work – he's going to whisk me off and I'll disappear without a trace?"

Disappointingly, she didn't rise to my teasing.

"C'mon, gals. We all know his reputation; give him an inch, he'll take a mile. I still think Flora should have made him try harder before agreeing to see him. He's far too quick a worker."

But none of us could have realized just how quick.

I hate this obsession with clothes we females have. The way whenever something exciting or out of the ordinary happens, all we can think about is what we're going to wear. Or is it just me?

At four o'clock I had the entire contents of my wardrobe spread out on my bed. By five they were all on the floor, and I was no nearer deciding what to wear. At half past, Hattie came wandering in clutching a piece of paper.

"Blimey," she said, looking at the chaos. "Has a bomb gone off?"

I ignored that. "What do you want?"

"Nothing," she said, innocently. "D'you want a hand?"

I was instantly suspicious – my sister only offers assistance when she's after something. "No thanks," I said, briskly.

But she wasn't to be put off that easily. "Are you going out?"

"I might be."

"On a date?"

45

"Perhaps."

"Not with Danny Oldfield?" She sounded as excited as Nat had.

"None of your business."

It was no use, she'd seen my face go red. "It is, isn't it! I knew it! Oh, go on, Flora – let me help you choose something to wear." She darted forward and began sorting through my clothes, selecting a couple of tops and holding them up in the air in front of my chest like a pushy sales assistant. "This is nice, the colour suits you. Or – no, I know. This one. It's dead sexy, boys love stuff that shows off girls' boobs."

I was genuinely shocked. "Hattie!"

"What? It's true."

"Maybe it is, but you're not supposed to know about things like that, not at your age."

"Why not? I'm twelve."

"Exactly." I sighed. "Look, what was it you wanted? Only he's coming at seven, and I've still got to wash my hair and stuff."

"I'll help you, shall I? You can borrow those little glittery clips of mine if you like."

"Well, OK." I was puzzled by this sudden helpfulness, but it seemed genuine enough. Maybe she really was pleased I was going out with Danny – maybe it offered her some kind of reflected glory. "If you want."

"Give us a call when you're out the bathroom.

46

Oh, by the way." Here it comes, I thought. Astonishing how many of Hattie's little bombshells begin with those words. "Have you got a photo I can borrow?"

"A photo? What of?"

"Of you."

I laughed with incredulity. "Why on earth do you want a photo of me?"

"For my penfriend." She waved the piece of paper she was holding. "It's a project for school. We have to tell them about our family. I want to send some pix."

It seemed harmless enough. "OK, I'll dig one out for you. Later, though. I've got enough on my plate at the moment. He's going to be here at seven."

When Danny arrived, at a quarter to eight, I was wearing black jeans and the black top Hattie had picked out as being sexy. It was low-cut and tight – a bit too tight, to be honest; either it had shrunk in the wash or I'd grown since last wearing it – with the word "cherub" in silver glitter across the front. Danny smiled when he saw it. He put a hand on my left shoulder and stooped to read it for an unfeasibly long time, his head bent low so that his forehead practically collided with me. I could feel the warmth of his hand on my shoulder; the heat of it seemed to burn through the thin fabric to the flesh and bone beneath, as if when he removed it a print would remain, left behind like a brand on my skin. *This belongs to Danny Oldfield.*

"Love the top," he remarked, and straightened up. I was glad my clothes seemed to meet with his approval – first last night, then now. "Sorry I'm a bit late. You haven't been worried, have you?"

Worried didn't even come close. I'd been in bits, certain he'd stood me up, then imagining him in an accident – injured, paralysed, dead. I'd got as far as planning the hymns for his funeral when I'd heard the front gate squeak on its hinges, and sprinted to the door and opened it before he'd had time to ring the bell.

"No," I lied. "I knew you'd be here. So where shall we go?"

He gave me one of his wolfish grins. "Round to mine. My folks are away tonight."

It started off promisingly enough, with a couple of videos and an Indian takeaway. Danny took two bottles of Pils from the fridge. The counter was littered with empties, although there was no sign of any other debris from his party last night. Perhaps his mum had tidied up before going out and leaving him to make inroads into the liquid leftovers.

He handed the beers to me. "See to those, will you? There's a bottle opener in the top drawer."

I'm not really a beer drinker, I prefer wine, but it seemed churlish to say so. Obediently, I removed the lids while he piled the foil containers, two plates and a handful of cutlery on to a tray and carried it through to the sitting room. He lit some candles and closed the curtains. The atmosphere of the room changed immediately, became cosy, intimate. The food smelled delicious but I could barely eat a thing, my stomach knotted with a mixture of excitement, awe and something else I couldn't identify. I picked at a plate of basmati rice and beef madras while Danny shovelled in great mouthfuls of curry, washed down with huge slugs of lager, as if he'd been marooned starving on a desert island all week. He drained the bottle to its dregs and indicated my plate with his fork, swallowing.

"Don't you want any more of that?"

I shook my head and pushed the food towards him. He polished it off in moments; I half expected him to pick up the plate and lick it clean, but he stopped just short.

"God," I said, with fascination. Hugh is famous at home for his healthy appetite, but this display left him standing. "Doesn't your mother feed you?"

He belched by way of reply and stood up, waving the empty bottle. "Want another?"

I'd barely started mine. "No ta. This is fine."

We settled down on the sofa together. Danny put one arm round me and wielded the remote with the other, pointing it at the TV with a flourish.

"OK," he said. "Let's see what Arnie's up to. I haven't seen this one, have you?"

It had struck me that an action movie wasn't perhaps the most appropriate choice of background for a romantic first date, but as it turned out Arnold Schwarzenegger didn't get much of a look-in because, within moments and by mutual consent, we were locked together in a spot of tonsil tennis. He was a pretty masterly snogger, I'll give him that; but then, he'd had plenty of practice. Everything was going swimmingly until his hands became involved – not caressing me gently, which would have been acceptable enough, but tugging my T-shirt down. The stretchy Lycra gave, and I could feel my boobs spilling out over the top. I made a little noise of protest and squirmed out of his grasp, wriggling myself back into my clothes.

"Don't do that."

He stared at me as if I'd grown a second head. "Why not?"

Why not? The words "because I say so" sprang

into my mind, but I didn't think they would go down too well.

"Because I don't like it," I said instead.

Slightly to my surprise, he didn't look at all shamefaced or apologetic. He laughed. "Course you don't," he said, with a nasty leer.

I could feel his mood change, instantly; as if a fire had gone out, or a light switched off.

"I don't like being groped," I said slowly.

"Yes you do," he said, and that's when it all started going seriously wrong.

He made a grab at me, pinning me back against the sofa. I didn't stand a chance; he's well over six foot and must weigh thirteen stone or more.

"Girls don't wear tops like that," he panted, "if they don't like being groped," and then proceeded to peel said top off me, followed by his own polo shirt. He chucked both garments behind him, not looking, with the hand that wasn't holding me down, then manoeuvred himself half on top of me and stuck his tongue down my throat. I flailed beneath him like a fish on a line, moving my head from side to side and beating my hands ineffectually on his solid chest, but it only seemed to inflame him more. He pumped his groin against my thigh, all revved up and ready for action, and all I could think was that he was going to rape me.

Who knows whether he would have gone that far? I never found out because, mercifully, the phone rang at that point. It trilled out merrily, and Danny stopped as if he'd been shot. Swearing, he got up to answer it. I scrambled upright, my face aflame, my heart pounding with fury at what he'd been doing to me and fear at what he'd been about to do next. I felt suddenly exhausted. It was as much as I could manage to retrieve my top from where he'd lobbed it. I scrambled into it and sat with a cushion clutched to my chest, waiting for my heart rate to subside.

I could hear Danny's voice from the hallway. "Yes Mum," I heard him say, docilely. "Just got a mate round to watch a vid. Yeah, that's right."

On the TV screen, Arnie messily totalled a couple of villains while I reflected dully that Danny's idea of a mate wasn't the same as mine. Presently, he came back into the sitting room. Glancing over at me, bent to pick up his shirt and pulled it on over his head in that ungainly arms-in-first way lads always employ. He began collecting up the empty takeaway cartons and dirty plates, calmly, as if nothing untoward had happened. I couldn't let him get away with that.

I stood up.

"How dare you," I began to splutter.

He turned his eyes to mine, his face carefully

impassive. "What d'you mean, how dare I? You've been coming on to me for weeks – what were you expecting me to do, ask for your hand in marriage?"

He picked up his Pils and took a lazy swig, but I knocked it from his hand, incensed. The bottle fell to the floor, the golden liquid splashing across the sofa and pooling across the pale green carpet in a dark stain, and Danny gave a little cry of dismay and sank to his knees.

"What're you doing? My mum's going to go mad!"

"I couldn't give a bugger!' I yelled, tears of rage springing to my eyes. "You assault me, and I'm supposed to be bothered about the bloody *carpet?* What's the matter with you!"

He straightened up and jabbed at the spilt lager with his toe, ineffectually, as if hoping his trainers possessed some kind of magic capillary action that would suck out the stain.

"Nothing's the matter with me. It's what you do that's the problem."

"What's that supposed to mean? What do I do?"

"You put out, sweetheart. You can't blame a guy for trying."

"Put out?" I was baffled; frustrated. "I don't know what you're on about." How could he have got that idea? He barely knew me.

He sighed, as if tried beyond endurance. "You

go like a train, is the rumour. You *shag*." He spelled it out for me, leaving no doubt. I felt my face turn an unflattering shade of raspberry.

"Who told you that?"

"Adam Barnes. He said you were all over him when you two were seeing each other, wouldn't leave him alone. Like a rabbit, he said you were." He leered at me, unattractively, half drunk, and I felt the raspberry deepen to beetroot. The problem was, it was true. Not the train bit, or the rabbit – that was fantasy. But it was true that I'd slept with Adam Barnes; I'd fancied him, he'd been persistent, and I'd given in under pressure. It wasn't something I was proud of, but it'd happened, nonetheless.

"Yeah, well," I muttered, "you shouldn't believe everything Adam Barnes tells you."

"Well I do. I believe him more than I believe you, at any rate. You girls, you're all the same. You flutter your eyelashes, you flash your tits," (I was suddenly, uncomfortably, reminded of Harriet: *boys love stuff that shows off girls' boobs*) "and then at the last minute you back off. Oh no, I didn't mean it, go and have a cold shower. Well, it's not as easy as that."

"It doesn't mean I want to *shag*. As you so elegantly put it," I mumbled.

"Then you shouldn't send out the wrong signals."

"Oh please." I'd had enough of this. "Spare me the quasi-psychological crapola."

He looked at me, and there was real dislike in his eyes. "You're just a prick tease."

"Yeah? Well that must make you a prick, then."

And with that parting shot, I threw the cushion on the sofa and stalked out, with as much dignity as I could muster.

chapter four

I couldn't tell anybody what had happened.
Don't ask me why; I just couldn't. Vanity I
suppose, or embarrassment. Or both, probably.
I felt so stupid – stupid for agreeing to seeing
Danny in the first place, given his reputation for
being a stud, for collecting scalps. Stupid for
allowing it to happen, for going round to his
place knowing we'd be alone, for wearing that
ridiculously provocative top (currently residing
in the bin; no way would I be wearing *that*
again).

I kept imagining people saying I told you so,
and muttering things about pride coming before
a fall, even though deep down I knew that pride
had naff all to do with it, and anybody who cared
about me would be as appalled at what Danny
had done as I was myself. But my conscious
reasoning was that I'd somehow deserved what
had happened; that my preoccupation with how
impressed people would be at knowing we were
together had somehow caused it, and it was
therefore my own fault. I'd brought it upon
myself. The idea of telling anyone what had

taken place in Danny Oldfield's house that Sunday evening made me feel physically sick; so much so that I stayed in bed the next morning, pulling the duvet around my head and pleading illness. It's not like me to skive school, so Mum didn't question me, just brought me some Nurofen and a bottle of water and left me to it.

Once everyone had gone, I wandered dispiritedly round the house feeling sorry for myself and unable to settle to anything. Until the phone went. I toyed with the idea of not answering it, but realized it was probably going to be for me, as everybody else was out.

It was Ruby.

"Oh, *there* you are," she said. "I've been trying your mobile for ages, but I keep getting the voicemail. What's up?"

"You don't want to know," I replied, grimly.

"Yeah, I do. What's wrong?"

"Two words. Danny. And Oldfield."

"Aha. So it didn't go too well last night, then."

There was a long pause.

"Don't say it, Rube," I groaned.

"Say what?"

"I told you so."

"I wasn't going to say that, hun. I was just wondering what he'd done to you to keep you off school, and why you didn't ring last night to tell me about it."

I gave her the brief details. "I was going to tell you, honestly. I just feel such a prat."

"What for? You ask me, he's the prat. He's lucky you didn't knee him in the goolies and report him to the cops for assault."

"Yeah, but. . ." I trailed off, pathetically. "Don't tell Nat, will you?"

"Why not? You've done nothing to be ashamed of. She'll be concerned about you, like me."

"I know, but. . . " But what? It was hard to explain just why I felt so stupid. "I'd just rather tell her myself, OK? In due course. I need some time by myself right now to get my head back together."

Ruby agreed not to tell Nat, but she did manage to convince me that the only thing to do was to write the whole thing off as experience, to put a brave face on it and to go back to school the next day. After all, she reasoned, I couldn't avoid Danny for ever. It didn't mean I had to make public the gory details of what had happened between us.

It never occurred to either of us that he might make it public on my behalf. And when I say public. . .

The weird thing is that I didn't spot it at first, even though all my senses were on red alert when I walked into the sixth-form common room the next morning. I was too busy looking out for Danny so I could promptly go in the opposite direction to pay much attention to the unusually large knot of people clustered around the noticeboard. The penny didn't even drop when one or two of them turned away from it, grinning, and then, seeing me making my way across the room, looked decidedly embarrassed and avoided my eye.

"Hiya Flora, are you feeling better?" It was Nat, entering the room behind me. "I was going to call round after school last night, only Rube said you were feeling really lousy when she rang and thought you needed some peace and quiet."

"It was just a migraine," I lied. "I'm fine now."

"So how did it go on Sunday with *Danny*?" She mouthed his name excitedly. "I've been dying to find out. Where is he, anyway?" She looked round the room as if she'd been expecting to see us locked together in a tender embrace. So Ruby had stuck to her promise not to tell her, then.

"It's a long story," I started to say, but was interrupted by a yell of outrage. It was Ruby, standing by the noticeboard.

"What a bastard!" She put up a hand and ripped down a white sheet of A4 paper that was pinned right in the middle of the board, high up, for maximum attention-grabbing value. Two drawing pins popped out on to the floor, but she ignored them. "OK," she said fiercely, to those who still stood there, watching her with amused interest. "You've seen enough. You can go now. Go on – *bog off!*"

Nat and I hurried over. "What is it?" I asked her. "What's the matter?"

For answer, she roughly screwed up the paper she held, then changed her mind and opened it up again, slowly, not looking at me.

"You're not going to like it," she said. She sighed. "But I guess you've got a right to see it. After all, everybody else has." And she handed it to me.

At first sight, it looked like a kind of Valentine's poem – ODE TO FLORA, it said at the top – a few weeks late. A pleasant, jokey little thing. Then my eye was drawn down, and down even further, and I realized to my horror it was no joke. Or if it was, it was wholly at my expense.

ODE TO FLORA
Oh beautiful Flo-Flo
With your top cut so low-low
And your cleavage on show-show;
How the boys adore you!

With your succulent beauty
And your ways oh-so-cutey

You make us feel fruity –
You know that you do.

You act oh-so-flirty,
Talk raunchy and dirty,
And then go all hurty
As our balls turn quite blue.

You make us feel silly
With brains empty and frilly,
Obsessed with our willy
And a pin-up or two.

Now you're making it clear
That you want me near –
Quite frankly, my dear,
I'd rather snog Hugh.

Oh beautiful Flo-Flo
With your titties a-go-go:
I'm afraid it's a no-no
'Cos I don't fancy you.

It was signed "From a secret non-admirer." I felt
as if I'd been kicked in the stomach. I glanced
up, my face aflame, and saw Nat; she'd been
reading it over my shoulder and was now
looking at me, her eyes and mouth perfect
round "O"s of horror and disbelief.

"Who wrote that?" she whispered, and at that moment the door opened and in strolled Danny, a smug self-satisfied expression on his face. As our eyes met I had no doubt that he was the author, and I daresay he instantly understood that I had read it. For the first time in my life I felt a stab of pure, corrosive hatred. I didn't even stop to think about what I was doing; I crumpled the poem up, shoved it into my pocket and fled, out of the common room, down the stairs and out of school, as if pursued by unspeakable demons.

I was still running when I reached the shopping mall, quarter of a mile away in town. All I could think about was my public humiliation, and getting as far away as possible.

I shot through the open doors of the mall, my breath coming in shallow gasps, a stitch in my side and a burning pain in my chest. People hurriedly got out of my way; couples parted as I approached them at full tilt, mothers with babies in pushchairs moved hastily aside, suspicious wary looks on all their faces as if I was some kind of a danger, a threat. To be fair, that must have been how I appeared; how were they supposed to know I wasn't a madwoman, bent on a mission of destruction, but just me, harmless me, trying to escape from Danny and his vindictive handiwork?

I didn't even see him. Not Danny – a total stranger. Perhaps he was coming out of a shop and didn't see me either, until it was too late. Or maybe he was lost in his own thoughts. Who knows. At any rate, I cannoned into him with a force that knocked the remaining breath from my body.

"Whoa!" he said. He took hold of my upper arms, in a reflex action. "Steady on!"

"Sorry," I said. "I'm sorry." At least, that's what I intended to say, but it came out as a muffled sob. I threw my head back – to catch my breath, to look at him, I can't remember why, it doesn't matter – and I realized that he wasn't a stranger at all, that I knew him, or rather I recognized him. He was the guy from Mum and Dad's party, the one who'd sent the flowers. Max.

At that exact moment, he said, "It's Florence, isn't it? Florence Wilcox?" He was frowning, not altogether certain.

I nodded, took a huge shuddering gasp, and then – well, embarrassing though it is to relate, I burst into tears on him. All over him. I leant my face against his expensively be-jacketed front, and howled and howled as if my heart was breaking. Which I guess it was, only he wasn't to know that. He just had this sobbing female hurling herself at him, dribbling inarticulately.

He coped really well, fair play to him. As if he

63

had hysterical women draped across him on a regular basis. Perhaps he did. He didn't seem at all nonplussed, just put his arms round me and let me lean and dribble, and made soft "there there"-type noises. His front seemed so solid and capable, his arms around me so reassuring. He even smelled comforting, the fresh and faintly sharp scent of a doubtlessly expensive aftershave or eau-de-something-posh. But I was beside myself, and far from consoling me, his quiet sympathy seemed to make me worse. It was the humiliation that was the worse thing – Danny's macho posturing, making out it was me who'd done all the running, on top of what he'd done to me. I couldn't seem to stop.

Inevitably, though, the sobbing at last changed down several gears, and when I was at the deeply unattractive snivelling stage he led me through the mall, outside to the small memorial garden next to the Catholic church. Scrubby flowerbeds bore a few early daffodils, their yellow heads nodding bravely in the keen north-easterly breeze. Pigeons strutted and pecked between the benches. There was no one around; nobody else was the slightest bit interested in watching my shameful blubbering, and the realization made my embarrassment shrink to more manageable proportions.

He led me to one of the benches, like an invalid, and sat me down solicitously.

"Better now?"

I nodded; sniffed, rummaged unsuccessfully for a tissue.

"Here." He produced a handkerchief that was a masterpiece of dazzling snowy whiteness, a tribute to his brand of washing powder (or rather, as I was later to discover, his laundry service). I put out a hand to take it, but he ignored it, and wiped my tears gently from my face. It could have been an overly intimate gesture, sleazy even, but it wasn't. He was as concerned and careful as a favourite uncle, and it made me feel like a little girl again. I sniffed, pathetically.

"I need to blow my nose." He stopped short of doing that for me, handed it to me instead. I duly blew. "Thanks." I held the hanky awkwardly, twisting it between my fingers, not knowing what to do or say. "I suppose I should tell you what it was all about."

"Only if you want to."

I sniffed again. "Not really." I looked at him. "Sorry."

"What for?"

"For being such a plank."

"You're not a plank."

"Yes I am." Gloomily, I thought again of

Danny. I'd known perfectly well what he was like; how could I possibly have imagined he'd been interested in anything other than my body? And why had I let that stupid poem affect me so much – why couldn't I have just laughed it off? A plank was exactly what I was.

"Florence." He leaned forward, looked into my eyes. Dimly, my brain registered that his were exactly the colour of treacle toffee. "You're not. I've met some planks in my time, and you're definitely not one of them. Trust me."

"Well I feel like one."

"No need. You were upset."

I sniffed again. "Slight understatement."

"Yeah, OK. You were totally out of your tree. I thought you had a leak." He was trying to be kind, making light of it to save my blushes. I attempted a smile, but it got stuck around my mouth and turned into a grimace. Bang on cue, my mobile started to ring. I fumbled around in my bag for it, my fingers stiff and unwieldy with cold and uselessness.

"Here – let me." He took it from me. "Hello, Florence's phone? Yes, she is, but she's not feeling too well at the moment." A pause, while he listened and I wondered who was on the other end. Could it possibly be Danny? No, that would be too much to hope for, that Danny should ring to beg my forgiveness and be answered by an unknown man. . . "Me? My name's Max Cooper, I'm a friend of her parents. Don't worry, I'll make sure she gets home safely." Another pause. "Yes, OK – I'll tell her. Thanks. Bye." He pressed End, and handed the phone back to me. "Someone called Natalie. She wants you to know she's thinking about you."

Nat. Worried about me, no doubt. Well, of course she was. I'd have been worried too, if our roles had been reversed.

"Oh, bless," I said. Annoyingly, my eyes filled up with tears again. What *was* the matter with me? I dabbed at them, and shivered as the chill wind cut through my thin sweater straight to my bones.

Max stood up decisively. "Come on."

"Come on where?" I stood up too, but with hesitation.

"We can't sit here, it's far too cold. I'm buying you a coffee."

"But—"

"No arguments. You look like death. On second thoughts, we'll start with a brandy. You can't beat it for shock."

I'd never sat in a pub drinking brandy at half past eleven in the morning before. It felt dead cheesy, sitting up at the bar of the Crown and Anchor on one of those high padded stools, clutching the ridiculously over-sized brandy balloon as if my life depended on it. But Max had been right about it being good for shock. Just two sips and I felt instantly better. He had one too, to keep me company, or perhaps to deal with his own shock – having me crashing into him like that, as elegant and subtle as a bulldozer, couldn't have done his equilibrium much good.

After the brandies we sat down at a smeary glass-topped table, and the barman brought us a tray of coffee. One of the cups was chipped, and the other had a faintly visible lipstick stain adorning its outer edge. Max pulled a rueful face at me behind the barman's retreating back.

"Bit of a dive," he whispered. "Sorry."

"Don't worry," I whispered back. The Crown isn't noted for its social niceties. I moved the overflowing ashtray to the adjacent table. "This place is always like this."

"Yeah? It's changed, then. It used to be quite upmarket." He wielded the coffee pot, and indicated the two cups. "Chip or lipstick? Or shall I complain?"

"No, don't worry." I couldn't bear the thought of any fuss; I'd had quite enough for one day. I took a folded napkin from the glass on the table and polished the edge of the cup until the lipstick disappeared. "I'll have this one."

"It looks like it's had – whatever the opposite of a facelift is. A facedrop, I suppose. I used to live round here, years ago. I've just moved back," he explained.

"I know. Mum told me, after their party. When you sent the flowers. They were fab, by the way. She was dead chuffed."

I took a mouthful of the coffee, which surprisingly was quite good.

"Are you OK now?" Max asked me. "You've got a bit more colour, at any rate."

"Have I?"

"Mm-hmm. It's green, but at least it's colour."

I couldn't help smiling. Just a tiny smile. "Thanks."

"What for?"

"Oh, you know. This. The brandy."

"The certain death by chipped cup."

"That kind of thing." I fished around in my pocket and withdrew the screwed-up piece of paper from within. "Here, you may as well read this."

He smoothed out the poem and read it, and I scrutinized his face as he did so, ready to take offence at the slightest hint of a smirk, but none came. He remained totally straight-faced, even when he pushed it back across the table to me.

"It's a bit harsh, isn't it. Hurt male pride, I presume?"

"Something like that. He pinned it up on the noticeboard."

"Ouch. Now that *is* harsh."

"He's a tosspot," I muttered.

"He sounds it." He picked up the crumpled paper and glanced at it again. "Actually, I suppose it's quite clever, in a tosspotty kind of way. Who's Hugh?"

"My brother. They're mates, him and Danny."

"Danny being the tosspot?"

"That's right."

"I see." He handed the poem to me. "And are they still mates?"

"Dunno." I blinked. It hadn't occurred to me. "I don't know if Hugh's read it."

"Then maybe he should. I only say that," he went on casually, topping up his cup of coffee, "because if somebody wrote that kind of thing about *my* sister, I'd want to read it. I remember Hugh now. Large lad, isn't he? Useful to have as a brother, I should imagine."

I smiled. "Maybe." I understood perfectly what he was getting at. The thought of Hugh locked in mortal combat with Danny because he'd insulted me was quite funny. We were close, as brothers and sisters went, but not *that* close. Especially given that, large as Hugh was, Danny was even larger. My brother's never been much of a one to risk his own personal safety.

Max put his hand over mine where it lay on the table, and patted it in a gesture of solidarity.

"Stuff him."

"Yeah."

"Death to all tosspots."

"Absolutely."

He took his hand away, looked at his watch and frowned. "God, is that really the time? I'm going to have to go shortly, I'm supposed to be five miles away in ten minutes."

I remembered how Mum had said he had this glamorous job in television, and felt immediately guilty at taking up his time with my stupid little problems. Although he hadn't made me feel they were stupid; quite the reverse.

I stood up. "I must just go to the Ladies. But look, you go on – you've been really kind, but I don't want to make you late for your meeting."

"Don't worry, it's not that important. Besides, I'm not abandoning you here by yourself after forcing strong drink on you – I'm too afraid of your dad!"

Inside the loo, I rang Nat. I was hoping she'd have her mobile switched on, as by my reckoning it was a study period, but no such luck. I wanted to speak to a person, not leave a message, so I tried Ruby instead. She answered at once.

"Hiya Rube. It's me," I said.

"Flora!" She sounded dead relieved to hear my voice. "Are you OK?"

Was I? I wasn't sure. Max had helped, but I couldn't in all honesty say I was OK. It was going to take a long time to get over Danny's treatment of me, both in private at his house on Sunday and then publicly today. It seemed too complicated to say all that, though.

"More or less," I said instead. "I was just ringing to see if you if you could tell school what's happened; I don't want them getting all heavy with me for bunking off."

"I already have: I said you still weren't feeling well and we all thought you should go back home."

"Ah, thanks, Ruby. You're a pal – I owe you one."

"No you don't. You'd do the same for me, wouldn't you."

"Course I would."

"Nat knows," she said suddenly. "That it was Danny who stuck that pile of crap on the noticeboard. I had to tell her, it didn't seem fair to keep her in the dark when I know what's been going on."

"What did she say?"

"She was convinced it couldn't have been him, that you and he were a real item. So I told her that he'd given you bother on Sunday night.

I didn't tell her the full story though – I knew you wanted to tell her yourself. But she's bound to ask you about it, is what I'm saying."

"It's OK, Rube. Don't worry about it." The door opened and I heard somebody come in. "Oops. Gotta go. Listen, why don't you and Nat come by after school? I'll fill you both in on all the gory details then."

Max was waiting for me outside. "So they call you Flora now, do they? I remember you as Florence. It's bizarre, I haven't set eyes on you in years, then I bump into you twice in one week. Literally."

"I stopped being Florence when I started at secondary school," I told him. "I hate it. Only my grandfather calls me it any more, but I'm working on him."

"Come on then, Flora." He smiled at me, and his eyes crinkled at the edges. "Much as I'd like to stay here all afternoon, I really should be getting along to that meeting. I'd better get you home."

chapter five

When Hugh got home that afternoon he had a split lip and a livid red-and-purple bruise on his right cheekbone, which he said he'd acquired playing rugby. He seemed unusually reluctant to talk about it though, just grabbed a Fanta and a handful of biscuits and disappeared up to his top-floor eyrie.

But when Nat and Ruby arrived, ten minutes later, they had a rather different explanation. They burst through the front door, the pair of them, agog and fairly frothing with the drama of it all.

"Guess what? Hugh beat Danny up," Nat declared, without preliminaries.

"You're *kidding*!"

"I'm not, honestly! Am I, Rube?"

"She's not," Ruby confirmed. "Is he home yet?"

"Well, yeah, but –" I thought of what Max had said earlier, about Hugh being useful to have as a brother. I'd thought it was ludicrous, his implication that Hugh might stick up for me with his fists. It had never occurred to me that

Max could have been right. "He said he'd been playing rugby," I explained, rather lamely.

"So you've seen his war wounds, then," said Ruby. She sounded satisfied, as if it was her honour that had been avenged, rather than mine.

"Yeah," I said, wonderingly. "God. What did Danny look like?"

"Worse," Ruby pronounced. "Far worse. He had a black eye."

"And he was telling everyone Hugh had broken his nose," Nat added.

"*God!*" My brother, breaking somebody's nose because of me! I knew I shouldn't approve of violence, but I couldn't help feeling pleased. Just the teensiest bit. Actually, I lie. I was thrilled to bits, over the moon that Danny had got his comeuppance.

"It wasn't broken," Ruby was saying, with scorn, "it was just a bit – you know. Bent."

"So what happened?"

"Hugh just went berserk," Nat breathed, dramatically. "At lunchtime. He came into the common room, went over to where Danny was sitting, and knocked him off his chair. I mean, literally. Like, *Pow*. Bruce Willis, eat your heart out. Then he piled into him on the floor."

"Really?" I turned to Ruby for confirmation. You could always rely on her to provide a detached viewpoint, a balance to Nat's more sensationalist reporting style.

She nodded. "Pretty much. They were giving it large for about five minutes – nobody dared go near them to break them up. It was full-on warfare – I mean, forget bundles in the playground, this was more like they were re-enacting a scene from *Gladiator*. Then in came Fozzy and pulled Hugh off Danny, and bawled them both out. Well embarrassing."

"And what happened then?"

"Nobody knows," Nat said. "Well, Mr Fosdyke told them both to go and report to him afterwards, but nobody knows what they said to him."

"Or what he said to them," said Ruby. "Nobody saw either of them for the rest of the day. For all we know they've both been suspended. Where is he, anyway?" She craned her neck towards the stairs, as if hoping to catch a glimpse of him. (My brother. My hero. . .)

"Upstairs. In his room. But I'm not going to go and disturb him. I'll ask him about it later on, after you've gone." I knew there was no way Hugh would tell me what had happened while Ruby and Nat were earwigging on the stairs.

"What I don't understand," said Nat, pulling out a stool and sitting on it, "is why Danny wrote that thing in the first place. I mean, the last time we saw you, you and he were like the Romance of the Century; then all of a sudden it's all off, he's bad-mouthing you via the sixth-form noticeboard, and your brother's knocking seven shades of poo out of him. It's like the Montagues and the Capulets all over again."

"No it isn't," I protested. "Romeo and Juliet were in love: Danny and I aren't."

"Well, whaddya know," said Ruby, darkly.

"You are sure it *was* Danny who wrote it?" Nat said. "Not somebody just wanting to stir up trouble?"

"I'm sure," I said, grimly, and then I told them both exactly what had gone on at Danny's on Sunday. I didn't spare any details, and once again I felt so stupid for not seeing it coming. Stupid and gullible. Predictably, though, Ruby was furious all over again on my behalf.

"He is such a sleazebag! He just assumes you'll be up for a quick shag, and then when you tell him to get lost he says *you* came on to *him*, and he never fancied you anyway!"

She has this knack, does Rube, of getting down to the nitty-gritty. Put like that, I could see she had a point; that it was Danny who had the problem, not me.

"That's about it, yeah."

"Forget him," Ruby declared, with a toss of her head. "He might be gorgeous, but he's toxic.

You can do better than that. There's loads more guys out there."

"Talking of which," said Nat, "who's this Max who's been answering your phone?"

For a split-second I couldn't think who she meant. It seems incredible, given the galvanizing effect just the mention of his name was to have on me only a short while later; but then, at that time, my head was too full of other thoughts. But when I remembered the events of earlier – me cannoning into him, his kindness to me – I felt an unmistakable but inexplicable blush spread up my neck.

It wasn't wasted on my friends.

"Eh up. Someone interesting, by the look of things," Ruby observed drily.

"Calm down. He's a friend of my parents, they've known him for years."

"That's why she's going red," Nat told her, meaningly.

I ignored her. "He just made sure I was OK, that's all. He's off limits; for a start, he's years older than me."

"That's a big turn-on for some men. You know – the whole Lolita thing."

I hadn't detected anything of the kind from Max. I shook my head. "Nope. Not Max. It wasn't like that – it wasn't, Ruby. Don't look at me in that tone of voice."

"So how old is he, then?" Nat is obsessed with men's ages, she sorts them into categories of suitable or unsuitable depending on their dates of birth, as if that's the only important factor.

"Haven't a clue."

"Well, roughly."

I hazarded a guess. "Twenty-four, twenty-five?"

"It's not that much older."

"Yeah it is. Anyway, forget it. I'm not interested; and even if I was, he certainly isn't. He was just doing the decent thing. He's my parents' friend, for God's sake; it would almost be like incest."

I meant it, too. I really did. I told myself he had simply done what any respectable family friend would have done under the same circumstances – picked me up, dusted me down and set me back on my feet again. Ruby and Nat were creating a liaison where none existed, and there was nothing remotely intriguing about what had happened. Nothing at all.

After they'd gone, I went up to Hugh's room and knocked on the door.

"Yeah?" came the mumbled reply. He was clearly eating something. Again.

"So what's all this I hear about you and Danny?" I said, going in and sitting down on the beanbag by the window.

He was working at his desk, textbooks spread out in front of him. "How d'you mean?" he said, cautiously, and took another bite from the monster sandwich he was holding.

"It's OK, Huge. Rube and Nat have told me all about it."

He swallowed, and looked at the sandwich as if trying to work out where it had come from. "Told you what, exactly?"

"That you got into a bundle with him."

He gave a short laugh, and tore off another mouthful. "Bundle doesn't even come close," he said indistinctly, through the crumbs. "He is such a loser – I destroyed him."

"So I gather. Broke his nose, or so Nat said."

"Yeah, well. That'll teach him to mess with my family."

Bless. . . "Look," I said, "I'm really grateful to you for defending my honour and all that, but there was no need for you to get into trouble over it."

"It wasn't your honour," he growled, "it was mine. I don't want people going round thinking I've got a slag for a sister." I'd embarrassed him by thanking him. Inside that hulking rugby-playing exterior there lurks a sensitive soul. Well, sometimes, at any rate. "And there was no trouble. Fozzy basically smacked our wrists and told us not to do it again, and that was that. But

I tell you what; you're better off without Oldfield. Clare told me he was a bastard, and she was right."

"What did he do to her, then?"

"Dumped her by text. Amongst other things. Anyway, there's plenty more fish in the sea, blah blah blah."

"Yeah, that's pretty much what Rube said."

"She's right. Forget him, Flo."

"I already have."

Actually, I blame Ruby for what I did next. For putting the idea into my head: before she'd started going on about Lolita, I hadn't given Max a second thought. Well OK, maybe a second one, but certainly not a third. Now, though, I kept running through events in my mind. Me crashing into him. Him steadying me, taking me outside. Drying my face. Taking me to the pub, and then walking me home. He'd been nothing short of the perfect gent; he'd even apologized for not being able to drive me, explained his car was being serviced. It hadn't mattered to me, it's only a ten minute walk, but he'd still apologized (*and* he hadn't smirked when he'd explained about his car, in that suggestive way lads of my age always do when there's any mention of the word "service"). He'd even been late to his meeting because of me.

It had all been perfectly innocent and respectable, and the least I could do, I concluded, was to ring to thank him.

So far, so reasonable. What it doesn't account for, however, if it was all so innocent, is why I didn't just explain to Mum what had happened – leaving out the actual events with Danny of course, no need to go *that* far – and ask her for his number. But I didn't. Something stopped me; some tiny little doubt in my brain, a protective instinct maybe. Perhaps I realized even then, on a deep subconscious level, that there had been more to our meeting than met the eye. Or perhaps I wanted there to be more, despite my protestations to the contrary to Nat and Ruby.

At any rate, I didn't ask Mum for Max's number. Instead, after my little chat with Hugh, I went downstairs and rifled secretly through the small leather-bound address book that lives beside the telephone in the hall. At first I thought it wasn't there – there was no sign of it in the "C"s, which took up four pages – but I eventually spotted it at the beginning of the "D"s, squashed in as if written in a hurry. No address, but a phone number, and a mobile one too. I started to copy the BT one down, then changed my mind and wrote down the mobile instead. At this time of the evening, I guessed he was more likely to be at home to answer the phone, and determined as I was to ring, I felt suddenly shy at the prospect of talking to him live, as it were. Far better to ring his mobile and leave a message on his voicemail.

It didn't quite happen like that. He picked up his mobile on the first ring.

"Max Cooper." Curt, businesslike, with an upward inflection at the end, as if frequently hassled with queries and accustomed to inviting callers to keep it brief.

I was immediately thrown, couldn't think what to say.

"Hi Max, it's me." Oh, dur. How was he supposed to recognize my voice? He barely knew me. "Flora," I added, into the silence that confirmed he was trying to work out who "me" was.

The silence continued. He'd obviously forgotten me already. So much for Ruby's Lolita theory.

"Florence Wilcox," I said, feeling stupid. What had I been thinking of, ringing him like that?

"Oh, hello," he said. "How are you?"

"I'm fine. That's why I'm calling, actually. To tell you. That I'm fine, I mean." I was burbling. This was ridiculous; I'd only rung to say thanks, and now here I was feeling as nervous as if I was asking him for a date. I took a deep, calming breath. "I just wanted to say thanks."

"What for?"

What *for*? He *had* forgotten!

"For earlier. For being so kind."

"Oh. Right." He sounded perplexed, but not in an amused kind of way. I could imagine him standing there, wherever he was, mobile clamped to ear, scratching his head and thinking *I've got a right one here.*

"I really appreciated it," I added.

"That's OK. Look, can I possibly call you back? It's difficult to talk, I'm in a meeting."

Oh no, not that old chestnut – the meeting cliché. How many times had I heard Dad use that excuse to fend off people he didn't want to speak to?

"Yes, sure," I said, and rung off hastily. I felt stupid: for having crept furtively up to my room to make the call, as if I'd been doing something daring and forbidden; for having called at all. Why on earth had I thought he might have been pleased to hear from me?

Which only goes to show how easy it is to misread situations and people's reactions to them; especially over the phone.

Gran and Grandpa were coming to stay for the weekend, which meant that Mum was having a panic. Let me explain about my father's parents, and my mother's relationship with them: she has this idea that they think she's – well, too good for them, I guess is the simplest way of putting it. Seems back-to-front, doesn't it; I mean, the usual thing with in-laws (or so I'm told) is that they don't think their darling child's partner is good enough. But Dad's parents are working-class and Mum's background is middle-class, or so they both claim, which seems to make her feel she has to be apologetic the whole time for having more than they had, or giving us more than they could give Dad, or some such.

Don't ask me to explain. This whole area of class is foreign to me; I don't understand why so many people get their knickers in such a twist about it. The way I see it, Dad has worked bloody hard to get where he is – editor of local paper, nice big house, etc. etc. – and Gran and Grandpa are proud of him and the fact he did it all without the benefit of university or anything else. And that's it – no resentment, directed at Mum or anybody else. But that's not the way Mum sees it. Not that she's ever said as much. I just know. I can tell by the way she carefully avoids talking in front of them about anything involving money, as if she's desperate not to attract accusations of flashing it about. Like the year she told them about the weekend we'd had in a cottage in Dorset but not the two weeks in Cyprus later, and let them think the Dorset stay was our summer holiday. Like the way she always uses the everyday plates and glasses and stuff when they're staying, and not the posh stuff all other visitors get. Like the way our diet changes when they're around; out go pasta and curry and chilli – normal stuff, in other words – and in come pies and roasts and hearty stews, all home-made, as though she's metamorphosed into a fifties housewife with nothing better to do than spend all day chained to the kitchen stove. I don't think the others even notice: Hattie's too full of her own concerns, and Hugh – well, Hugh's a lad. As long as the food appears on the table at regular intervals, and there's enough of it, he doesn't notice what it is. I sometimes think you could serve up roast rat with onion jam and he'd still shove it down his gullet in thirty seconds flat, look up and say "Mm, great, any more?", just like he always does.

Anyway, Mum's obsessing about the grand-parents' visit on this occasion wasn't about going downmarket in order not to offend them, but about wanting us to play Happy Families. Put simply, it was Gran's birthday over the weekend, and Mum was trying to organize us all to go out for a meal on Friday evening to celebrate.

"No way," said Hugh, immediately.

"Why not?" Two little vertical lines appeared

between Mum's eyebrows; a bad sign, it means she's annoyed but trying to maintain control. She's not much good at maintaining control; I don't know why she doesn't just let rip at the outset and be done with it.

Hugh just gave her one of his oh-for-God's-sake looks. I thought I'd better step in, for the sake of family harmony.

"I don't think going to the Merry Yeoman with the grandparents is Hugh's thing any more," I said, as reasonably as possible. It isn't mine, either, it must be said. The Merry Yeoman is naffness squared, it has wallpaper, carpets and chairs all with different busy patterns, is always packed with the over-60s and families with troops of small yelling children who run about constantly, and serves food like old-fashioned school dinners – roast beef, shepherd's pie, treacle tart, semolina pudding. It's where Gran and Grandpa always insist on going, presumably for the food rather than the ambience.

"And what's so terrible about spending an evening with your grandparents once in a blue moon?" Mum demanded.

"Here we go," Hugh muttered.

"I just think Gran would appreciate it, that's all. It is her birthday."

"Come off it, Ma," he retorted. "She doesn't

want to spend an evening with me. She and Grandpa would only go on like they did last time, about the good old days when lads my age used to wear a shirt and tie to go out of an evening, and why did I want to go and get my eyebrow pierced. Anyway, I'm already going out on Friday. You'll have a much better time without me. You can all slag me off behind my back then," he added, and slipped deftly from the room before any more could be said to him on the subject.

Sensing defeat, Mum turned to me. "How about you, Flora? Will you come, or is the Yeoman too uncool for you now, too?"

What did she mean, *now*? I sighed. "Hugh has got a point, you know, Mum. Their relationship does work best at a distance."

Mum pursed her lips together, what Hugh calls her hen's bottom impression. "They're his *grandparents*," she insisted.

"Yeah, but he's outgrown the doting grandson thing, hasn't he? He is fond of them, in his way, but they do – well, pick on him a bit. Don't they?"

"I'll come out on Friday," Hattie piped up. "I'll always enjoy being with Gran and Grandpa, even when I'm a horrible teenager like Hugh and Flora."

"That's because they give you money," I

growled. "You just suck up to them, it's vomit-inducing. Anyway, I can't come – I've already arranged to go round Nat's on Friday after school."

"Well, thank you, Hattie," Mum said. "I'm sure your grandmother will appreciate having at least one of her grandchildren to celebrate her birthday with." She turned to me. "She's going to be very disappointed, you know, Flora. I really do think you could make an effort, and spend some time with your family rather than your friends for once."

"I'm not going to socialize – we've got English coursework to hand in on Monday. But I'll tell you what. . . " My conscience kicked in – I am still fond of my grandparents, even if the prospect of the Merry Yeoman was too much to handle. ". . .why don't you all go out on Friday as planned, and then we could have a birthday lunch here on Sunday? I'll give you a hand with the shopping and everything. And look, I'll even have a word with Huge and talk him into showing his face. How's that?"

Mum was mollified, but in the event Nat cancelled because she wasn't feeling well. I didn't let on to Mum, though – I knew if I admitted to planning a night in instead she would somehow coax me into joining in with the party, and like Hugh I couldn't face it.

Besides, I still had an essay to finish: I'd got behind with work the past week or so because of all the Danny-related trauma, and the prospect of having the house to myself for once was very tempting. I'd be able to play music very loud without anyone yelling at me to turn it down, have my pick of the leftovers in the fridge, *and* get my head round the complexities of "The Importance of Marriage to Jane Austen's Heroines", all without interruption. What more could a girl ask for?

Gran and Grandpa arrived on Friday evening as planned, and by seven-thirty the house was quiet and empty – all apart from me, that is. I was just settling down to some serious CD-and-snack-choosing when the doorbell rang. I immediately felt uneasy – our house is set well back from the road, a good fifty metres from the next-door neighbours; I was alone, and it was pitch dark outside. Lots of thoughts jostled for position in my brain, none of them pleasant – half-remembered images from horror films I'd enjoyed well enough at the time, visions of schizophrenic stalkers and psychotic serial killers.

Chiding myself for having too much imagination, I peered cautiously down the stairs. I could just make out a shadowy figure standing on the doorstep, illuminated through the stained

dear life, with my mouth hanging open like a carp.

"Um, er, yes," I muttered, trying to rearrange my features so that I resembled half a dork, rather than a total one.

"What a night," he said, indicating the blackness behind him. I could see long shafts of rain lit up in the pool of light spilling from the porch and I realized that his hair was wet, the shoulders of his pale-grey overcoat speckled with damp. I grunted. *Grunted!* Like some kind of farmyard animal. Here was my parents' old friend, metamorphosed on my doorstep into Mr Sex On Legs, and what do I do? Grunt. *That's after I weep all over him a couple of days earlier, of course. Boy. Do I know how to make an impression or what?*

I stepped back into the hallway, opening the door wider.

"You'd better come in." Even to my ears it sounded ungracious. But that's nothing to what came out of my mouth next. "You never rang me back," I said, and then immediately cringed inside as I realized how accusing it sounded. *Oh God! Now he's going to think I'm Miss Teenage Strop. How attractive, how alluring, how—*

"I'm so sorry. You must think I have appalling bad manners," he said. I looked at him with suspicion, thinking he must surely be taking the piss – drawing attention to my impolite behaviour by mentioning his own. But no. He just looked genuinely apologetic. "It's partly why I called round."

"Only partly?" *Buggeration!* I was doing it again! I forced myself to smile: it felt horribly rictus-like, not a smile at all but a grimace. "Look, come on in, don't stand there in the wet, let me take your coat, you must be freezing, would you like a coffee or something?" Now I was going too far the other way, prattling on like I had verbal diarrhoea. Luckily, he didn't seem to notice.

"No, I can't stop – I was just on my way home, but I wanted to drop this off for Julia. Is she around?" He peered round me, and I noticed for the first time the plastic carrier bag he was holding. From Harrods – serious class, just like the flowers he'd sent after the party.

"She's not, I'm afraid. She and Dad have gone out."

He looked really put out, as if he'd set his heart on seeing Mum, and it crossed my mind at that point that he might fancy her. I banished it at once; there was something faintly ludicrous about it, the notion of this wildly attractive guy with a crush on my mum who, much as I love her, isn't really the kind of woman likely to float younger men's boats. She's just not the toyboy type.

"What a shame," he said. "In that case, would you give it to her when she gets back and tell her I called?"

"Sure." I put out a hand and took the bag. "What is it?"

"Just a book we were talking about, I said I'd look it out for her and drop it in next time I was passing."

I looked inside the bag: it was *Bridget Jones's Diary*. "Oh, cool! I loved the film. Can I borrow it after Mum?"

"Of course." He smiled again; it did peculiar things to my insides. "And I really am sorry I didn't call you back, I honestly did mean to but life has been really hectic the past couple of days. Like I said, it's partly why I called round. To apologize."

Miss Teenage Strop disappeared and I regressed even further into Miss Bashful Eleven-Year-Old, going red and staring at the ground. "Oh, that's OK," I muttered, twirling a strand of hair around my index finger.

"So you're fully recovered from the Tosspot Experience now, are you?"

"Pretty much."

"That's good."

He looked at me, and I looked at him, and suddenly neither of us were smiling. He was scrutinizing my face minutely, as if looking for something. I remembered the new and particularly disgusting zit that had appeared on my chin that morning, and put my hand over it.

"Are you sure you wouldn't like a coffee?" I mumbled, to distract him from my acne.

"Positive, thanks. Coffee hypes me up, and I need to chill. Especially after the week I've just had. I'm going home for a huge gin, closely followed by another one." He ran a hand through his damp, dishevelled hair in a gesture that turned my already disordered insides to mush.

I don't know where my next words came from; only that they changed things for ever.

"I don't suppose you feel like some company, do you?"

Well, what can I say? That I felt sorry for him, standing there in the hallway looking rain-splashed and knackered and somehow vulnerable, and that's what made me volunteer to accompany him? I could say that I suppose, but it would be a load of spherical objects, as Nat – who's more ladylike than me – would doubtless say. Fact was, at that moment I fancied him so much I'd have offered to go with him wherever he was planning on going – home, Outer Mongolia, Outer Space. Me, who famously never hits on guys first (whatever

Danny bloody Oldfield might be saying to the contrary), inviting myself to this man's house! When I thought about it later on, back at home and alone in the safely non-judgemental darkness of my room, my brazenness made me squirm with a mixture of horror and excitement.

As it happened, though, we didn't go to Max's. He didn't seem to think me at all brazen, just said that actually, he really didn't feel like drinking by himself and he'd love some company. So I followed him slavishly down the path to his car – a sleek streamlined sporty number with a soft top, squashy leather seats and an unmistakable air of lavish indulgence – and he drove us to a wine bar in town that I'd never even heard of, let alone visited, despite having lived round here all my life. Like Max's car it reeked of luxury and no-expense-spared – all pale wood floor, huge yielding sofas and discreet low-key lighting. I could see why he'd thought the Crown a bit of a come-down, if this was the sort of place he was used to. Two women sitting together on one of the sofas near the door stopped talking as we entered the place, looking at Max with undisguised appreciation, and one of them stubbed out the cigarette she was holding and fluffed up her hair in an unconsciously coy way. Or perhaps it was deliberate flirting. It was only after he sat me down solicitously in an unoccupied corner and went off to the bar to get some drinks that I realized I was still wearing the same clothes as when he'd come ringing the doorbell twenty minutes earlier, my Friday night chill-out uniform of baggy jeans and even baggier sweatshirt. Not only that, but I'd left the hi-fi blaring and the back door unlocked. Mum and Dad were going to go ape, if they got back before me.

Max returned from the bar with a bottle in a wine bucket filled with ice (a wine bucket! – how swank was that) and two glasses which he held upside-down, the stems between his fingers.

"I thought you said you wanted gin?" I said, taking the glasses from him and setting them down on the table.

"Yeah, I know, but I can safely have a couple of glasses of this and still drive. Gin just makes me want to crash out. Chardonnay OK for you? I don't know what you like, but I thought it was a safe enough bet. Even if it is a bit Bridget Jones-y these days."

He grinned at me, and poured wine into the glasses. I took a sip from the one he held out to me; it was astonishingly good, like no wine I'd ever tasted before.

"Mmm, gorgeous," I said, trying to sound as

if I knew all about Chardonnay. "Look, I'm so sorry."

"What on earth for?"

"This." I grabbed a handful of my sweatshirt and pulled a face. "I look pants. I should've got changed first."

"You look fine to me."

"No I don't. Those two –" I indicated with my head the two women by the door, who were still glancing surreptitiously at Max – "they look fine. I look shocking. *Flora is wearing the Bag Lady Look.* It's doing your street cred no good at all, being seen with me."

"You look fine," he repeated. "The bag lady look suits you. I thought it was great, the way you came out just as you were."

"Did you?" I hid my surprise by taking another giant slurp of wine (it really was very moreish). "I bet Venetia never goes out just as she is. She seemed very glam."

"Oh, she is," he agreed. "Glam's her middle name. Just hasn't got much between her ears, unfortunately."

"Ooh, Max, you bitch!" It must have been the wine, I'd never have dared say that kind of thing to him otherwise, but he just grinned again.

"Yeah, I know. Bitchy, but true, sadly."

"So are you still seeing her, then?" There I went again! What was the matter with me? It sounded like I was blatantly checking out his availability. He didn't appear to take it like that, though.

"Nah," he said, wrinkling his nose. *God he looks cute when he does that!* "It was doomed, really. As a relationship, I mean. It was a bit of a rebound thing, to be honest."

"You or her?" I sat up, interested. Did I sense a bit of a history here? *Well of course he's going to have a history, a man of his age!*

"Me. Perhaps her as well, I never got round to asking. To tell you the truth, it was when she said that thing to you at the party about grown-ups that I realized enough was enough."

"Honestly?" I was delighted that he'd thought her remark as pathetic as I had.

"Honestly. I hate it when people say things like that. It's so patronizing – I mean, for heaven's sake," he said mildly, "it's not even as if she's that much older than you."

We caught each other's eye, and there was a tiny beat. He looked away first.

"I guess not," I said, softly.

"So what were you up to when I turned up on your doorstep, then? Obviously not out on the Friday-night razz with your mates." He refilled both our glasses, his voice slightly over-loud.

"I should be so lucky. No: homework."

"How d'you mean?"

I wasn't sure which bit of the word "homework" he didn't understand.

"English coursework," I elaborated. "'The Importance of Marriage to Jane Austen's Heroines'. It's OK, you don't need to say it. Only saddos stay in doing homework on Friday nights."

He looked slightly nonplussed. "So what's the homework for, then?"

"English A-level." My heart sank slightly. Don't say he was going to come over all uncle-y on me. He'd be asking me what I wanted to do when I left school next. "I'm doing three: English, French and Media Studies. I've just remembered – you're in The Meeja, aren't you? Mum told me. Perhaps you can give me some tips."

I was burbling, talking too much to cover how his presence was making me feel, but I suddenly noticed he was sitting stock still with his glass held to his lips, his eyes wide and fixed as if he'd seen something scary.

"Perhaps," he said eventually. His voice sounded quite normal. Perhaps I'd imagined it, then. Maybe someone had come in he hadn't expected to see: an old flame, a blast from his past.

"That'd be cool," I said, turning round to look behind myself. I couldn't see anybody, and anyway, he looked fine again now. Perfectly normal.

"So are the A-levels this year?"

"Next. I'm only Lower Sixth. It's AS this year. Hugh's doing his As this year, though – absolute nightmare, he's getting so stressed about them. Hey, you'll never guess what – you were right about him and that poem. He only went and duffed Danny up over it!"

"Told you. I know about these things." Max raised his glass to his lips and took a slow, careful sip, then set it back down on the table, equally carefully. "So if you're in the Lower Sixth that makes you – what? Sixteen?"

"Seventeen. Last September."

He fiddled with the stem of his glass for a bit and looked away towards the bar, distractedly, as if wondering what he was doing there with me when he could have been at home making inroads into the gin bottle.

"Right," he murmured. "Seventeen, eh – I thought you were older."

"Did you?" I was pleased – well, who doesn't like being thought older? Who under the age of twenty-five, that is, when it seems to reverse for some reason.

"I lost track of time, I guess." He looked back at me, and the crinkly eyes were back in place. "I couldn't remember how old you were when I was working with your dad, but I imagined you must be about nineteen or twenty now."

"Well, there's not that much difference. People often think I'm older, I haven't been asked to prove my age in pubs since I was fourteen."

"You've been going into pubs since you were fourteen?" He sounded alarmed, and I laughed.

"Calm down! Only occasionally. Didn't you used to, when you were young? Younger, I mean," I corrected myself, hastily.

"Can't remember much about when I was young. I'm a *grown-up* now, remember?" He mimicked Venetia, and I laughed again.

So we finished the Chardonnay, although I seemed to drink most of it, and when we got up to leave I noticed the two women by the door watching us again. I indulged in a tiny fantasy that Max and I were a real couple. Well, why not? He was good fun, not to mention drop-dead gorgeous; and anyway, I needed a bit of an ego-boost after the way Danny had treated me. Why shouldn't I go out for a drink with a good-looking man who was good company as well? And that's all it was at that stage, I swear. Just a drink.

I beat everybody back home by a short head. Everybody except for Hugh, that is, who came down the stairs as I shut the front door behind me.

"Cool car," he said. "I saw it from upstairs. I didn't know Nat's dad had a Jag."

"It wasn't Nat's dad. It was Max."

"Who?"

"Max. Max Cooper. Friend of Mum and Dad's from the Good Old Days. You remember, he was at their do on Saturday."

Hugh raised an expressive eyebrow. "Oh yeah? Friend of the parents, eh. Sugar-daddy material, is he?"

I ignored the jibe. "He came round with a book for Mum, and was at a bit of a loose end. So we went out for a drink."

"Well, he has to be a better choice of drinking buddy than Danny 'I'm Too Sexy For My Shirt' Oldfield, doesn't he?"

To tell the truth, I was relieved Mum and Dad weren't back home, as I'd been wondering how I was going to explain away an evening's studying at Nat's without any books. Telling them the truth – that Max had turned up and we'd gone for a drink – just wouldn't have been an option.

Just a drink or not, I couldn't seem to get Max out of my head over the weekend. Thoughts and images of him lurked at the edges of my consciousness, like when you have a strange dream that leaves you feeling edgy and unsettled for a day or two. Not that the thoughts of him were unpleasant; far from it. His hair, his eyes, his mouth. . . (*Oh boy. His mouth.*) It did occur to me that perhaps it wasn't really very – what's the word? – very *savoury*, to be thinking about him in the way I was thinking about him. Not quite nice, as Gran would say. I mean to say: he was, after all, Mum and Dad's friend. Having him constantly occupying my thoughts seemed as unlikely and distasteful as if I'd found out Dad was fantasizing about Nat or Ruby. But I couldn't help it. Max was just *there*, occupying my mind, and there seemed to be nothing I could do about it.

"So what's happening in your life then, Florence?" Grandpa asked me at breakfast-time on Sunday. "Anything exciting?"

"She's going out with Danny Oldfield," Hattie said, squinting sideways at me and spreading a thick layer of butter on a doorstep of toast.

"Who's Danny Oldfield?" Grandpa asked her.

"Mr Sex of the Upper Sixth. Hugh reckons he's working his way through all the girls in the sixth form, just because he knows he can."

Grandpa cleared his throat. "I'm just going to, er, find your father," he said vaguely, getting up from the table. "Something to discuss." And he drifted out of the room.

Gran chuckled. "It's the S-word," she said. "Embarrasses him. Folk of our generation aren't used to discussing such matters in public."

"What S-word?" Hattie asked brightly. "Do you mean sex?"

"You must excuse Harriet," I told Gran. "She was at the back of the queue when tact was handed out."

"Gran doesn't mind me talking about sex," Hattie said. "Do you, Gran?"

"Well, it takes a bit of getting used to," she said, smiling at Hattie. "But I'm naturally nosy, you see, so I make the effort. Anyway, I'm broad-minded."

"You have to be with her," I said. "And for your information, Harriet, you're way out of date. I'm not going out with Danny Oldfield. Not any more."

Hattie scowled. "Why does Gran have to be broad-minded with me?"

"Because you're a total embarrassment."

"No I'm not! You are such a scuzz, Flora."

"And you," I told her, with a sweet smile, "are a sad tragic little person."

"Girls, girls," said Gran, pinching half Hattie's toast from her plate and taking a bite. "No bickering allowed. It's my birthday weekend."

But Hattie was determined to take offence. She pushed her chair back with a toss of her head and flounced dramatically from the room.

I picked up the other toast half and crammed it into my mouth. I hate waste.

"So come on," Gran said, leaning forward, a twinkle in her eye. "Spill the beans about this Danny Oldroyd, then."

"Oldfield," I corrected her, automatically. What could I tell her? Broad-minded she may be, but I doubted she was *that* broad-minded. I thought of Danny jumping me the day after his party, his revelations about what Adam Barnes had said about me – the poem, the implications. Tell my grandmother he'd thought I was easy and then dumped me publicly, so the whole sixth form knew? I thought not.

"Nothing to tell," I said breezily, through the toast crumbs. "He's history."

"So did you blow him off," she asked earnestly, "or was it the other way round?"

"Er, no." She does love to use trendy terminology, does Gran. Trouble is, she doesn't always get it quite right. "No, he dumped me I'm afraid."

"Shame."

"Not really. He was bad news. Hugh tried to warn me, but I didn't listen."

"Too much in love?"

"In lust more like." God, just listen to me. Why was I telling her all this? I'd never divulged this kind of thing to her before.

"Is he a – what's the word you girls use – a hunk?"

"Kind of. Everyone else seems to think so, anyway. Including Danny himself. Not my type though, if I'm honest."

"Aah." Gran nodded, wisely. "Always a mistake, that. Doing things because of what other people would do. Or think you should do."

"You think so?"

"I do, aye. Or not doing them, for that matter. You be true to yourself, my love. That's what counts in this life."

I was intrigued. "It sounds like you're speaking from experience."

"Oh, I am that. Well, you'd expect it, wouldn't you? Old bird like me. More experiences than you can shake a stick at, good and bad."

"So what are we talking about, then? You and Grandpa?"

"Not really. Although there were those who were against us being together."

"Yeah?" I hadn't known. "Why's that?"

"No reason at all, far as we could see. But it was the age thing."

"What age thing?"

"He's eight years older than me."

Max. He sprang into my mind again. Strange, that Gran should be telling me this now, of all times.

"That's not much of a difference."

"We didn't think so, either. Other things matter much more, we thought. You can't help who you fall in love with, after all. We knew we were meant to be together, but others didn't see it that way. See, I was only nineteen when we met, and he was nearly twenty-seven. My parents thought that meant there was something wrong with him, that he'd have been wed years since if he was normal."

"*Normal?*" My voice rose; I couldn't help it. "What on earth d'you mean, normal?"

"Twenty-seven was quite old to still be single in those days. Folk did tend to get married younger then."

"Even so. Implying he was abnormal – that's really harsh."

"I know. That's what I mean, love. About being true to yourself. Here's your grandpa and me now, fifty-odd years down the line." She laughed. "We've proved them wrong, all the nay-sayers, haven't we?"

The timing of our conversation seemed spooky in view of the circumstances, a real coincidence. (Nat always says there's no such thing as coincidences. Synchronicity, she calls it. Yeah, right, Rube and I say. Synchronicity. Whatever.) But it did seem peculiarly appropriate to my situation, even though I kept telling myself there was no situation. *We just had a drink. That's all; just a drink.* And then in he would float again, Max, into my brain, my thoughts, my life. He was seriously messing with my head. There was only one thing for it: Mate Therapy.

chapter seven

Nat was out, but Ruby came round like a shot when I rang her.

"What's the story, then?" she said, once up in my room with fortifying supplies of Red Bull and Pringles. "Bloody hell. Something's put a smile on your face."

I looked in the mirror; she was right. I had this great big cheesy grin spread right across my chops.

"Come on then, babe." She popped a can of Red Bull, leant back against the bed headboard and crossed her legs. "Tell Auntie Ruby who he is."

"God, Rube," I protested. "Talk about a one track mind. Why does it have to be a he?"

She eyed me beadily. "Don't give me that. I know you too well."

"Yeah, OK," I conceded. "You do."

"So, tell me all."

"Well." Where to begin? "He's coolness on legs, and lush like you wouldn't believe."

Ruby grinned approvingly. "So you're, like, over Danny, then?"

"Pretty much."

"So where d'you meet him?"

"Ah. That's the snag." I took the lid off the Pringles and offered them to Ruby, who took a handful absent-mindedly. "He's a friend of my parents."

Ruby snapped her fingers triumphantly. "I knew it! It's the Lolita man. The one who picked you up and brought you back home after your wobbly over Dan the Man and his tacky little poem. I knew there was more to all that than you were letting on. What's his name again?"

"Max. Max Cooper."

She leaned forwards conspiratorially. "So are you seeing him, then, or what?"

"No way!" I protested. "He's out of my league."

"Now Flora." She nibbled her way delicately round the edge of a Pringle. "I keep telling you not to sell yourself short."

"I'm not. He's too classy, too experienced – too everything."

"Too old?"

"Yeah, that too, I suppose." I sighed. "So why do I fancy him so much, when he's not going to look twice at me?"

Ruby pulled a face. "You know that for sure, do you?"

"What?"

"That he's not going to look at you twice."

112

"Well, yeah, it stands to reason. Why should he be interested in someone like me? He's not shown any signs, and I've seen him twice now – socially, kind of thing. No, three times, if you count the parents' party."

"What d'you mean, *socially*? Is that as opposed to anti-socially?"

I ignored that. "I mean, surely I'd know if he fancied me back?"

"I want to know what you mean by socially," Ruby persisted. "When is it you've seen him, exactly?"

I sighed. She's hard work when she's being obsessive. "Once at Mum and Dad's party." I ticked off on my fingers. "Once after that Danny poem thing. And we went out for a drink on Friday night."

"Phew-ee!" Ruby whistled. "Well, that proves it! Why didn't you tell me you'd been out on a date?"

"It wasn't a date," I protested. I tried to tell her how it had been, that he'd just happened to turn up, but she wasn't having any of it. "Anyway, I'm telling you now, aren't I?"

"You've been out for a drink together, that means he's interested."

"I don't think so." I was sceptical. I can usually spot interest from twenty paces, and I hadn't sensed any from Max. Not the type of interest we were discussing, at any rate.

"Look, think about it. He's older than you, right?"

"Right."

"Fun?"

"Yeah."

"More experienced?"

"Of course he is – he's older than me."

"Loaded?"

"Looks like it – well, maybe not *loaded*, exactly, but—"

Ruby held up a silencing hand. "And doesn't exactly resemble the back end of a bus?"

"No, he's gorgeous, like I said."

"So why, pray, would he choose to spend his Friday night having a drink with you if he's not interested? I mean, the way you describe him he sounds like a cross between Robbie Williams and Hugh Grant – a man like that's bound to have women queuing round the block for the chance to have a crack at him."

"Actually," I mused, "he does look a bit like Hugh Grant, now you come to mention it. A much younger version. More articulate, too. Max doesn't do all that mumbling stuff."

"Flora," Ruby said, leaning towards me, "you are missing the point."

"Ruby." I leant forwards too. "What is the point?"

"The point is, and I'm surprised you need me to tell you." She crammed the rest of the Pringles into her mouth and made me wait while she crunched on them noisily. "The point is, what are you going to do about it?"

I blinked. "How d'you mean?"

Ruby sighed impatiently. "What. Are. You. Going. To do. About it," she repeated slowly, as if to an imbecile.

"Yeah, I heard what you said, I just didn't understand what you meant. Why should I do anything about it?"

"Are you serious? Robbie-Hugh Williams-Grant sweeps you off your feet, takes you out for a drink, and you don't know if you should do anything about it? Go for it, girlfriend! Get in there, quick, before somebody else beats you to it!"

I looked at her, part of my brain ticking away all by itself. The part Max had been inhabiting for the past forty-eight hours.

"Do you think I could?" I said at last.

"Of course you could! You're gorgeous too, don't forget."

"Oh Ruby, I never knew you cared."

"Of course I care; you're my mate. I care that a bastard like Danny Oldfield has been giving you grief, and I think it's time your luck changed."

"Yeah, but. . ." I hadn't even considered what she was suggesting. As far as I'd been concerned, my preoccupation with Max could only possibly be one-sided. It had never occurred to me that the attraction might be mutual, and I certainly hadn't been thinking how I might develop it further. Not until that moment; until Ruby had sown the seed. "Do you think I should?"

"Do I think you could, do I think you should," Ruby said, raising her eyes heavenwards. "Never mind what I think. What do *you* think?"

"I think," I said, slowly, "that I can't get him out of my mind. That nobody's ever affected me like this before. That's what I think."

"Then there's your answer." Ruby chuckled. "Want to know what I think? He's not going to know what's hit him!"

Why is it I always think of loads more to say to my mates after they've gone home? No sooner had Ruby gone sashaying down the path than I thought of a million and one things I wanted to ask her. Like, why was it that impossible things seemed possible when I was with her, but preposterous once she'd left. Like, just how did she think I was going to make my move on Max, exactly. Like, how on earth was I supposed to face him again afterwards, when he called to see

116

my parents, if he did what I thought was inevitable, namely laugh in my face. How could I cope if he did that?

"Oh Rube," I sighed to myself, "you have this talent for setting cats amongst pigeons, and then scarpering and leaving the poor little sods to fend for themselves."

I couldn't even ring her – my mobile needed a new top-up card, and there was no way I was having *that* kind of conversation on the other phone. E-mail, I decided; that's the thing, and headed off for the computer.

Hattie was on it, tapping away on the keyboard. She started, guiltily, and the picture on the monitor diminished and shrank to the bottom of the screen as she pressed Minimize.

"What's that?" I asked her, curious. "What were you up to?"

"Nothing," she mumbled.

"Yes you were. If it was nothing, why don't you want me to see it?"

I craned my neck, and the screensaver burst into life.

"C'mon Hat – fess up. Were you looking at something smutty on the Net?"

It seemed unlikely, and more Hugh's province than my sister's, but her face turned crimson.

"Ooh, you little raver! What was it, then – Super Studs On Parade?"

The crimson deepened. "Piss off, Flora," she muttered. "You don't know anything."

I don't often manage to embarrass Hattie; it was deeply satisfying. I leant across her, swiped the mouse from under her hand and clicked on Restore. The image that filled the screen, far from being Super Studs, was quite clearly a chatroom.

"Oho!" I crowed. "So this is what you've been up to when you've been pretending to do homework, is it? So what's the site, then – Pre-Teen Dur-Brains Exchanging Fatuous Observations?"

Hattie snatched the mouse from my grasp. "You think you're so clever, don't you?"

I considered her question carefully. "No," I said. "I know I'm so clever. Unlike you. Mum and Dad'll throw a mental if they find out you've been visiting chatrooms on the sly. You know what they think of them."

"That's because they don't know anything about them. They just assume there's something wrong with them. It's not chatrooms that's the problem, it's the people who visit them."

"Exactly."

"You know what I mean. You're not going to tell on me, are you?"

"Dunno." I shrugged. "Depends."

"God, Flora," Hattie complained, "you're such a *teacher*!"

"Yeah, sure I am," I agreed, unperturbed, "and you're such a – oh no, Hattie! You're not really Britney, are you? Tell me it isn't true!"

She looked where I was looking, at the list of participating names on the right-hand side of the chat screen, and flushed again.

"So?" she said, defensively. "I can call myself whatever I like. I can be whoever I want. It's the whole point of chatrooms."

"Yeah – that's what Mum and Dad are worried about," I pointed out. "Look, far as I'm concerned, you can do what you like. You can make contact with all the pervs in the whole of Southern England if you want – just don't come running to me for backup when Mum and Dad find out. Now shift – you've been on here long enough, and I want to send an e-mail."

Slightly to my surprise she did as she was told. I was half-tempted to log back on to the chatroom site and become Britney myself, but I couldn't really be bothered. Sounding out Ruby's advice on the Max situation was far more important, and besides, I told myself, Hattie was too judgemental and too naturally suspicious of her fellow human beings to endanger herself in a chatroom. Which only goes to show, I guess, how little I know my sister.

Once alone, I dashed off a quick mail to Ruby – *Re Max – How to proceed? Please advise asap! F x :)* – and hit Send and Return. A new one appeared in my Inbox, as brief as the one I'd just sent to Rube and so totally unexpected that I sat in shock in front of the screen long after I'd read it and absorbed its contents.

Great evening on Fri, thanks for your company!
Hope the school work is going well.
Love Max
PS: How about dinner some time?

It was as if that e-mail was the green light I'd been waiting for. Having him contacting me first was a huge shock, but I felt a bubbling excitement as well, as if I was on the verge of a big adventure. All I had to do was take the next step, respond to his mail, agree to a date, and off we'd go. Like a rollercoaster ride. I even had the accompanying butterflies in my stomach. It was all so thrilling and unexpected that it never occurred to me to wonder how he'd got hold of my e-mail address.

I kept hearing Ruby's words: "he's not going to know what's hit him". It was almost as if he'd overheard our conversation and this was his way of proving her point – that he was indeed interested in me. *How about dinner some time.* *Love Max.* All thoughts of a relationship between us being impossible had gone, flown out of the window; after the way he'd filled my mind over that weekend, not only did I want him, but I wanted to prove that I could get him. *I'm young, I kept telling myself, I'm single, I'm available – how can he resist?*

I could go on about how long I sat in front of that computer before finally replying to his e-mail; about how I wondered as to his motivation for suddenly asking me out like that, about how I felt during the intervening week before seeing him again, about how I instinctively kept both the fact of our meeting and my growing feelings for him a secret from everybody – absolutely everybody – without really knowing why. But I won't go on about all of that. I'll just cut to the chase.

I'd suggested meeting up on the Friday evening at the same wine bar as before, mainly because I didn't want Mum and Dad to see him turning up to collect me – it was a measure of how much my own motivation had changed that, whereas before I'd just instinctively felt they would disapprove, I now *knew* they would, without a shadow of a doubt. I wasn't surprised when Max didn't insist on picking me up, but just went along with my proposal. Apart from a small flurry of e-mails between us to confirm plans and times, we had no other contact during the week; and as I sat in the taxi that carried me to him, in my carefully-chosen Miss Sophisticate ensemble, I have to confess to a brief moment of panic. *What the hell am I doing?* I asked myself. But then the taxi pulled up outside the wine bar, and I didn't have time for panic.

I was late – not intentionally, the cab just hadn't turned up on time – and Max was already there. It was only half-past seven, the place hadn't hotted up yet, and I could see him standing at the bar. Even though it was only his back view I knew instantly it was him, and my stomach contracted with desire. He turned, saw me and smiled, and I had to flex my thigh muscles to stop my knees from giving way. I know, I know – corny or what – but it was the oddest sensation. I'd never felt it before.

"Hi," he said, coming over. "What would you like to drink? I've booked a cab for eight thirty to take us to the restaurant, so we've plenty of time."

"No Jag tonight?" Even though it solved the dilemma about me getting home without the parents noticing the flash car and asking awkward questions, I couldn't help feeling a tiny bit disappointed. The only car-owning lad I'd been out with up to then was Adam Barnes (apart from Danny, of course, and I wasn't counting him), and he drove a clapped-out old Golf. Not quite as much cachet as a Jag, somehow.

Max shook his head. "I want a drink. Safer not to risk driving."

"Ooh, Max," I teased him. "So socially responsible!"

He didn't laugh back, and I felt a pinprick of – what? Mild alarm, I think. Which increased with what he said next.

"Should I get you a soft drink?"

"You're joking!" I pulled a face. "I'll have some wine, please. Some of that Chardonnay we had before, if that's OK. You can't come to a wine bar and drink soft drinks!"

"It's just –" Here it came. The under-age lecture. I hadn't thought he was like that. "You are only seventeen. I don't want your dad to accuse me of leading you astray."

He smiled, to soften what he'd said, but I was stung. It felt like he was pulling rank, implying that he knew best because he was older than me.

"You didn't say that last week," I accused him. "You were pouring wine down my throat like it was going out of fashion then."

"That's before I knew how old you are," he said, softly, and our eyes met. He held my glance for a fraction of a second longer than was comfortable.

"It's no big deal." I shrugged. "I'll be eighteen in six months. All my friends have a drink now and then – it doesn't mean we're turning into closet alkies."

So I got my Chardonnay, but in a glass rather than a bottle this time because Max was on the gin. He had three large ones by the time the taxi came to take us to the restaurant; not that he seemed drunk or anything, but I couldn't help noticing how much he was putting away. Probably had a bad week, I thought, as the cab took us off to where we were eating.

Max had booked a table at a little Italian pizzeria that was so smoky we could barely see across the room. It had drippy candles stuck in old Chianti bottles on the tables, giant displays of artificial fruit stuck to (for some reason) a fishing net suspended from the ceiling, and a huge and deeply horrid mural of an Italian fishing village painted across the longest wall. When the waiter showed us to our table he had to clear the dirty plates away before we could sit down, and the checked red tablecloth was sprinkled with salt and stained here and there with red wine.

Max pulled a face as we sat down, and asked the waiter to change the cloth.

"Shades of the Crown," I whispered to him, across the table.

"Sorry?" he said, frowning. He seemed distracted. "What crown?"

"The Crown and Anchor. The pub, you know." Light still didn't dawn. I elaborated. "Where we went? After the Tosspot Experience?"

"Oh, right, yes. Sorry. Look, d'you mind if I smoke?"

I hadn't known he did. I felt another twinge of something unpleasant – disappointment, let-down. The evening wasn't turning out quite as I'd anticipated.

"Course not, go ahead."

He shook out a cigarette from a pack of a brand I didn't recognize, and lit it. He seemed a bit more focussed after a couple of good drags – maybe that had been the problem, nicotine withdrawal.

"I don't really do this any more," he commented, waving the cigarette, as if reading my mind. "I gave up years ago. I just went out and bought some during the week. I'm ashamed of myself, to tell the truth."

"Had a hard week?" I sympathized. So I'd been right about that, then.

"You could say that, yeah." He took a couple more drags and then mashed it out in the ashtray. "Look, I'm sorry about this place. I've never been here before, but a work colleague recommended it."

"Is this a colleague who hates you?"

He laughed. "You'd think so, wouldn't you?"

"It's OK. It's fine." *It's just nice to be with you.* I just stopped myself saying it, wanting to play it cool. I didn't want him to cotton on to how I had been feeling about him – not yet.

"I thought it'd be a pretty safe bet," he went on. "You know – pizza."

"How d'you mean?" Now it was my turn to frown. I felt myself becoming defensive. "Are you saying you thought, hey, all teenagers like pizza, let's take Flora there?"

"Of course not." He half-reached across the table, as if to take my hand, then changed his mind and withdrew it. "I didn't mean that at all. I just meant, most people like pizza."

I looked at him, right into his eyes, to try and determine whether he really had been implying something about my age again, or if I was just being over-sensitive. Then he smiled at me, and somehow it didn't matter. Being in his company was enough, and having him look at me like that. As if I was the most important and fascinating person in the world.

"OK," I conceded. "You're right. Most people do. I do, at any rate."

"I absolutely don't think of you as a teenager, you know. I have to keep pinching myself to remember that you're only seventeen."

"Yeah?" I was ridiculously pleased, even more

so than when he'd first told me I looked older.

"Yeah. And I'll tell you something else."

"What's that?"

He leaned closer to me, across the table. "You look really nice tonight. I should have told you at the wine bar, but—"

"I didn't give you the chance," I interrupted him, and tutted. "Typical me, that is – too busy being defensive to let a guy compliment me."

And suddenly the tension between us that had been there from the beginning was gone. The tackiness of the pizzeria didn't matter any more – it was as if we'd begun the evening again, and it was just so good to be spending time with him. Time we'd planned, rather than accidental time, as our previous meetings had been. It seemed so natural – *normal* – to be with him that I even forgot about how bloody attractive he was, until he smiled again or looked into my eyes with those deep brown melting pools of his (forget treacle toffee; this was serious Mills & Boon stuff) and I just melted all over again. I'd never felt this way before about anybody – both completely relaxed and light-headed with the nearness of him, that magical combination of genuinely enjoying his company and fancying him like mad. I suppose that's on account of me having only been out with boys before, and Max was, oh to hell with sounding cheesy, one hundred per cent man.

I was enjoying myself so much that I totally forgot about my conversation with Ruby and subsequent virtual deal with myself to net him. What I mean is, I wasn't sitting there flirting, or judging the right time to make my move, or anything like that. It never even occurred to me – like I said, it just felt natural to be in each other's company, as if we'd known each other for years. (Which I suppose we had, in a manner of speaking.) He seemed to be having a good time too; his distraction had vanished, he was chilled and relaxed, and great fun to be with. Which made what happened at the end of the evening, after he'd paid the bill (ever the gent) and escorted me out on to the pavement to find a cab, even more baffling.

It was one of those odd moments when the conversation just seems to dry up. Having been really animated with each other all evening, it was like we'd both run out of steam at exactly the same moment.

"Well," he said, after an awkward gap of what felt like five minutes but was probably only thirty seconds, tops. "Better get you home, I guess."

"Yeah." God knows what made me say what I did next. I still wonder whether things might have turned out differently if I'd kept my big gob shut and just rode out the awkwardness. "Max, can I see you again?"

The silence this time was truly deafening. It was too dark to see the expression on his face, but I could take a pretty good guess.

"I don't think so," he said, at last. Softly – sadly, almost. Though why *he* should be sad at knocking me back, I didn't know. "I don't think it would be a good idea."

It was no good – I had to ask, didn't I? "Why not?"

His face was illuminated by a passing car, briefly, the twin headlights reflected in his eyes.

"You know why not, Flora," he said.

"I'm too young, right?" It was a challenge.

"No, sweetheart. You're not too young. I'm too old."

"No you're not!" I burst out. "Anyway, what does age matter? We had a good time this evening, didn't we? *Didn't* we?"

I was pushing it, pushing him, all my usual playing-it-cool tactics with lads and dates forgotten, submerged under my overwhelming feelings of rejection and disappointment and, most of all, injustice. I couldn't help only being seventeen.

"Yes," he replied, quietly. "We did. I certainly did, at any rate."

"I thought you liked me."

"I do like you. Very much."

"So why can't we—"

"Flora," he interrupted me firmly, "the reason we can't see each other again is partly *because* we had such a nice time this evening, *because* I like you."

It made no sense to me. "What do you mean?"

"How old do you think I am?"

"Oh Christ," I groaned, "please, don't rub it in. You've made your point."

"How old?" he persisted. "It's important."

"How should I know?" I was getting angry now. "Twenty-three, twenty-four?"

He laughed, but it wasn't an amused laugh. "Not even close," he said grimly. "I'll be thirty in July."

He couldn't have startled me more if he'd told me he was a mature-looking twelve.

"Thirty?" I whispered, stunned. "That means you're—"

"Thirteen years older than you. Exactly. That's why I can't see you again, even though tonight has without question been one of the best evenings I can remember for a long time."

"But it doesn't matter." I could tell I was on a losing wicket, even though I meant every word. Every bloody word. "Age isn't important. Not when people get on as well as we do. Think

130

about it, Max. Think about what it's been like when we've spent time together. Think about this evening. It wasn't just good, was it? It was really special."

He turned his head away from me, and I knew I'd blown it.

"I knew it was a mistake," he said. "Sending you that e-mail. I shouldn't have suggested meeting up like this."

"So why did you go through with it?"

"I didn't want to stand you up. It didn't seem kind – you'd have thought you'd done something wrong."

"Oh right. So what am I supposed to be thinking now, then?" I was close to tears – stupid, little-girly, *needy* tears.

"I'm sorry. I truly am. Nothing you can say will make me feel worse about it than I already do." He raised a hand and hailed a passing cab. It pulled in to the kerb next to us. "But it's for the best. It couldn't have worked out between us."

And he helped me in to the cab, slammed the door shut and was gone, walking away fast into the damp, drizzling dark.

chapter eight

Perversely, it was only then, after I couldn't have him any longer, that I realized how much I wanted him. Somewhere along the line it had ceased to be anything to do with what Ruby had said to me, or what I'd said to myself. Although I'd never guessed just how much older than me he actually was, the age gap didn't matter to me. I'd really thought that meal was the start of something important, I'd felt the attraction between us so strongly; but Max had made it quite plain that it was the beginning and the end. And I didn't see how on earth I was going to be able to do a damn thing about it. How do you force somebody to see you, to have a relationship with you, when they don't want to? Answer – you can't.

To make matters worse, and with typical little-sister lack of sensitivity, Hattie was a total pain over the next couple of days. Everybody else seemed to sense I wasn't exactly feeling hunky-dory about life (possibly something to do with the way I kept shutting myself away in my room, playing profoundly gloomy music) and kept enquiries to a minimum, but not Hattie. Oh no. She wouldn't notice anyone being down about something until they topped themselves from misery under her nose. Everywhere I turned, there she was – making stupid comments, gurning in the background, just generally getting in my hair.

"What's the matter with you?" she asked me eventually, standing in my bedroom door, on the Sunday evening. Forty-eight hours after The Great Knock-back.

"Nothing I want to share with you," I growled, from the depths of my duvet.

"Ooh, Flora – is it the time of the month?"

I felt like hitting her. "What would you know about that?" I demanded. "You're just a kid. Anyway, for your information, no it's not."

"A boy then," she declared loftily, with all the benefit of her twelve years' experience of these things. "It must be a boy. I don't know why you let them get to you so much."

I thought of Max, for the umpteenth time. "It's definitely not a boy," I said. "Why don't you just sod off back to your little pals in the chatroom, *Britney,* and leave me alone?"

That did the trick. Off she flounced, muttering stuff about not being a kid, and left me to my thoughts. They weren't exactly great company. I tried ringing Ruby and Nat but they

133

were out, their mobiles switched off. Then into my head came an idea, though from where heaven alone knows because there was no precedent. I decided to ring Gran. *She'll understand,* I told myself; *she'll be able to advise me whether to persevere with Max, or cut my losses and run. I don't need to say who he is – just that he's older. She'll identify with that.*

But, wouldn't you just know it, Gran was out too.

"She's away for the weekend," Grandpa told me, down the line from Durham. "Out on a spree with her friends from Bingo, spending all my money." He chuckled. I felt horribly let-down, although her not being there was hardly his fault. Neither was it hers – she wasn't to know I was going to ring, was she?

"Do you know when she'll be back?"

"Haven't a clue. Is everything all right, Florence, pet? You sound down."

I was tempted, just for a moment, to confide in him instead; but then I remembered how embarrassed he'd been when they were staying just by idle talk of boyfriends, and stopped myself in the nick of time. *Phew. Lucky escape.* What had I been thinking of, to even consider offloading on to Gran and Grandpa? I didn't want to risk even telling my parents about Max, let alone my grandparents. How could they possibly understand? When all was said and done, they were just too old.

I told Grandpa that I was fine and would catch up with Gran later, and hung up. Just then, bang on cue, the bedroom door opened, and Mum popped her head round it.

"Knock knock," she said. I hate it when she says that. It's as if it exempts her from actually knocking, like she's respecting my privacy when in actual fact she isn't.

"What is it?" I said. That did it, I'd never fob her off now. I should have just ignored her, then she'd have got the message and gone away.

Sure enough, she came in and sat down beside me on the bed.

"What's wrong, Flora?" she asked me. "It's not like you to shut yourself in here for so long."

"Nothing," I sighed. "Just having an off-day, that's all. If that's allowed."

"It's more like an off-weekend," she pointed out. "I'm worried about you."

"No need. I'm fine."

"You're not fine, love. Look at you. Hattie's worried too. She said you were all wrapped up in your duvet and just lying on the bed."

"Oh, *Hattie*," I repeated, scornfully. "Since when has she cared about anyone except herself?"

Mum looked at me, hard, but I could see the

anxiety behind her eyes. "Have you been – well – doing anything you want to tell me about?"

I sighed, and sat up reluctantly. "Is this the drugs talk? It's OK, Mum – honestly. I can get pissed off with life without drugs having to be involved, you know."

"I know." She patted my hand, awkwardly, trying to reassure me, "I didn't mean drugs. I just wondered if you wanted to talk about whatever it was that's bothering you."

"I'm fine," I repeated, and got up and went over to my desk in an attempt at ending the conversation. I knew she was only trying to help but I didn't see how she could, unless she was going to offer to ring Max and persuade him that he and I really should become an item, and that was likely, wasn't it? Not. She didn't seem convinced that I really was all right, but took the hint nevertheless. After a few more comments of the "well-if-you're-sure" variety, she went and left me to it.

It was then that I decided I'd had enough of drooping around uselessly. I'd had Mum and Hattie both on my case, as well as bothering Grandpa needlessly. It was time to *do* something about it. So I found Max's mobile number once more, sent him a short but to-the-point text message asking him to get in touch with me urgently, and drew an emphatic line under the weekend by going to bed.

Max was waiting for me after school on Monday, standing in his designer suit outside the main entrance with his top shirt button undone and an anxious expression on his face. He was absolutely the last person I was expecting to see at school, so out of context that for a moment I didn't recognize him. When I did, I couldn't make out why he was there.

"I'm parked round the corner," he told me. "I didn't know whether I'd be able to spot you." He indicated the stream of kids pouring through all the doors and surging across the tarmacked car park.

"What's wrong?" I could only imagine there must be something wrong for him to turn up out of the blue like that. "Is it Mum or Dad?"

"No," he said, and frowned. "You texted me, didn't you? Last night? I thought it was easier to come and see you rather than ring."

We walked rather hurriedly to where he'd parked the car. Whatever I'd expected his response to my text to be, it hadn't been this. I felt strangely revved-up, as if something exciting was about to happen, and as I got in I was aware of the curious and admiring glances of some of the lads from school as they checked out the Jag.

"Thank God you're not wearing school uniform, anyway," Max said, as I threw my bag into the back and climbed in beside him. "I was rather dreading you might be."

I didn't understand what he meant. He gunned the engine into life, and we pulled away.

"Sixth-formers can wear what they like," I told him. It seemed utterly bizarre to be sitting next to him in his car in the middle of the day, straight from school, talking about school uniform. I couldn't imagine why on earth he'd come. "So where are we going?" I asked him, brightly.

"Let's go for a coffee," he said, and then almost immediately, "Oh hell, no, let's not. Let's just go and sit somewhere quiet. Somewhere we can talk."

So that's what we did, drove out to a half-built business park miles away from town and found a brand-new office block right at the far end. We sat there in his car in the middle of the empty car park, and he switched off the ignition.

"I can't stop thinking about you," he said, all at once.

I blinked, startled. It was weird, totally unexpected – as if he was speaking my lines, the words that had been playing in my head, over and over. "How d'you mean?"

Max passed a hand over his eyes, wearily, but didn't look at me.

"I can't get you out of my mind. Everything I do, you're there. I've tried to forget you, but I can't. It's doing my head in."

"But. . ." Whatever I'd been expecting him to say, it certainly hadn't been that. I was utterly nonplussed, and couldn't think how to respond. "But what about what you said the other night? About being too old for me?"

He said a lot more then, about wanting to do the right thing by me and trying to deny his feelings, and as it slowly dawned on me what he was saying I could feel a grin sliding across my face, as sweet and satisfying as syrup melting on a pancake.

"But that's fantastic!" I exclaimed. "It's exactly how I've been feeling!"

"It's not fantastic." He looked at me then. "It's not fantastic at all. I'm thirteen years older than you. But I can't pretend any more."

I could scarcely take in what he was saying. It seemed inconceivable, too good to be true. Never in a million years had I imagined that someone like him could be feeling like this about someone like me, no matter what Ruby had said.

"So are you saying you've got feelings – for me, I mean?"

"Feelings?" He gave a short laugh. "Yeah – sure I've got feelings. I've had feelings ever since I saw you at your parents' house-warming, and wondered who the beautiful girl was. Even when I realized who you were, Roger and Julia's daughter, the penny still didn't drop. I'd lost track of time – I thought you were older."

"But Max – my age doesn't matter, don't you see? What you're saying, it's exactly what I've been feeling too!" I leaned towards him excitedly, sideways, and put out a hand to touch his face. He caught my wrist before I made contact.

"Of course it matters," he said, roughly. "I've been feeling like some kind of pervert, ever since I found out how old you are. And you can bet your life your parents will think it matters," he added.

I still don't know what made me say or do what I did next, where it came from. It was as if I was acting out a scene in a film I'd seen, long ago. All I know is, it felt absolutely right.

"I don't give a shit," I said softly, "about what my parents think matters. It's how we feel that counts."

And I put my other hand up to his face, gently, and drew it to mine, and kissed him.

He pulled away after a few seconds. "Flora," he muttered, "oh Flora. Flora."

I wanted to laugh out loud with happiness.

"Oh Max, Max," I teased him. "What's wrong? Don't you like it?"

"Oh yes. I like it," he said, and pulled me back to him and kissed me again, only not gently like the first time. Not gently at all.

Well. What can I say? That it was amazing, unimaginable? That the most I'd dared hope for was that Max might answer my text and agree to come out for another date or two, and that suddenly finding myself sitting in his car listening to him telling me all this and kissing him – I mean, my God, *snogging* him – was completely beyond anything I'd dared hope for? All of that, and more. He'd been thinking the same things as me, feeling the same feelings – it was incredible. In-bloody-credible. Yet, apparently, true.

We clung to each other as though we were drowning, for who knows how long. Eventually, he drew away from me. My mouth felt sore, my lips bruised with passion.

"We have to think if we can make this work," he said, carefully. "We need to talk about it."

"OK," I said. "Let's talk!" I was dizzy, light-headed with joy; I'd never felt like this before with anybody, like we fitted together so perfectly. I just knew everything was going to be all right –

how could it be wrong, when we both felt like this about each other?

"You say you've been feeling the same way?" He wasn't looking at me again, was sitting with his hands carefully placed on the steering wheel, looking straight ahead through the windscreen.

"Can't you tell?" I demanded. "Or do you think I just snog anybody who comes along and picks me up after school?"

"No, of course not. I'm sorry." He inclined his head slightly, contrite, but still didn't look at me. "But this is important. I don't want to get it wrong."

So to make him feel better I told him everything, about the effect he'd had on me when he'd turned up on my doorstep that evening, about how I'd been able to think of nothing but him since.

"It's been the same with me," he told me. "Since I saw you at that party. You were lit up, glowing – I couldn't take my eyes off you. Then when we bumped into each other and you told me what had happened with your boyfriend I thought this is it, it's a sign, the way is clear for me. But at the back of my mind has always been the fact that you're Roger's daughter – I didn't want to go rushing in like a bull at a gate with you, I wanted to get to know you in a subtle kind of way, but I couldn't think how. I was getting desperate. I felt like a lovesick fool, if you want to know the truth. So that's why I ended up coming round with that stupid bloody book."

"What – Bridget Jones? I thought you'd brought it round for Mum."

"I'd gone out and bought it that day. It was just an excuse to see you. I told you, I was desperate – I thought I might just catch a glimpse of you in passing. I never thought you'd be there by yourself, or that we'd end up going for that drink." He regarded me solemnly. "And I certainly didn't expect you to tell me you were only seventeen."

"I didn't know, Max. I knew the thoughts I was having about you, but I never thought you might be feeling the same way. Why didn't you just tell me? We could have skipped all this, we could have avoided wasting all this time." I reached for him again; he was so gorgeous, I just wanted to touch him, to kiss him again, but he fended me off once more.

"If we're going to take this further I need you to know that I'm serious. That it's not just a physical thing."

"How do you mean?"

"I feel such a connection with you. We're on the same wavelength. You don't seem only seventeen – I have a niece who's sixteen, and you're so different from her. She seems a little girl by comparison. I feel – I feel *alive* when I'm with you. But ever since you told me how old you are I've been feeling like a total sleaze, lusting after my ex-colleague's teenage daughter. I have to keep reminding myself that it's not like that, that it's not just the –" he moved his hands apart, made a sweeping gesture – "the peripherals, although the peripherals are very nice of course. Oh hell, I'm burbling again. I sound like a computer salesman." He passed a hand across his eyes. "What I'm trying to say is, it's you as a person I'm attracted to – the whole Flora. And I need to know that it's the same for you. Otherwise I don't think I can go through with it."

"Go through with what?"

He looked into my face, deep into my eyes. "You know what, Flora."

A little thrill passed through me, of lust and excitement, and fear too. Fear of what, I didn't know. The unknown, probably. Nothing like this had ever happened to me before, and I didn't have a clue how we were going to proceed. All I knew was that I wanted to, in a way I'd never wanted anything before.

"Yes," I told him. "Yes, I know what. And yes, it is the same for me."

"I was so sure you were going to tell me to get lost," he went on. "When I sent you that e-mail,

I mean. I spent hours composing it. Hours, for – what? A couple of sentences? Trying to get the tone right. Whether I should put 'love' or 'best wishes' at the end. And shilly-shallying about whether I should actually send it, and then after I'd sent it, convincing myself that you'd ignore it, that you'd be wondering how on earth I'd got your e-mail address; think I was some nutter, stalking you."

Of course, he was right: I'd never sent him an e-mail for him to reply to.

"So how did you get it, then?"

He laughed, guiltily. "When you answered the door to me that time, you were carrying a whole pile of papers. I don't suppose you remember, but you put them down on the hall table when I handed you the book. There was an e-mail for you on top – I just happened to notice it."

"And you memorized my address?" From just one glance – I was impressed.

"Well, Funky Flo at Yahoo isn't especially hard to remember. It's very you." He smiled at me then, his customary warm crinkly-eyed Max-like smile, and my heart turned over. Not to mention my insides. He took my hand. "Are you terribly shocked by all these revelations?"

"I'm not shocked at all. I think it's brilliant."

"And are we going to go through with this?"

"I'm game if you are." I smiled back at him.

"Even though I'm practically old enough to be your father?"

It was my turn to laugh. "Come off it, Max! You'd have to have been a pretty young starter to be my father."

"There's still a huge age gap. That's why I tried to put a stop to it, after we'd had that meal; although I thought I'd already blown it, to be honest. That awful Italian place, and you getting in a strop about pizza being for teenagers." He grinned at me. "But then we ended up having such a good evening, and when you asked to see me again. . ." He shook his head. ". . .I suddenly felt really bad about what I was doing. I felt I had to end it, before we got in too deep. I didn't want you to get drawn in to something that was going to be difficult for us. We're bound to come up against some opposition from other people, like it or not. They're going to think it's wrong."

I thought of Gran, of what she'd told me about her and Grandpa. I leant towards Max, and touched his leg. I felt his thigh muscles contract beneath my hand, and lust jumped within me again.

"We can't help who we fall in love with," I said slowly, holding his gaze as I spoke. "I've already told you, I don't care what other people think. Let them think what they like. We know the truth; we know that the feelings we've got for each other are special. Don't we?"

And then we fell on each other again; and I knew that whatever happened, we were going to be all right.

chapter nine

You know those fairy tales you read when you're little, about wishes being granted and dreams coming true? That's exactly how I felt when Max and I got together. I was wafting round in a state of continuous joy, blissed-out, and everything around me seemed oddly dreamlike – brighter, clearer, more vivid.

Yeah, yeah, I know. I know it makes me sound as if I was taking mind-altering substances, or at the very least like I'm some kind of dumb man-centred airhead. But I wasn't taking anything, and I'm not. An airhead, I mean. I have plans for my life: A-levels, university. Interesting job. Don't get me wrong. I'm not a swot – I mean I like to think I have balance in my life – but, unfortunate episode with Danny Oldfield notwithstanding, I'd never allowed men to come between me and my focus for my future. Yet here I was now, floating along on Cloud Nine, or possibly even Cloud Ten, a fully-fledged member of the Loved-Up Club, and all because of S-E-X.

Before I go any further, I have to make it plain

that I never thought Max was doing anything wrong. Not once. Although his own instincts apparently told him that, given the difference between our ages, coming on to me was somehow sleazy – he kept using that word, sleazy – I never felt there was anything remotely improper in us having a relationship. How could there be? He wasn't a figure of authority, a teacher, or a doctor, or whatever. He hadn't seduced me – quite the reverse, in actual fact. Look at how I'd fallen on him in his car, and how he'd tried to hold me at bay. And besides, I never felt he *had* been coming on to me: it seemed to me that I had been doing all the running, and all the attendant agonizing because, up to the moment he confessed all to me, I'd genuinely had no idea he had been feeling the same way. But now he'd made his feelings quite plain, and all I knew was that this lovely, funny, completely respectable, totally *gorgeous* guy, who I'd believed thought of me fondly, like an uncle (if at all), couldn't get me out of his head. I mean to say, how flattering is that? How completely, head-turningly certain to make me fall into his arms? That's not why he told me what he did, though. I'm absolutely certain of that. He told me how he felt because he was honest and sincere and, like he said, denying his feelings was doing his head in.

I did fall into his arms, though; of course I did, although it was some time before our relationship moved up a gear, physically speaking. This surprised me, to be frank – I mean, he was of an age where sex was part and parcel of a relationship, and as for me, I just fancied him so much I couldn't resist him. But I soon realized that he was holding off to try and prove to me that his motivation was sound, and that we should get to know each other first. But it was unnecessary, to my mind. I already felt I'd known him for ever and, every time I was with him I just wanted to tear off some clothes, his and mine, and get physical.

God. Just listen to me. I'm really not that kind of girl, honestly. It was just the effect he had on me. He was so careful too, making sure we met in public places at first so that we didn't get "carried away", as he put it. But we both knew it was just putting off the inevitable, and that knowledge hung between us like smoke every time we met.

I was desperate to tell Ruby and Nat about Max and me as soon as possible; I wanted their opinion, sure, but most of all I wanted to re-live the thrill of it all in the way that only sharing every little detail with your mates can provide. So I tried ringing them, the same evening as all his revelations to me; but Hugh had a mate round for supper, Mum was sorting out the airing cupboard and lurking annoyingly on the landing outside my door, and Hattie was in one of her oh-go-on-Flora-please-let-me-borrow-that moods, popping in and out my bedroom what seemed like every thirty seconds. Not exactly conducive to having a private chat with my mates about how I'd just hooked up with an older man. So I had to satisfy myself with sending them both a text saying I had something important to tell them at school the next day but not to ring because it was difficult to talk, and left it at that.

"So how long have you been seeing him?" demanded Ruby as soon as I walked into the sixth-form common room the following morning.

"Keep your voice down!" Wanting to wait until we were by ourselves. Huh. Vain hope. Once Ruby gets on to something she's as tenacious as a ferret.

"C'mon, Flo. Quit stalling. I know what's been going on – I saw you getting in this well flashy car after school yesterday."

"Oh, right."

"I'm right, aren't I? You've finally got it together with whatisname – Max – haven't you?" she boomed. I put a finger in my ear and wiggled it, pulling a meaningful face.

"Ssh," I told her, urgently. Her voice has the power to slice through glass, and a couple of people were already looking curiously at us across the room. Including my brother. "I don't want it being common knowledge."

"Why not?" She lowered her voice by about half a decibel.

"Because. . ." I looked round, to check that nobody was standing close enough to hear. "Because he's thirty. Well, almost."

"*What?*" The force of her yell made the windows rattle, I swear it. Then her face unexpectedly creased into a huge grin. "Cool!" she exclaimed.

"Has she told you what that text was about yet?" Nat came over, drawn by the prospect of some juicy gossip. "Why all the mystery, Flora? What've you been up to?"

"She's only dating Hugh Grant, that's all."

"Hugh Grant?" Nat looked blank. "How did you get to meet Hugh Grant?"

Ruby sighed impatiently. "Not really Hugh Grant, Natalie. A rich looky-likey."

"He doesn't look like Hugh Grant," I objected. "Only a little bit. Just round the eyes, kind of. And a similar smile. Anyway, Hugh Grant's far too old for. . ." I tailed off, and my eyes met Ruby's.

"What?" said Nat, mystified. "What are you

two on about? I mean, don't take this the wrong way, but is there something you want to tell me, at all?"

"Flora's dating that Max guy," Ruby said, slowly, still grinning, not taking her eyes off me. "Apparently, he's loaded, and he's gorgeous. Oh yeah, and he's thirteen years older than her."

Nat's eyes grew round as saucers. "Oh," she said. "D'you think that's – you know. Wise?"

I went immediately on the defensive. "What's the problem?" I asked her. "Don't you approve?"

"It's not that I don't approve. Not exactly."

"So what's the problem?"

"Anyway, it's not up to me to approve or disapprove, is it?"

"Oh come on, Nat." I was getting exasperated with her. She does this to me sometimes. "You sound like my mother when I ask her how I look and she says, *Well it wouldn't be my choice but it's up to you.* I just want your opinion, that's all."

"Well. . ." She pulled a rueful face. "I'm not sure you're going to want to hear my opinion on this."

"Go on – shoot."

"I just think it's a bit of an age gap."

"Oh, Nat!" Ruby screeched. "You're so *reactionary*!"

Nat turned her pale-blue gaze on Ruby, quite unoffended. "It's only my opinion. She doesn't have to listen to it. What do your parents say?" she asked me suddenly.

It threw me for a moment. "Well, actually, the thing is," I started. "The thing is, we haven't actually told them yet."

"Ah," said Nat, and nodded her head sagely.

"Whaddya mean, *ah*?" I wanted to know, but Ruby flapped a dismissive hand at me.

"Never mind her," she told me, her eyes gleaming. "Just tell us all the details. Have you got jiggy with him?"

Nat let out a snort of laughter. "Rube, you are unbelievable," she giggled.

"No!" I protested. "Not yet. Give us a chance – we only got together yesterday."

"Not yet? Not *yet*?" Ruby teased me. "So it is on the cards, then?" I felt myself blushing, a guilty stain spreading across my face, although heaven knows why I felt guilty. We hadn't done anything to feel guilty about.

"I've just realized who he is," Nat exclaimed. "He's the guy who answered your mobile, isn't he? When I rang you after that Danny thing." She inclined her head towards the door, where he was standing surrounded by his usual cluster of adoring females.

"That's right."

"So was that when it started, then?"

"God, no," I said, heatedly. "I was far too cut

up about Danny at the time. It wasn't a rebound thing – I've known Max for years, he's a friend of the family. I had this big crush on him, but what I didn't know was he was feeling the same."

It seemed simpler to put it that way, to condense the relevant time period, not to mention the intervening years when Max had lost touch with our family. But Nat's eyes widened even more.

"Boy," she said slowly. "Are your mum and dad going to go ape, or what."

That's precisely why we didn't tell my parents from the start. Part of me genuinely felt what I'd told Max, that I didn't care what they thought, but another part – the larger, more unignorable part, the bit known as my brain – knew that they were not going to be happy about it. That's why we began meeting in secret, although Max didn't like doing it that way at all. He felt we were deceiving them. But I managed to convince him that the time wasn't right, and we should hang fire until it was.

"OK," I said to him, a few weeks in. "If you feel so strongly about it, come in and tell them when you take me back this evening."

I didn't mean it really; in truth I'd have died if he'd taken me up on it, but I was getting fed up with him continually mentioning it.

155

"All right," he replied, mildly, "if that's what you want me to do."

"Of course I don't want you to! We agreed, didn't we – we agreed we wouldn't tell them just yet."

"I know we did. I just don't feel doing it this way is right – it's like we're going behind their backs, like naughty children. I'd rather we tell them, face whatever their reaction is, and deal with it. Doing it this way makes me uncomfortable."

It wasn't like that for me at all. If I'm to be perfectly honest, the secrecy added to the deliciousness I felt when we were together; it made our relationship daring and illicit and even more exciting. I didn't tell Max that though. I somehow didn't think he would have approved of my motivation.

"I know," I told him instead. "And we will tell them soon, I promise. Just not yet."

Max lived in a flat in the smart bit of town, a two-bedroomed jobbie on the top floor of an old converted warehouse. We'd been seeing each other for some time before he took me there; he didn't tell me why it took so long and I didn't ask, although I wanted to. I wanted to know everything about him, in that way you do at the start of a relationship, and that included seeing the place he called home. You can tell a lot about people by observing the stuff they choose to surround themselves with.

The first time I went there was after a meal together one Saturday evening. It was still quite early, and as we got into Max's car outside the restaurant he asked me if I had time for a coffee. I had plenty of time: Nat was my alibi, I'd told everyone I was studying with her that evening, and if it had been true there was no way I'd be home before midnight. My heart rate quickened. The casual question seemed to signify we were subtly moving on to another level, and I didn't want to blow it by appearing too keen. So I agreed, as casually as he'd asked the question, and off we went.

It was a fab flat, an eclectic mix of traditional and modern, antique and trendy.

"This is wicked," I told him, as he opened the door from the hallway into the split-level sitting room. Acres of pale cream carpet spread away in front of me, and the lights of the town glittered below and beyond through a huge picture window with a wrought-iron balcony like a ship's prow on the other side.

"Thank you," he said, formally. "It's a bit yuppified, but I like it." He took me by the shoulders and led me gently towards the window. "This is the best bit. The view. At night it's like being on top of the world, and in the daytime you can see the Downs in the distance."

I had a sudden, romantic image of us sitting on the balcony together on a summer's morning, with nobody else up, the sky streaked with pale pink and gold and the dawn chorus serenading us. A tray of freshly-brewed coffee, grapefruit and croissants sat on a table between us, and Max was pointing into the distance with a long artistic forefinger. It was like a scene from a commercial. I could hear the voiceover in my head: "Welcome the day together with Gold Blend"; "New Dawn Fresh body spray from Impulse, for that tingly summer morning feeling"; "All-night protection from new Always with wings." Music swelled in the background, accompanying shots of a woman running along a beach in skimpy white shorts and then doing cartwheels, to show just how protected she was. . .

Aaarrgghh! What on earth was I doing, spoiling my lovely fantasy with such thoughts? I blinked, several times, hard, to clear the vision.

"Have you had this place feng-shuied?" I asked him, to change the subject.

He laughed. "No. Are you into all that?"

"Kind of," I admitted. I felt suddenly embarrassed. All my mates were into feng shui and horoscopes and stuff, and it felt like it was a really teenagey thing to confess to.

"So are some of my colleagues," Max told me, and I felt instantly better. "My PA Mel does a bit of feng shui on the side, so to speak, and she keeps offering to come round and get me sorted."

"Cool! You should let her." I moved to a small table underneath the window, covered with silver-framed photographs of all shapes and sizes, and picked one up at random. It was of a small child of indeterminate sex, bundled up in a snowsuit and offering something invisible to the camera with a mittened hand and a huge delighted smile. "Who's this?"

Max glanced at it. "My nephew, Barnaby. My sister's son. It's a bit out of date, he's six now."

"Phew, that's a relief. For a moment I thought you had a secret kid." I didn't know what made me say it; I hadn't thought that at all, it was just something to say. Max smiled at me, but his smile seemed a little forced. I wondered if coming to his flat had been such a good idea after all. He didn't seem entirely comfortable having me there and his discomfort was rubbing off on me, as if we were embarking on something more intimate than either of us was ready for.

He picked up another photograph: a couple with a young boy, grinning broadly against a backdrop of yacht masts and a cloudless summer sky. All three were clad in shorts, T-shirts and bright orange life jackets.

"This is Barney again, with Pippa and Guy – my sister and her husband. It's a bit more recent, I took it last July when I went down to stay with them."

"Down where?"

"Cornwall – Falmouth. We'd all been sailing, hence the life jackets."

"Sailing? Cool!" I'd never considered sailing cool before – in fact, I'd never thought of it in any terms before – but it suddenly seemed to be a fabulously elegant and desirable pastime: a day on the foamy briny (was that the phrase?), at one with the elements, pitting our strength against the sea and the weather; and then whiling away endless summer evenings together in a succession of picturesque little harbour-side pubs filled with eccentric old sea dogs, who entertained the assembled company with their amusing tales of a life on the ocean wave. . . On the other hand, maybe it didn't sound that cool after all; perhaps it was just because I fancied Max so much that everything about him seemed to be imbued with a certain magic and charm.

He glanced at me. "Do you sail?"

"No," I admitted. "Not as such. But I've, er – I've always liked the idea." Well, that wasn't too much of a fib, was it? I did like the idea, even if it had only come to me thirty seconds previously.

"That's great. I'll have to take you some time, you'd just love it," he said. "Pippa and I grew up down in Cornwall and we could sail practically as soon as we could walk – she's brought Barney up the same way, and it's really great to see." His eyes took on a faraway look, as if remembering the carefree sailing days of his boyhood. Where he lived now didn't offer a great deal in the way of yachts, unless you counted the boating lake in the middle of Alexandra Park. Not quite the same appeal.

"Sounds fab."

"OK – it's a date! In fact, we've been talking about taking a month off one summer and going round the Greek islands – perhaps. . ." He trailed off, awkwardly. *Perhaps you'd like to come too*; I knew it was what he was going to say. I didn't know why he didn't complete the sentence, only that his discomfiture was back.

"It's a great place you've got here," I enthused, trying to get things back on course. "Can I have a nosy round?"

"Sure." Max laughed, slightly to my relief. "Want a guided tour? Or can you find your way round by yourself?"

"Oh, I think I can manage," I replied breezily. "I'm an expert at looking round houses. All those years of being dragged round National Trust places by the parents."

"I'll go and put the kettle on for that coffee, then. Give us a shout if you get lost in the west wing."

I prowled round, in and out of rooms, admiring his taste in interior décor and art. There were full-to-overflowing bookcases everywhere and loads of pictures on the walls, from arty black and white photographic posters to framed reproductions of French impressionists and other stuff I didn't recognize. One wall of the tiny spare bedroom was filled with old school and college photos; I picked him out in each of them, an ever-maturing Max amidst groups of lads in caps and blazers, teenagers in formal suits and young men in cricket whites and rugby gear. There was even one of him with what looked like a rowing team, all dressed in long shorts and high-necked pale-blue T-shirts and holding one oar aloft. Perhaps the others had fallen into the river. WOLFSON COLLEGE FIRST EIGHT, said the legend, rather incomprehensibly, with a date ten years ago. Ten years. I was seven then. It was like having a glimpse into another world. Max was pretty tasty even then, though; even in the ones from his prep school, or whatever it was, I could recognize the smooth regular good-looking features of the man he was now.

I went back into the main room, where all the latest high-tech toys held centre stage – a state-of-the-art hi-fi, widescreen plasma TV, Sky box, dual DVD player. Hugh would be in his element here, I thought, rifling idly through Max's CD collection, which comprised everything from drum 'n' bass to Debussy.

He came through from the kitchen carrying a tray with a cafetière, two bone china cups and saucers, and a small silver jug and sugar bowl. The bowl was full of those pale brown unrefined sugar lumps that look like sweets, with a pair of silver tongs resting on top, and the cups had scrupulously accurate butterflies painted on them. Coffee at boyfriends' houses in the past had been Nescafé slopped into mugs in the kitchen after parental lights-out, a preliminary to and excuse for a mammoth snogfest in front of the television carefully set at a volume high enough to mask our sounds of passion but low enough for us to hear the arrival of any enquiring parent. I was slightly disappointed to realize that coffee at Max's meant just that – coffee. Otherwise, why would he have gone to so much trouble?

"They're pretty." I indicated the cups. Something to say again. "What butterflies are they?"

Max looked at them as if seeing them for the first time. "Haven't a clue. They were a present. I think there's some biscuits somewhere, shall I. . .?"

He left the sentence unfinished. This was terrible; the atmosphere between us felt more like two people who had only just met, not an established couple. Friends. Undisputed soon-to-be-lovers.

"No, don't worry. I'm not really a biscuity person."

Not really a biscuity person. What the hell was that supposed to mean? I groaned inwardly. Max started to pour the coffee.

"Cream? Sugar?" He pushed them across to me. It wasn't my imagination, he did seem very on edge.

I'm not really a creamy person. I'm not really a sugary person. I cast round the flat for a topic of intelligent conversation, desperate for something to say other than the silly meaningless words that I could feel forming on my tongue. My eyes lit on a piano in a corner of the room.

"Do you play?" I asked him, indicating the instrument with my head.

"I did, once upon a time. Hardly ever any more – I don't seem to have the time."

"You know Mum plays the piano?"

"Of course. It was one of the first things we

talked about when your dad invited me to supper for the first time, all those years ago. Bach versus Mozart, as I recall."

He smiled at me properly then, that wonderful crinkly-eyed smile that transformed the way he looked. Max's face in repose was serious and beautiful and almost cruel, as if he was capable of doing great damage, but when he smiled it made me feel I could wait my whole life for a man to look at me like that again.

"Will you play something for me?"

I half-expected him to demur, to say oh no I'm so rusty I couldn't possibly, or even to go all coy on me. A lad of my own age probably would have, but Max didn't. He walked over to the piano, lifted the lid, and tried a few experimental tinkles and flourishes. Then he sat down, and began to play properly.

I'd been expecting something classical, probably because of him having mentioned Mozart and Bach before, but he played some jazz. I didn't know the piece – my knowledge of jazz is on a par with my knowledge of The World's Greatest Golfers – but it was slow and smooth and smoky. It was also incredibly sexy. I closed my eyes and leant back and let the soft coaxing harmonies wash over me. It made me feel unbelievably sophisticated, sitting there in Max's plush flat, having him play jazz to me.

"What was that?" I asked him, when he finished.

"'The Nearness of You'," he said, with an apologetic little smile. "I know it's corny, but I just love the tune. I used to play it at parties at university, it never failed to get the attention of my passion of the moment."

"I'll bet. Where did you go to uni?"

"Cambridge. For my sins." Another oddly apologetic look, as if going to Cambridge was something to be ashamed of.

"Yeah? That's where I want to go." I was enchanted. It seemed like another connection, another bond between us. "Did you do English?"

"No, music."

"Oh, right. Yeah, the piano and everything. I just assumed you'd done English, as you went into journalism. Mum told me that you used to work with Dad; that's how you know each other."

"That's right. My first job after I graduated, as a matter of fact." He laughed. "God, I was green. Roger was brilliant, he taught me so much. I really looked up to him – he was a kind of father-figure, I guess. But I left the paper after eighteen months or so and went into TV production, starting pretty much at the bottom and working my way up. That's what I'm doing now."

"For the BBC?"

"No, an independent company. I produce and direct drama, mostly. Although we're not above doing the odd commercial – they pay better."

It sounded wonderfully glam, just the sort of prestigious and exotic thing Max would be doing to earn a living. I realized for the first time just how little I really knew about him, about his life. It excited me to think of how much fun we were going to have finding out about each other.

"God, how fantastic," I said. "It makes me feel my life's really boring by comparison."

"Ah, but you have your whole life ahead of you," he replied. "That's the really exciting thing. The world is your lobster, as someone I once knew used to say." He patted his trouser pockets as if trying to find something. "Look, would you mind awfully if I just popped out for a moment? I've run out of cigarettes."

I didn't really like him smoking but I didn't see how I could object, especially not in his own flat. It wasn't as if he smoked much, anyway – just the odd one every now and again. He told me to make myself at home, picked his jacket off the back of the sofa where he'd thrown it and went, slamming the front door behind him.

After about thirty seconds the phone began to ring. The timing was curious, it was almost as if somebody had been watching for him to leave.

I tried to ignore the slight feeling of impending menace that crept up my spine and touched the back of my neck with chill fingers.

Ring ring.

I waited for the answering machine to cut in, but it didn't.

Ring ring.

I got up and went over to the phone, as if looking at it would will it into stopping.

Ring ring. Ring ring.

Ten double rings. Max must have forgotten to set the machine. I gave in, and picked it up.

"Hello?"

"Hello? Maxim?" A woman's voice; impatient, slight foreign accent, I couldn't tell what.

"No, I'm sorry, he's not here right now. He's just gone out for something, he won't be long. Can I get him to call you back?"

A silence, then she sighed, an annoyed exhalation that gusted into my ear.

"I suppose so."

"Who shall I say rang?"

"This is Marina. His wife."

chapter ten

Who knows what might have happened if I hadn't taken my shoes off. My instinct was to run, to flee, just as I had after reading Danny's poem; to get as far away from that flat and Max as possible, although I daresay psychologists would have a field day about what that says about my capacity for facing up to things, for dealing with problems. But I couldn't run anywhere, for the simple reason that, faced with all that immaculately vacuumed ivory-coloured carpet on entering the flat, I'd taken my shoes off, like the nicely brought-up girl that I am, and in the heat of the moment hadn't the faintest idea where I'd left them. I cast around for them, wildly, my palms damp with perspiration and my heart beating so fast it felt as if it would burst right through my chest.

I finally located them by the door from the hallway into the sitting room, but it was too late. I heard a noise, the unmistakable rattle of Max's key in the lock and froze where I stood, clutching the shoes to my front as guiltily as if I were the one in the wrong.

"Hi," he called, breezily. "Sorry I was so long, there was a. . ." Catching sight of my stance, my face, he tailed off. "Flora, what on earth's the matter? You look as if you've seen a ghost."

For a reply, I threw one of the shoes at him.

"You bastard!" I yelled. "You total fucking bastard!" And I lobbed the other shoe at him, as hard as I could. He put out his right hand to catch it, but it caught him on the knuckles and fell uselessly to the floor.

"What are you talking about? What's going on?" He rubbed his injured hand with the other one, wincing slightly. I take a size seven shoe, and my taste in footwear is for the solid and chunky, not delicate little Cinderella-type slippers. It must have hurt, and I was glad – I wanted to hurt him, to injure him, to hurl myself at him and tear him limb from limb for having deceived me in such a humiliating, obvious bloody way. Of course he was married; no man with his very apparent attributes would have made it to the age of nearly thirty and remained single.

"You prey on me," I spluttered, so furious I could barely get the words out, "you drive me around in your fancy car, you lure me back here to your love-nest, and all the time you're just a bloody *fucking*. . ." I ran out of both words and breath and, spying the coffee things still sitting on the table where we'd left them, strode over and overturned the tray with a violent sweep of my arm. Then I snatched up a large vase from another table next to the sofa, and raised my arm to throw that at him, too.

Max was before me in a second. He grasped my upper arm, tight.

"No you don't," he commanded. His voice wasn't raised at all, but cool and measured and full of authority. "Stop it, Flora. Put that down, calm down, and tell me what's happened."

I looked at the vase, still clutched in my hand. It was a pretty vase, blue and white and Chinese-looking. It was also around half a metre tall, and heavy as a lump-hammer. Heavy enough to smash Max's head in. Our eyes met and locked, for all of ten seconds. I counted them, along with a clock that was ticking ponderously somewhere in the background, incongruously tranquil. Slowly, I handed the vase to Max, and equally slowly, he released his grip on me.

"All right," I said, flatly. "OK. I'll tell you what happened. Your wife rang. While you were out. *Marina.*" I spat the name out, with venom, but Max didn't turn a hair.

"I might have guessed," he said, with the tiniest resigned sigh.

"Is that all you can say?" I snarled, the fury flaring up again. "You might have guessed? How about, oh shit, that's torn it? How about oops, sorry Flora, forgot to mention I've got a secret wife stashed away?"

"I didn't mention her because she's not my wife," he said, with a composed equanimity that made me want to grab the vase from his hand and beat him over the head with it until his brains turned to butter.

"Oh really," I yelled, glaring at him with hatred. "Well, isn't it funny that she seems to think she is!"

"She knows damn well she's not my wife. Not any more. We're divorced."

"Oh, how convenient – you're divorced!"

"It's true. I wouldn't lie to you." He gestured with the vase. "Look around you – do you see any signs of a wife? Did you notice anything when you were looking round just now – clothes in the bedroom, cosmetics in the bathroom?"

"No," I conceded, with ill grace, "but that doesn't mean a thing. You could have tidied everything away before I got here."

"I could have," he agreed, "but I didn't. Because I didn't have to. This is my flat, I bought it with my share of the proceeds from the sale of our house. She's never even been here, Flora. And look – what about Venetia?"

"What about her?"

"You knew I was with her at the party; you saw us together. I wouldn't have been with her if I was married to someone else."

"If you say so."

"I do say so," he said, "because it's true. You must know me well enough to know that I wouldn't lie to you. I promise you, the decree absolute came through four weeks ago. Marina and I are as divorced as it's possible to be."

Four weeks ago was when we'd gone to that seedy Italian place, when he'd seemed so on edge. I'd thought it was because of the uncertain way things were between us at the time.

"Was that why you started smoking again?" I shot at him. Stupid thing to say, under the circumstances, I know; irrelevant, trivial. He looked slightly taken aback.

"Well, yes. Partly. She wasn't making things easy, right up to the end; she'd agree to things and then she. . ." He passed a hand through his hair; he looked rumpled, dishevelled, careworn. "Then she kept changing her mind," he finished.

I was beginning to be swayed. But I had to make sure, had to be certain. I just couldn't run the risk of getting embroiled with a married man.

"Why didn't you tell me about her?" I challenged him. "Right from the start?"

"I should have, I realize that now," he said.

"And I would have got round to telling you. But I didn't tell you at the beginning because I didn't want to give her an importance she doesn't have. She's irrelevant to us – she doesn't matter."

"Of course she matters!" I roared, beside myself at his inability to grasp this simple, fundamental point. "You should have told me about her. She's part of your history – part of your baggage. How can you say she doesn't matter!" And to my horror I began to cry, huge fat splashy tears, in a kind of illogical jealous grief that I wasn't the first person he'd cared deeply about, that he must have loved this Marina or why else would he have married her. Illogical, like I say. But impossible to do anything about.

I felt his arms go round me, in an action replay of our first contact outside that shop, and just like then I subsided weakly against him. He felt the same as then, he smelt the same.

"Ssh," he murmured reassuringly in my ear. "It's OK."

"You should have told me," I repeated into his front, still sniffling.

"I know. I'm so sorry. I wish you hadn't found out like this, it seems so unnecessary. It's typical Marina behaviour, though – hears a woman's voice answering my phone, and can't resist stirring it by referring to herself as my wife."

I perked up slightly at the artless way he'd called me a woman. (*A woman.* Not a girl, a woman.) Only slightly, though. I was exhausted from the expenditure of all that emotion, done in. I leant away from him and looked into his face.

"Is she still in love with you?"

He grimaced, and shook his head. "Not Marina. One of the more unpleasant things I've come to realize over the years is that the only person she really loves is herself." He touched my face, gently, and smoothed the hair from my forehead. "I'm sorry, Flora. Truly. You do believe me, don't you? That I'm not married any more?"

"I guess." I disengaged myself from him, and noticed for the first time the wreck of the coffee tray I'd knocked on to the floor. Both cups had smashed, the cream jug sat upside down with its contents pooled stickily around it, sugar cubes were scattered as far as the eye could see, and the cafetière was lying empty on its side, grounds spilling from it, a large dark patch seeping out from it across the carpet which was immaculate no longer.

"Oh my God!" I put my hands to my face in dismay. "Look what I've done! All that mess on the carpet!"

"It's OK. It's what I pay the cleaner for."

"But your beautiful cups!" I was appalled at

what I'd done – this, throwing my shoes, threatening him with that vase – it wasn't like me at all. I'm not normally given to violent behaviour.

"It doesn't matter. You were upset, you didn't mean it."

"But you said they were a present."

"A wedding present."

He looked at me, and I looked at him, and suddenly I started to laugh. Well, not laughing, exactly. More giggling weakly.

"Well that's all right then." I made an involuntary snorty noise, like a pig.

"Glad to be shot of them, to be honest. I always thought they were hideous. There's four more in the dresser, I don't suppose you feel like obliging?" Then he started to laugh as well. "Your face when you were holding that vase. You looked as if you were all set for a spot of serious GBH."

"I was. Was that a wedding present, too?"

"No. I'm actually quite fond of that vase."

"It's just as well you took it away from me, then."

Then he started laughing so hard I could barely make out what he was saying. "My love-nest," he spluttered. "You called my flat a love-nest!"

"I know," I joined in. "And I said you'd been preying on me."

"No, love-nest is the best. Love-nest!"

He was so tickled with the phrase, he kept repeating it and sniggering.

Eventually, we both sobered up and stopped laughing. I don't think either of us had thought it was that funny, to be honest. It was just a release of tension.

"So are you going to tell me about Marina now?" I asked him.

"What would you like to know?"

"Everything."

So he told me everything: about how they met at Cambridge, when he was an undergraduate and she was a postgraduate, how she was older than him, Italian and effortlessly sophisticated.

"I just fell in love with her," he said, simply, "the first moment I saw her." (Again that nasty twist of jealousy in my stomach. But I said nothing, I let him carry on.)

They started living together during his final year, sharing a flat with some other students and then moving to their own place after Max had graduated. He told me that he asked her to marry him countless times, and she always refused, saying it would change things between them – spoil things. Then, after they had been together for five years, she finally agreed.

"I'd worn her defences down," he said. "But she was right. It did change things. Nine months after the wedding, we were separated."

"But why?" I didn't understand. "Why did she say she'd marry you, after all that time, and then leave you?"

"She didn't leave me. It was a mutual decision. Things just weren't working out. It was as if getting married forced certain issues, brought stuff out into the open that had been ignored or brushed aside."

"What kind of stuff?"

"Lots of things. She wasn't faithful, for a start. She never had been, I knew about it but thought I could cope with it, but once she was my wife I realized I couldn't."

"You mean she had affairs?" It seemed incredible to me that anybody, having Max, would want other men too.

Max shrugged. "Affairs, flings. Whatever. It's just the way she was, she couldn't seem to function without a lot of male attention. Then there was the children issue – I wanted them, she didn't. Her career was too important. That was a shock, she came from a very close Italian family to whom children were clearly very special and important. Not Marina, though; she said she wasn't interested, and never would be. Basically, I think we both came to realize that we were two very different people who wanted different things from life. And like I said, I began to understand that she herself was the most important person in her life, and always would be."

"She sounds very selfish."

"I suppose she was. She didn't seem so at first, though. Just very confident, sure of herself and where she was going. It was very attractive."

"It sounds like you really loved her. You must have been devastated when you split up."

"It wasn't the best time of my life, that's for sure." He looked at me, his eyes meeting mine. "But it's over now. In the past. It's the future that matters now, not the past. I've never regretted anything I've done in my life, however painful it might have been at the time. Only things I haven't done. Wasted opportunities. Missed chances."

And that was the night we became lovers.

After all that, I began to agree with Max that we shouldn't keep our relationship hidden from my parents any longer. I didn't want them to find out about us in the same way I'd found out about Marina, by accident, especially as we had now moved on to an entirely different level. I'd rather we told them ourselves. Not that I had any intention of spilling the beans about everything. I mean, there was no need to go into details about exactly how close we were, just to

tell them that we were seeing each other.
Although Max said they'd know anyway about
us sleeping together.

"Why should they?" I wanted to know. "They
might guess, I suppose, but there's no way they
could *know*. Not for sure."

"They will," he said, grimly. "Trust me on this
one. Or at least, your father will, at any rate."

"But *how?*"

But all Max would say was "because he's your
father".

"It's a guy thing," Ruby declared. "Radar, I guess.
Instinct. Max has deflowered his little girl, and
he'll just sense it."

Nat looked shocked. On the other hand,
perhaps she just didn't know what deflowered
means. It's sometimes hard to tell with Nat.

"He hasn't *deflowered* me," I snorted. "Don't
look like that, Nat. For God's sake, close your
mouth – you'll be catching flies on your
tongue."

"You know what I mean," Ruby said, airily.
"Your dad's the Alpha Male, and Max is
encroaching on his territory. Face it, girl; he's not
going to like it."

"Well, thanks a bunch for the vote of
confidence," I said tartly. "You've made me feel
a whole lot better about telling them. Anyway,

I'm not Dad's territory, as you so delightfully put it." It made me sound like the Sudetenland, with Max in the Hitler role.

"I suppose you do have to tell them?" Nat sounded doubtful. "Couldn't you just – you know, carry on the way you have been?"

It was what I'd have preferred, to be perfectly honest, but I'd promised Max.

"I wish we could," I admitted. "It's ridiculous – here I am with this proper, grown-up bloke in a proper, grown-up relationship, having to confess to the parents as if I've done something naughty."

"Try not to think of it like that," Nat urged me. "If you think negatively, you'll most likely attract negative energy back from them. They might not react in the way you think. After all, you did say they like him, didn't you?"

"Yeah, but as one of their friends. Not necessarily as my boyfriend."

"Well," she mused, thoughtfully, "you have to see their point."

"Here we go," I exclaimed. "The 'he's too old for you' routine again. Well, ta very much, Nat. At least you're giving me a taste of things to come."

"I didn't mean it like that," Nat began to protest, but it was no use. I'd wanted my mates to understand and be sympathetic, but here one of them was predicting how direly my dad was going to respond, while the other was coming out with all her New Agey crap about energies, interspersed with saying she understood why. Not exactly guaranteed to make me feel supported.

"Now, now," Ruby chided me. "It's no good getting out of your pram, Flo. We're on your side, remember. All we're saying is, don't forget your crash helmet when you get round to telling them." She went into her Mystic Rube mode, something she often does to wind Nat up but on this occasion it had the same effect on me. She half-closed her eyes and swayed from side to side, humming under her breath. "Aah yes, I see it all clearly now, here in my load of crystal balls. I predict a mighty explosion coming to the Wilcox household in the very near future."

chapter eleven

Max and I walked through the front door together, hand in hand. I could feel his warm solid bulk next to me, and his presence comforted and reassured me. *It'll be all right*, I kept telling myself. *They won't be angry, they'll be perfectly understanding.* Although I was beginning to regret wearing the wedding dress – I couldn't remember where I'd got it, but somewhere at the back of my mind was the thought that I'd bought it for a fiver at the local Oxfam shop. It was possibly not the best choice of attire for telling Mum and Dad that Max and I were an item, especially as Max was clad by contrast in a pair of cut-off jeans and nothing else. I caught a glimpse of the two of us in the hall mirror as the door closed behind us: we made an oddly mismatched couple, Max looking as if he'd just stepped off the beach, bare-chested, tanned, healthy and smiling and looking full of confidence that we were doing the right thing, and me in the long white lacy gown that was slightly too big for me, with a faintly apologetic look on my face. But it was too late to get changed now. I pinned on a smile, pulled the veil down over my face, and in we went, still arm in arm.

Mum and Dad were in the sitting room, next to each other on one of the sofas. Dad stood up angrily when he saw us, and pointed an accusing finger at Max.

"Before you start," he said, in a voice that was quivering with rage, "I want to know what on earth you think you're doing."

"Now, Roger," said Mum, bossily, and plucked at his free arm. "Don't get upset. Come and sit down and finish watching *Bridget Jones's Diary*."

Dad ignored her. "Well?" he demanded of Max.

"I'm not doing anything," Max said. He took his arm away from mine, guiltily, took a step away from me, and began to talk very fast. "Honestly. It's Marina and Venetia's fault, they dared me to. We met in a chatroom and it was the peripherals that I fell for, but I can see now I made a mistake. We shouldn't have slept together. Anyway, I'm thirty years older than her and I don't even like pizza."

He shouldn't have admitted that we'd slept together. Dad would never let it rest now. I had to get him out of there, as quickly as possible.

"Max," I said, and took his arm. "Come on. We've got to go now."

He looked at me as if he didn't know who I was. I had to admit, it was a brilliant piece of acting.

"What are you doing here?" he said. "You're not Marina."

"Actually," I said, "I am." I suddenly had this brilliant plan – if I pretended I was Marina we'd be able to escape and Mum and Dad would never know what we'd been up to. But Dad was already striding across the room towards us, the finger now pointing in my direction. He looked like the Harbinger of Doom, his face stern and unforgiving.

"I know exactly who you are," he said, in a terrible voice. He pulled off my veil triumphantly. "As I thought. It's you, Flora."

I suddenly felt really scared, absolutely terrified. I looked over at Mum for support but she was engrossed in *Bridget Jones,* laughing uproariously at Renee Zellweger's antics in a bunny girl costume, and apparently oblivious to the real drama that was unfolding before her.

I took a deep, calming breath. "Look, Dad," I said, reasonably. "It's not what it looks like."

But Dad was beyond reason. "I just don't know how you've got the brass neck," he yelled, in my face, "to wear that dress. Brides wear white for a reason, and *you're not even a virgin!*"

And then I was suddenly running along the

road, without any memory of having left the house or the room, in that curious disjointed way events have in dreams; only it wasn't the road outside our house as you'd expect but a busy dual carriageway and I was running along the hard shoulder the wrong way, and as I glanced down I saw I was wearing trainers on my feet, huge fluorescent orange jobbies, and the last thought I had before I woke up was *trainers with a wedding dress, omigod, how tasteless is that. . .*

We agreed that Max would call round over the weekend, as we felt daytime revelations would probably be easier for the parents to take on board than evening ones, when they'd be tired after a day's work etc. etc. The plan was he'd come after Sunday lunch when Dad (in particular) was full of good roast dinner and mellowed out by half a bottle of claret. So I duly sneaked upstairs and rang Max when we were all done, and sure enough, twenty minutes later the doorbell chimed.

Mum looked up from loading the dishwasher. "Who's that at this time on a Sunday afternoon?" she said, sounding slightly peeved.

"Someone for Flora, I expect," Harriet smirked, with a little sideways glance in my direction to see how I'd react. But I didn't have time to react, because at that moment in came Hugh, fresh (if that's the right word, and I don't think it is) from rugby practice, followed by an ever-so-slightly-sheepish-looking Max.

"Look who I found lurking on the doorstep," Hugh bellowed. He always speaks at top volume after rugby, like all the testosterone swilling around has caused his vocal chords to go into overdrive. He made a beeline for the chicken carcase on the counter and tore off a chunk, cramming it into his mouth and devouring it as if he hadn't eaten for a week. "Mmm, chicken. Any left for me?" I do find it rather worrying the way my usually perfectly civilized brother turns into Cro-Magnon Man after a couple of hours of contact sports.

I carefully avoided looking at Max. I knew if I did I wouldn't be able to stop myself from hurling myself at him, throwing my arms round his neck and pleading for reassurance that everything was going to be all right. I had a nasty sinking feeling in the pit of my stomach that, in fact, everything was going to be far from all right.

Mum straightened up from the dishwasher and kissed him, a smile of genuine pleasure on her face.

"Hello, Max. How lovely to see you. Would you like a glass of wine?" She put out a hand and without looking slapped Hugh, who was still making inroads into the leftover chicken, on the wrist. "Leave it alone. Yours is in the oven. There's some blackberry crumble too, Max, if you'd like any. Red or white?"

"Oh, er, thanks. Red, please." He looked slightly discomfited, as well he might. Given what he'd come round to divulge, he hadn't expected to be greeted with kisses and offers of wine and pudding.

Mum handed him a giant helping of crumble, smothered with cream, and a large glass of wine.

"There you are, love. I'm not quite sure where Roger is, but let's go and find him."

"He's in the sitting room, reading the paper through his belly-button," Hugh put in helpfully.

We all trooped through – I mean *all* of us: Mum and Max with his hands full of goodies, Hugh with his plate, greedily forking food to his mouth as he walked, Hattie with – well God knows why she had to follow, sheer nosiness I imagine – and me, bringing up the rear with my heart in my mouth. Dad was in his chair in his customary post-lunch position, glasses pushed down his nose, slippered feet stretched out, *The Sunday Times* across his front and his arms folded across his belly. He snorted and harrumphed as we entered, and rearranged the paper with a great deal of rustling, pretending he hadn't really been asleep.

"Hello there, Max," he said, smiling matily, and stood up. "To what do we owe this pleasure, then?"

I didn't dare look at him, at either of them. I wished Hugh and Hattie would go, just bugger off – it was bad enough having to go through this with just Mum and Dad present, let alone the whole family. *Oh well*, I thought. *In for a penny*. . .

I took a deep breath, just like in my dream. "Actually," I began, "he's got something to tell you."

Max shot me a quick look, the visual equivalent of a kick on the ankle. *Shut up,* the look said, *and let me handle this*.

"That sounds ominous," Dad said, with a hearty laugh.

"It's not," said Max, quickly. "At least, I don't believe it is. Look, Roger – Roger and Julia, I should say, I want you both to know this – the fact is. . ." He swallowed. It was the most nervous I'd ever seen him, and it made me all the fonder of him. "The fact is, Flora and I have – well, we've been seeing each other."

"Seeing each other?" Dad's face was blank. "What exactly do you mean by seeing each other?"

He looked at Mum, for translation or

elucidation or something, but she was just standing there, seemingly frozen to the spot. *Oh shit. She's in shock. Bloody fantastic.*

"Are you telling me you've been dating?" *Dating.* Well, at least he didn't say courting. That was something.

Max nodded eagerly, relieved that he'd been understood. "Yes, if you like. Yes."

"Well, since you ask," Dad said, slowly, "I don't like. Not at all." His accent thickened to deepest Geordie, as it always does when he's angry or tired or emotional – or all three, as he clearly was now. *Oh double shit. . .*

"Now, Roger," Mum muttered, snapping out of her coma.

"Now nothing. He's twice her age, and he's divorced. Am I supposed to like that, then?"

"I do understand your point of view," Max said, his voice loaded with reasonableness.

"Oh, do you!" Dad scoffed. I realized Max was still clutching his plate of pudding and glass of wine. It put him at a definite disadvantage. "Do you, indeed!"

As if reading my thoughts, Max bent and deposited the plate and glass on a nearby table. "Roger," he said, a note of appeal in his voice. "You know me. You've known me since I was twenty-one. You must know I'd never do anything – anything *dishonourable*."

"It's not you I'm worried about," Dad said. "It's her." And he flicked his head in my direction.

It sounded like criticism, a censorious comment on my choice of men or my lack of common sense or something. Red rag to a bull time, in other words.

"Oh, thanks very much!" I shot at him.

"Well look at him." Dad turned to me, waving a dismissive arm towards Max. "Little Lord Fauntleroy, rolling in money and reeking of charm. How's a child like you supposed to resist a fellow like him, eh? How are you supposed to recognize wrong from right, when it's all wrapped up in a fancy bloody package like that?"

I was aware of Hugh and Hattie, standing open-mouthed with shock in the background; although whether shock at Max's news or Dad's words, I wasn't certain. For my part, I'd never heard my father say anything so offensive to anybody. Afterwards, I thought perhaps I should have told him so. Or maybe I should have realized there was no reasoning with him in that frame of mind, should have calmly left the room – should have done anything apart from what I did, which was say "I'm not a child!" in the most childish way possible. Short of stamping my foot and throwing myself down on the hearthrug, I couldn't have reacted in a less mature way.

"Roger." Max spread his hands appealingly, ignoring me. "Please believe that I care about Flora, very much. I'd never do anything to hurt her. I do understand how you feel, honestly. It's what I expected you to say – I'd probably be the same if I had a daughter who was going out with a man thirteen years her senior."

"You mean you know how old she is, and you've still been – what was it you called it? – *seeing her*? Aye, and we all know what that means, don't we," he added, grimly, under his breath. "What's the matter with you, man? Can't you get a woman of your own age?"

"Don't, Roger." Mum stepped forwards suddenly, unexpectedly, and put a hand on Dad's arm. "Please don't. Max says he cares about Flora. Surely that's what really matters."

"Well, thank you," I muttered. "At least someone's got some sense round here."

Dad and Max glared at each other like two stags about to engage in a spot of antler-locking. Or rather, Dad glared at Max; I couldn't see Max's face because he had his back to me, but the set of his shoulders looked pretty damn glarey. In fact, it looked like a stand-off to me.

Abruptly, Dad moved away. "So tell me," he

said, in a bitter distasteful voice. "Just how long has this little liaison been going on?"

I could see Max struggling between telling the truth and wanting to make it seem as innocent as possible.

"Not long," he said, at last. "But long enough to know that my feelings for Flora are genuine; I really want you to understand that. Although I quite see why you find it difficult to accept the idea of us having a relationship."

Dad looked at him for an endless moment, his nostrils flaring with the effort of remaining composed. "Is that right," he said, sourly. "Well, I'm not going to forbid you to see her. That's not the way I operate."

Max inclined his head in acknowledgement. "Fair enough."

"But I'm not going to approve of what you're doing, either." Dad folded his arms mulishly. "I can't do that. You're too old for her – it's as simple as that."

"We're not asking for your approval," I put in. "Just so long as you know we're together; that's all." I was furious with him. Didn't he realize how worried I'd been about him being told, how much courage it had taken Max to stand there in front of him like that?

"Flora," Max said, gently. "Take it easy." He came to stand beside me, and gently touched my shoulder. It was possibly the least sexual gesture he could have made, but it seemed to drive Dad into a frenzy.

"Now don't you go groping her!" he roared. "Not right in front of me! That's really rubbing my nose in it!"

Max dropped me as if I were red-hot. "I'm sorry," he said, but to Dad, not me. "Look, I've said what I came to say. I think I'd better go."

"Good idea," Dad retorted. "Before I knock your smarmy block off."

Somehow I got Max to the front door without Dad accosting him.

"So," I said to him, breezily. "That went well, didn't it?"

He put out a hand and tucked my hair back behind my ear. "You can't blame him for being protective of you. He said pretty much what I expected. Anyway, at least he didn't ban you from seeing me."

"I'd like to see him try."

"You don't want to fall out with them. That really would make things awkward."

I shrugged. "I don't care. Just so long as we can be together."

"At least we've got over that hurdle. I'm sure they'll come round, eventually. Once they see I'm serious about you."

Back in the sitting room, after he'd gone,

Mum and Hugh and Hattie were standing around like leftover guests at a party, in varying states of agitation.

"Bloody hell, Flo," Hugh exploded, "you sure know how to make a Sunday afternoon go with a swing. How long have you two been at it, then?"

I pulled a face at him. "Long enough. Like Max said. Where's Dad?"

"Gone out for a walk," Mum said. She looked flustered and angry. "He wanted some fresh air. I think I might go and join him."

I caught hold of her sleeve. "Hang about. You don't think it's so awful, do you? Me and Max? Can't you talk Dad round?"

"I really don't know, Flora."

"But you said the age thing doesn't matter, didn't you?"

"I didn't say that at all. I said that what matters is that he cares about you."

"Oh, right." I'd thought she was on my side. I could feel exasperation flare up again inside me, and forced it down, out of sight. "So you *do* think it matters, then."

Mum pursed her lips. "To be honest, I don't know what I think. It's been an enormous shock. I've always had a soft spot for Max, but I'd certainly never thought of him as boyfriend material for you. You don't know what you're getting yourself into – at his age he's going to want totally different things from a relationship, and I'm frankly worried about it."

"But Mum!" My voice rose by several decibels. "Can't you hear yourself? You like him, you've always been fond of him – what better boyfriend material could there possibly be!"

"One who's nearer twenty than thirty, for a start," she replied, tartly. "Look, Flora, I really don't feel up to this discussion right now, OK? We'll talk about this later, but right now I need time to think. I'm going to find your father and try and calm him down."

"You won't let him talk you round, though, will you?" I called after her, as she left the room, but she didn't answer, just closed the door behind her.

"For Christ's sake," said Hugh, as soon as she'd gone, "why can't you quit while you're ahead?"

"What d'you mean?"

"She already said she likes the guy, but that's not enough for you, is it? Oh no. You've got to push her, to try and get her to say his age doesn't make any difference."

"But it's so ridiculous!" I fumed. "They know him, they know what he's like, but all of a sudden he's a big no-no just because he's older than me!"

"Thirteen years older than you. That's some age gap."

"Oh God," I groaned. "Not you as well!"

"What? You mean you really didn't think people would care? Or maybe you thought they just wouldn't notice?"

"I knew people would notice. I just hoped they might not be so petty as to think it was the only thing that mattered."

"Oh, come on, Flo! Of course it bloody matters! I mean, tell me honestly, just what is it you think a thirty-year-old guy sees in a seventeen-year-old girl?"

"He's not thirty yet," I muttered. I wasn't at all sure I liked the direction this conversation was taking.

"Sex," Hugh said, confidently, supplying his own answer. "He's knocking on middle age's door, then along comes this foxy young babe offering it to him on a plate. What's he going to do, say no thanks? I don't think so."

"It's not like that," I protested.

"Yeah, it is. I know – I'm a guy too, remember?"

"You shouldn't judge other people by your own standards. Anyway, I've not offered him anything on a plate." Was that what my brother really thought of me?

Hugh looked at me, beadily. "You're telling me you're not sleeping with him?"

I couldn't look him in the eye, far less answer him. How could I? He'd only take it as confirmation of his nasty little theory. But he took my silence as confirmation anyway.

"Aha!" he exclaimed, with triumph. "I knew it! He's screwing you, and what's more Dad knows he's screwing you – no wonder he went ballistic."

It was exactly what Max had said. What was it with these men, so in tune with each other's mentality when it came to matters of sex? Or was it just that they kept their brains permanently in their trousers, as Ruby always maintains?

"You're disgusting," I said, slowly. "If you really think that's all there is to Max and me, then you're disgusting."

Hugh stood and looked at me, for a long moment. "No. My mind might be, I'll grant you that, but I'm not. I'd never take advantage of a young girl like he has. He's the disgusting one." I started to protest, but he wasn't listening. "I thought you'd learnt your lesson after Danny Oldfield, but you obviously haven't. You must be attracted to scumbags, that's all I can say. Because that's what your darling Max is – scum. A *dirty old man*. With the emphasis on the old."

And he turned on his heel and slammed out of the room.

Which left me with Hattie. Harriet, the best, most understanding younger sister anybody could ever hope for. Not. What ammunition she'd have gathered, and in such a short space of time – enough to snipe at me with for the rest of our lives, probably. How she must have loved it, how she must be gloating, how she must—

"I don't think he's a dirty old man," she said, unexpectedly. "I think he's cool."

"What?" I spun round, ready to deflect whatever smart-arse comment she was going to follow up with. She was clearly just trying to soften me up, getting me to drop my guard before pouncing with the killer blow. "Don't even bother," I said, caustically. "I'm not in the mood."

"He doesn't look thirty," she carried on. "I think he's well fit. I'd go out with him, if he asked me."

"Oh yeah, that's likely, isn't it?"

"Course it isn't." She shrugged. "I'm just saying, I would if he did. That's all."

It began to dawn on me what she was saying. "So don't you think I should stop seeing him, then?"

"S'up to you. But I wouldn't if it was me. Not just because Dad doesn't agree with it. I mean, Max is really nice. And anybody can see he really likes you, too."

I could scarcely believe it – my irritating little sister, alone of all my family, giving me her seal of approval.

"And you don't think the age difference matters?"

Hattie pursed her lips and shook her head. "Nope."

I could feel tears – tears of relief, that someone was finally on my side – prickling behind my eyes. I blinked, hard, and picked up Max's discarded glass of wine and drained it to its dregs. Boy, did I need that drink.

"Hattie," I said, "you don't know how good it feels to hear someone say that for a change."

Even if that someone was only twelve. Hey, everyone is entitled to their opinion, right? And I needed all the support I could get.

chapter twelve

So that was it, then. We'd told them, just as Max wanted. And what had been achieved, exactly? My father now saw Max as some kind of devil incarnate, flashing his money and charisma around to bedazzle and seduce poor innocent little me (yeah, right), my mother wasn't sure what she thought, having apparently judged him as being pretty much perfect up to then, and as for my brother – well. Best not even go there. The only ally I appeared to have was Hattie, and what use was she, when all was said and done? Not a lot, really. I mean, she wasn't exactly likely to get the rest of them to change their minds, was she? She wasn't really up to getting Mum to revert to her original, rosy-spec'ed view of Max, single-handedly. She was hardly going to be able to persuade Dad or Hugh that, in actual fact, much of our time together was spent discussing intelligent topics like two civilized adults and not, as they appeared to imagine, getting down and dirty as often as possible.

No, Hattie's more reasonable point of view was really only useful for moral support.

Cheering though it was that at least one of my family didn't think Max was trying to corrupt my mortal soul, if I didn't use my little sister's championing of my cause as much as I might have done it was for the simple reason that I just wasn't used to having her on my side. As a rule, we don't get on – we argue, we bicker and fight. That's our relationship, that's what I was used to, not having her playing Agony Aunt to my Misunderstood of Surrey.

And anyway, all of that aside, none of my family's reactions to me and Max's little bombshell actually impinged on me that much. Because I decided I wasn't going to let it. It was my life, wasn't it? My life, my responsibility, my decision who I was going to see or not see. Mine. Not Mum's, or Dad's, or – God forbid – Hugh's. The way I saw it, I'd gone along with Max's wish to tell them about us, and now we were free to get on with things the way we wanted to. Max seemed happy that we were no longer going behind their backs, and I – well, I started keeping a very low profile at home. I didn't see any point in putting myself in the way of disapproving looks or comments, so I began to stay out as much as I could. My impending AS-levels provided the perfect excuse; most days I pretended I was going round to Nat or Ruby's after school, on the pretext of revising with them, but in actual fact I'd catch a bus or a cab straight to Max's. Occasionally, if he wasn't working, he'd collect me from school. Not often, though. I didn't want Hugh to spot me getting into the car, the flash fly Jag he'd so admired when its owner's relationship with me was innocent and wholesome and altogether more acceptable.

There were times when Max was working late or at the gym or having an after-work drink with his colleagues, and seemed surprised that I still wanted to go to the flat. I always did, though. Even with him being absent, it was still better than being at home, with the atmosphere of continual and growing chilly repression. I was never sure whether Mum and Dad really bought the revision excuse, but even though they never actually challenged me about where I was going or where I'd been, they never seemed to look at me these days without an expression of deep disapproval.

On those occasions when Max was late home we only saw each other for a short time before he took me back, but he always did take me home, late back or not. He insisted on waiting outside in the car for me to go up the path and let myself into the darkened house (it was always darkened: my parents go to bed early and, anyway, I got into the habit of making sure

I got back late enough to avoid attracting hassle) before pulling away with a wave and a dipping of headlights.

Truth to tell, I enjoyed being in his flat when he wasn't there almost as much as when he was. Does that sound awful? I hope not, after all it's not a reflection on how I felt about his company. The solo enjoying of his flat was a different thing altogether. It was a kind of sybaritic appreciation of the finer things in life, I guess – the things that Max had, and had opened my eyes to the possibility of obtaining. It was blissful to sit and relax in peace and quiet, away from the relentless thumping of Mum's piano pupils, Hugh's nerdy techno tracks and Hattie's moronic little friends as they trailed their endlessly chattering way up and down the stairs. It was good to be able to fix myself something to eat when it suited me from the upmarket heat-and-serve contents of Max's American-sized fridge (he apparently shopped for food entirely at the chill counter of Marks and Sparks and Waitrose); and as the days drew into late spring and the evenings began to lengthen, I would open a bottle of wine and take it and two glasses on to the balcony, and watch the sky darken and the lights come on across the town as I waited for Max's return. Sometimes I'd indulge in a little fantasy – oh God, I can hardly believe I'm confessing this – a little daydream that we were, ahem, married. How cringe-making is that? I think it was just the whole make-believe thing – playing house, enjoying the fruits of somebody else's labours, and appreciating the generosity with which he shared them with me.

Shortly after the Confessing to the Parents episode Max gave me a key to his flat, which I wore on a string round my neck so I wouldn't lose it. It was probably the most symbolic thing anybody had ever given me, and certainly the most significant. Its significance wasn't lost on Ruby and Nat, however, who thereafter kept pestering me to invite them round.

"Sure," Max said nonchalantly, when I asked him if it would be OK. "No problem. Would you like to have them round for dinner?"

"Christ, no!" I squeaked. I'd only meant a quick coffee after school, not a full-on dinner party. "Nothing heavy, I just want them to come round and check you out."

"I see," he said, solemnly. "Do you think I'll pass muster?"

"Oh, yes," I said hastily. God, had I offended him? "I didn't mean it the way it sounded. It's just they haven't met you yet, and. . ." I trailed off.

"It's OK. I was only teasing. I do understand that you want your friends to meet me – I want mine to meet you, too."

"Do you?"

"Of course I do. I want to show you off."

"And how about your parents?"

"I'm sorry?"

"Well, we've told mine about us – are you going to tell yours as well, take me to meet them and stuff like that?" Frankly, the very thought appalled me, but it seemed important to see what his response would be.

"Ah. That might be a bit more difficult."

"Why?"

"Because, my sweetheart. . ." *Oh no*. An icy finger of dread brushed against the nape of my neck. *He's going to tell me they'll disown him for going out with someone my age – no, he's going to say he's already told them, and they have disowned him. . .* "Because they're both dead."

"Oh God. Oh Max, I'm sorry."

"Don't be." He smiled, that smiliest smiley smile of his that made my knees turn to jelly and my insides to mush. "It was a long time ago. But you see, it does make telling them just a tad impossible."

"Yeah, I can see that. So when do I get to meet your sister and her family – Paula, is it?"

"Pippa." He grinned at me. "I'll have to get something organized."

"Cool. When can I get Rube and Nat to come round, then?"

"Who's Rubanat?"

"Ruby and Natalie. You know – my mates."

"Whenever you like. I want you to treat this like home, remember."

He meant it, too. It was amazing – I still couldn't get over the sheer novelty of going out with a guy with serious money. If that makes me sound shallow then I'm sorry, but come on – who wouldn't have found it all thrillingly impressive?

My reasons for wanting to invite Ruby and Nat round weren't just to impress them, though. Ever since Max and I had got together I'd been uncomfortably aware of neglecting them, in the way all the mags warn you against when you start dating hot new men. Don't neglect your friends, they warn, all metaphorical clicking tongues and shaking fingers; you never know when you might need them. I knew I needed them – they were my alibi, apart from anything else, as I've already said. But I had a kind of guilty awareness of not having actually spent much time with them recently. I'd told them about how Mum and Dad had responded to the news about Max and me, not because I particularly wanted to, but because I wanted the reflex sympathy I knew they would provide on account of my having been on the receiving end of parental stick. Well, it's what friends are for, right? When the going gets tough, your mates are supposed to come up with tea and sympathy by the bucketload. We'd always been there for each other in the past: when Ruby failed the entrance exam to the posh private school down the road, when Nat's Mum and Dad split up when she was in Year Seven. When Shane Spinks had been two-timing Rube with that stick insect Janey Sharpe in Year Nine, and when Danny Oldfield – well, I've already told you how they reacted to the Danny-and-me saga. We'd always provided the shoulders for each other to sob into.

But, you see, having been there for me when I needed them about Max, I now wanted them to see what it had all been about. I wanted to show them that I wasn't just hanging round with this older man in order to be provocative and get up my parents' noses. I wanted them to meet him, to judge him for themselves and see just why I was attracted to him in the first place. In short, I wanted the thumbs-up from them.

Pathetic, really, when you come to think about it. I mean, if I was so convinced that our relationship was sound, it shouldn't have mattered what anybody else thought, should it? So I guess I did want to impress them: with Max himself, but firstly with the outward evidence of his material success and worth. His flat, for example. It impressed the hell out of them when they did finally come round, one Friday afternoon when Nat and I had a double study period. Ruby was supposed to be in an Art lesson, but she sportingly skipped it so that I could show them the flat and get all the jaw-dropping out of the way before Max came home.

"Holy Moly," said Ruby, when I opened the front door. "So this is where Mad Max hangs out, is it?"

"It's fab, Flora," Nat said, in tones of reverential awe.

"OK, Nat, no need to whisper. We're not in church." Ruby strolled over to the window. "Sheesh, look out of that window! You pay a packet for a view like that. This place is way cool."

I preened ever so slightly with vicarious pride. Their response to the rest of the flat was similarly gratifyingly enthusiastic.

"This is so nice," Nat said. "What I wouldn't give to have somewhere like this to escape to."

"Nice?" Ruby queried, curling her top lip expressively. "Is that the best you can do, Nat? Nice?"

"Well, what would you call it, then, Ms Dictionary?" Nat always gets bristly with Ruby when she goes on one of her vocabulary crusades.

"I'd say it was a ringing endorsement for

going out with an older man," Ruby declared, pompously. "I bet it makes up for your dad's reaction, Flora. Being able to come here to chill out whenever you want to, I mean."

"You're so lucky," Nat sighed. "Going out with a guy with his own place must really move your relationship on to the next level."

"She means sex," Ruby guffawed.

"No I don't. Although it must make it easier for that, too – no more drunken fumbles in the back of cars."

"I wouldn't mind having a drunken fumble in the back of that particular car," said Ruby. "Have you seen it, Nat? Enough to rev anybody's engine." She can be so uncouth at times.

"Take no notice of her," I instructed Nat.

She didn't. "I mean, you've got the space here to get to know each other properly, without parents or nasty little kid sisters breathing down your neck. So you get to discover things about each other much sooner than you normally would, and you both get to feel you've known each other for longer than you actually have."

It was so near to how I was currently feeling that I was astonished Nat had the perspicacity to see it; dear Nat, who fond as I am of her is usually more preoccupied with the colour of boys' eyes or the size of their muscles than what goes on inside their heads.

"You're right," I said. "It's only been a few weeks, but I feel I've known him for ever."

"Well, that's good, isn't it?"

"I think so. I really think I understand how his mind works, that we're on the same level – it's weird, I've never felt like that about a lad before."

"Maybe because Max isn't a lad," Ruby observed.

"True. Although we're not always on the same level. He refuses point-blank to go to Checkers, says it's too teeny for words." Checkers is one of the local night spots; it has a reputation for not being too choosy about checking ID, if you get my drift. "Then he said he was taking me to a club the other night, so I spent ages getting ready – you know, the works – only to find when we got there that it was a jazz club."

"A *jazz* club?" Nat looked horrified. "What did he want to take you to one of those for?"

"He thought I'd like it." After my reaction to "The Nearness of You", he'd said. He'd meant it as a surprise, a sweet romantic gesture. "It's a long story, but he did have a reason."

"Aren't jazz clubs all full of middle-aged men in beards and black polo necks, clicking their fingers and saying 'hot'?" Ruby asked.

"Pretty much." The mortifying recollection of it spread across my mind like a stain – the startled look Max gave me when I took off my coat to reveal my hotpants and sparkly clubbing make-up, closely followed by the looks the beardy weirdies at the bar gave me. I felt myself burning with the memory of it, and pushed it firmly to the back of my brain. "It was fine." I shrugged, in an attempt at nonchalance. "Max thought it was quite funny, actually. We didn't stay long."

"You mean, he made you *stay*?" Nat managed to make it sound as if he'd tied me down and beaten me with a rubber hose.

"Only for a drink. We bumped into a friend of his, we could hardly go rushing off." I remembered his friend's face (Max had introduced him to me as Brian-from-work), his bemused but not entirely unappreciative expression as his gaze had travelled from my face to my legs, and then up again, slowly, taking in every detail of my totally inappropriate get-up. *Don't even go there. . .*

Ruby threw herself down with a whoop on to one of the pale sofas. "Well anyway, this place rocks. Even if Mad Max does make you go to jazz clubs. Does he keep anything to eat here?"

"Of course he does." That was the second time she'd called him that. It annoyed me; I knew she didn't mean anything by it, it was just Ruby being Ruby, but even so. It seemed a bit much to be calling him silly names when she hadn't even met him yet.

"Give the guy chance to get home before we start raiding his fridge," Nat said. "I can't wait to meet him. I saw all those pix in the spare room – he seems very sporty." So she'd clocked him in his college rugby kit, then. She always was a sucker for the well-exercised type.

"Well, all I can say is, he'd better live up to the build-up Flora's given him, or I'm going to demand a refund." Ruby struggled up from the depths of the sofa. "What did you say he—"

There was the sound of a key in the door and she stopped abruptly. Then it opened, and in he walked. Max. My Max. My stomach turned over with that omigod feeling I always got when I saw him. I went through to the lobby to greet him; he came towards me, walking that walk, smiling that smile, and I still couldn't believe my luck.

"Hi," he said. "Good day?"

"Yeah, cool," I said. "Got an A for that essay."

"See – I told you it was top stuff."

"So what have you been up to?"

"Oh, boring things – on the phone most of the day, sorting out location costs. Deeply tedious. You don't want to know."

He gave me a kiss, and Ruby coughed theatrically somewhere in the background. So I took him through and made all the necessary

213

introductions, and Max went off to get changed out of what he calls his work clothes while I went to make some coffee. Ruby and Nat followed me into the kitchen, uncharacteristically silent for once.

"Flora," Nat whispered, her eyes goggling, "he's *gorgeous*!"

"Told you," I said, carelessly heaping coffee into the cafetière. I glanced at Ruby, who was examining with casual studied nonchalance the cork noticeboard on the kitchen wall that Max fills with the postcards all his friends send from exotic locations. "What d'you reckon, Rube?"

"I've always wanted to go to Rio," she remarked. "I can just see me sunning myself on the Copacabana."

"She's jealous," Nat informed me authoritatively. "It sticks out a mile."

"As the actress said to the bishop," Ruby said. "Yeah, you're right, Nat. Course I'm jealous. I mean, just look around you. Swank flat, gorgeous man who adores her – who wouldn't be jealous?"

"Not me," Nat said definitely, and I for one believed her. She does the ditzy thing to perfection, but she doesn't have a jealous bone in her body. "I think she deserves it. You go for it, Flora."

"I didn't say she doesn't deserve it," Ruby

objected. "Just that you're right. I'm jealous." She flicked a careless fingernail against the postcard of Copacabana Beach, and turned to me. "You make the most of it, babe. While it lasts."

chapter thirteen

Back at school on Monday, I remembered Ruby's comment.

"So what did you make of Max?" I asked her, when we all converged on the sixth-form centre at break time.

"He's a babe. Total love ninja. Wouldn't mind having him as arm-candy myself."

"Then what did you mean about making the most of it while it lasts?"

She shrugged, and took a Mars bar out of her school bag. "Just a figure of speech, hun. I need a sugar hit – want some of this?" I shook my head, but Nat, who has a nose for chocolate like a bloodhound, came scurrying over.

I persisted. "It sounds like you think I'm going to finish with him."

"Well, looking at it logically, the odds are it will finish sooner or later, aren't they?"

"Oh, *Ruby*," Nat began, but I held up a suppressing hand.

"It's OK. Go on, Rube. Why do you say that?"

She bit into the Mars bar while she considered. "I read somewhere that in one sense all relationships are failures, because they all end eventually. Until you settle down in the one true lasting one. That's all I meant."

"So what makes you so certain this isn't the one true lasting one, as you put it?"

Even as I asked the question I knew that I was scarcely likely to be satisfied with the answer, but I couldn't help myself. Ruby's invariable tendency to see the glass as half-empty has the power to infuriate me on occasions, and this was one of those occasions. Sure enough, she looked at me with that half-amused, one-eyebrow-raised way that always precedes some scathingly sardonic Ruby-ism.

"So what are you telling me, that it is?"

"I don't know."

"Well there you go, then. You don't know."

"But neither do you."

She gave a fair-enough shrug. "True. I don't. But look at the facts."

"What, like he's older than me?" It just came bursting out. I couldn't help it.

"Bloody hell, Flora, take a chill pill! I'm on your side, remember!"

"It doesn't feel like it." I glared at her. A strand of caramel from the Mars bar adorned her lower lip and chin. It made her look ridiculous, like a greedy child who couldn't wait to cram her sweeties into her gluttonous mouth. Come to think of it, that described her perfectly.

In answer, she shrugged again, and turned on her heel.

"I'm not having this conversation," she threw over her shoulder. "Not while you're in this kind of mood. I'll see you both later."

I turned to Nat, exasperated. "What's her problem?"

"Don't worry about it." Nat, ever the peacemaker, put an appeasing hand on my arm. "I think she's feeling a bit sensitive because of Tom."

"Tom who?"

"Tom Sheldon. You know – your sister's mate Amy's brother."

"So why's Ruby upset about him?"

"'Cos he knocked her back at the weekend. At Kaz's party."

"Did he?" This was news to me. "I didn't even know she liked him. And I didn't know Kaz was having a party. I don't remember being invited." Not that I'd have been able to go even if I had been. Weekends were for spending with Max.

Nat gave me a look that, had it come from anybody else, I'd have thought odd. "She's been going on about Tom for long enough. Months, it's been."

"So what happened?"

"He was at Kaz's on Saturday night, and Ruby being Ruby, she decided it was now or never. She dragged him out to dance, and asked him for a date."

I could well imagine. Get a couple of Bacardi Breezers down her neck, and Rube thinks she can conquer the world. "But he didn't want to know?"

"To put it mildly. To add insult to injury, he was all over Kaz like a rash after that. Ruby was well cut up about it; she even took Kaz's present back."

It explained a lot. "So it's like you said on Friday. She's jealous. Because I've got a man, and she hasn't."

"Well . . . I don't think I'd put it quite like that."

"No, OK," I said, with a sigh of surrender. Unrequited love was pants; I remembered it well. It was such a relief to be shot of all that trauma and heartache. "I guess I'm being unfair. She just really winds me up when she gets all cynical and pompous."

"Yeah, me too. But don't be too hard on her. She's been really down."

"Has she? I haven't noticed."

She eyed me again. This time there was no mistake – it was definitely what Gran calls an old-fashioned look.

"What?" I said. "What's the matter?"

"Did you two fall out, or something?"

"Not that I'm aware of – why?"

"I just wondered why you didn't know about her and Tom. And why you don't seem to care how she's feeling about him."

"I do care!" I protested. "Of course I care! I love Rube – you know I do. She's my mate."

"But. . .?"

"Whaddya mean?"

"It sounded like there was a but. She's my mate *but*. . ."

"There's no but," I said, decidedly. "Well – only that all this stuff with Max has been taking up quite a lot of my time."

"So I noticed," she said softly.

"Look, Nat, what do you think about us? Honestly?"

"You do seem very happy."

"We are."

"And he's very good-looking."

"Yeah." I beamed. "He is, isn't he."

"So is he – like, you know –" She waved a vague hand. "Serious?"

"Serious?"

"Yeah. Like, has he told you he loves you or anything?"

"Not exactly. Although as a matter of fact. . ." I bent, and rummaged in my school bag. "He did give me this the other day." I dug around in the outside pocket and produced an envelope with a flourish. "Just don't tell Rube, or it'll be something else for her to get all pissy about."

"What is it?" Nat looked at it warily.

"It's a poem. A sonnet, to be precise."

"Is it Shakespeare?"

"No, Cooper. Max wrote it," I explained, seeing her blank face.

"For you?"

"Uh-huh. He said he wanted to redress the balance after Danny's effort."

"Wow." Nat regarded the envelope as if it was the Holy Grail. "Can I read it?"

"Sure – but not here. The bell's going in a sec, let's go outside."

We went down the stairs from the sixth-form centre, and paused in the stairwell below. I handed the envelope across, and Nat drew out the single sheet of paper. She began to read it aloud, her voice growing tender as she went on.

When I consider all that's passed before –
My empty life, so full of care and blight –
I marvel at the radiant face you wore
As, lovingly, you filled my world with light.
With heedless joy you strode into the frame;
You shone with childlike fervour from the start.

> *All pansy-eyed and satin-limbed you came*
> *And quelled the restless demons in my heart.*
> *You gave me but one look: I was enslaved,*
> *My soul at once set free and yet in chains.*
> *The poor wretch that was me has now been*
>   *saved,*
> *With passion to replace my bitter pains.*
> *Unwittingly you craft a silken noose*
> *And captivate my heart – my artless muse!*

"Wow," she said again, when she reached the end. She looked up at me, wide-eyed. "That is just so sweet."

"I know."

"You're lucky, you know that? To have a guy like Max, with all his—"

"Money?" I suggested, with a grin.

"Now who's being cynical? No, I was going to say qualities. All his qualities. *And* he writes you gorgeous poetry, too." She sighed fervently, moved to the bottom of her romantic soul. "You are just so lucky."

"I know," I assured her again. "I know."

By chance, Max was involved with location filming in a local park, and I decided to call by to see him after school on Friday afternoon. It was just one of those impulsive whim things that afterwards, in retrospect, I realized I should never have done. It was a classic case of our two very different worlds colliding, and I can see now that the collision had repercussions that I could never have imagined.

But that was afterwards. At the time it seemed like a great idea. It was a beautiful late afternoon in early June, the first really warm day of the year after a week of heavy showers. All the trees were laden with their fresh green leaf growth, the air heavy with flower fragrance and birdsong. I'd finally handed in my long-overdue English coursework, and a whole weekend of lazing around doing nothing other than a bit of light revision stretched ahead. In short, life seemed pretty damn fine. So I made my excuses to Ruby and Nat, who were lobbying for going into town and checking out the talent at a new café, and went to catch a bus.

"Sure we can't tempt you to a coffee? De luxe cappuccino with chocolate flake? My treat?" Nat wheedled.

"Leave it, Nat – she's got bigger fish to fry," scoffed Ruby. She'd been in an odd mood with me since Kaz's party: she was clearly still pissed off with me for not knowing she'd fancied Tom. I suppose I had been a bit insensitive, now I came to think about it. "She's off to meet Mad Max for a secret tryst in Allie Park."

"It's hardly secret," I responded. "We'll be

surrounded by a whole pile of actors, not to mention the camera crew."

"Are you going to a shoot?" Nat sounded impressed, and for a moment I was tempted to invite her along. But I didn't. Instead I said goodbye and hurried to catch the bus out to Alexandra Park. It was a double decker, half empty, and I found a seat at the top, from where the said actors, camera crew and assorted paraphernalia of the film shoot could clearly be seen as we approached along the main road. I got off at the bus stop outside the curlicued wrought-iron main gates, feeling suddenly ludicrously self-conscious. What should I do – sidle up to where the action was and lurk around until Max spotted me? Or march right in, announce who I was and ask for him? It struck me that I hadn't a clue what Max's job actually entailed, or what the protocol was for disturbing him at work. I wouldn't have dreamt of barging into, say, Dad's office and interrupting him, but all these people were outside in a public place and in full view to everyone. Surely that was different?

In the event I didn't have to do anything, because as I approached I spotted someone familiar. It was one of the sound men; he was holding a long pole with one of those huge grey fluffily-encased mikes on the end, the type that always look curiously like an archaic form of animal torture, with headphones around his neck and an expression of terminal boredom on his face. I recognized him as the guy we'd bumped into at the jazz club that time: Brian-from-work.

"Hi," I said, strolling over to him. Relief at seeing someone I knew must have made me sound more eager than I'd intended, because as he turned round a great big cheesy smile spread itself across his face that had nothing to do with recognizing me in turn.

"Well, hello darling," he drawled. I was suddenly aware of having unbuttoned my shirt much lower than usual – it had been stiflingly hot on the bus, the sun streaming in through the large windows – and he was talking to my chest rather than to me. He probably thought I was some kind of filming groupie, if such things exist, which they probably do.

"It's me," I said, intelligently, doing up another button.

"I can see that," he agreed.

"Flora?" I prompted him. I was beginning to feel a bit of a prat, to be honest. "Max Cooper's girlfriend? We met at that club the other night?"

All traces of leer disappeared immediately, as if wiped off.

"Right. Yes. Of course," he said. "Of course we

did. So what brings you here, then, Fiona?"

"Flora," I corrected him. "I just thought I'd drop by and say hello to Max. If he's not too busy."

"Sure. I'm sure he'll be delighted to see you. He's over there somewhere." He waggled the grey furry animal in the general direction of where everyone was standing around in little knots of three or four, nursing styrofoam cups, chatting and smoking. There didn't appear to be much in the way of filming going on, or indeed action of any kind. "Just look for all the totty, and he'll be in the middle of it all. He usually is," he added, gloomily.

Assuming it was his idea of a joke, I walked over. Sure enough, there was Max, holding a clipboard and with his back half-turned to me. My stomach did its usual backflip. As I approached, a girl with long red hair standing next to him threw back her head and laughed at something he said, something I couldn't catch. Her laugh was deep, husky and amused. She dropped the cigarette she was holding, trod it into the ground, laid a long-taloned hand on his arm in an annoyingly intimate gesture, and made to walk off.

"Hi, Max," I said.

He turned. So did the girl.

"So who's this?" she asked him, with a

conspiratorial smile. "One of your teeny admirers?"

Bloody cheek. That laugh was just one millimetre away from being a smoker's cough, and her hair had to be dyed. I linked my arm through Max's, proprietorially, and kissed him on the cheek.

"Flora!" he exclaimed. "How – er – how lovely. What brings you here?"

"I just thought I'd come and say hello. Surprise you."

"Well, you've certainly done that, honey," the girl drawled. "Catch up with you later, Max sweetie, OK?" And off she sashayed, into the fray.

"Who's your ginger friend?" I asked Max, stung by her familiarity and his taken-aback response at seeing me.

"Oh, just an actress," he told me, with an indifferent casualness that didn't fool me for a second.

"Oh yeah. Not Nicole Kidman, by any chance?" I scoffed.

He frowned, baffled. "Sorry?"

"The hair, the Australian accent. It's obvious who she's trying to be like."

"Actually, she's from New Zealand. Although you're right, she does rather fancy herself."

Not half as much as she fancies you, I

thought, but didn't say it. Consoling myself with the thought that, despite apparently being surrounded on a daily basis by more actresses than you could shake a stick at, it was me Max had chosen to be with, I tucked my arm further into his.

"So what's her name?"

"Hmmm?" He seemed very distracted. "Sorry? Whose name?"

"Ginger. The Nicole looky-likey."

"Oh, Sara something, I think. Something like that. Look, Flora." He looked at me properly, for the first time since I'd arrived. "Lovely though it is to see you, and much as I'd like to be able to drop everything, I am supposed to be working."

"I know." Was it my imagination, or did he sound just the teensiest bit irritated? "I'm not expecting you to drop everything. I just wanted to come and see you. You know, watch the maestro at work, kind of thing."

He laughed. OK – not irritated, then. Just unsure what I was doing there. "Hardly. No maestros here, I'm afraid."

"So can I stay?"

"Of course you can. Not that you're likely to see anything very exciting. If you go over to that van –" he indicated it with the clipboard – "you can get a cuppa and a sticky bun. Tell them I sent you. We should finish in about another hour or so, if you're quite sure you don't mind waiting."

"And then shall we go out for a meal?"

"Ah." He looked faintly abashed. "That might be a bit difficult. We've arranged to go for a drink, a whole pile of us; show our Antipodean friends Esher's finest drinking holes. I was going to ring you."

Now it was my turn to be irritated. "I see. And am I invited along, or will that cramp your style too much?"

"Of course it won't. Don't be daft. Look, go and get that cup of tea, and I'll see you afterwards, OK?"

Unappeased, I muttered something that sounded childish and ungracious even to my ears, and pulled my arm from his. Max caught hold of it, and lifted my chin with his thumb so my eyes met his.

"OK?" he repeated, softly.

"I suppose so."

"Don't be cross, Flora. I really am pleased to see you. Now go and get your tea."

He was right – I didn't see anything exciting. In fact, had I realized that gatecrashing a shoot would be so mind-numbingly dull I'd probably have thought twice about it. All that happened was a load of arm-waving and shouting,

229

followed by a few brief moments of silence during which time a camera on a kind of crane thing on wheels drove steadily backwards, followed by more gesticulations and noise. I couldn't see what part Max had to play in all this as he was lost to view. I didn't even see anyone famous, although the guy who presents that silly sports quiz on TV was in front of me in the tea queue. At least, I think it was him. It might just have been someone who looked like him.

"So what is it they're filming?" I asked the bored-looking girl who was slopping tea into cups with an air that all this was somehow beneath her.

"Dunno," she responded, with a shrug that said she couldn't care less.

"Shampoo commercials," said a more forthcoming older woman in a blue checked overall, opening a carton of milk and pouring it into an aluminium jug. "Australian, I believe. They've been at it all week, although two days of that was just standing round on account of all the rain. Leave that, Gemma, and take this tray over to Mr Cooper. He asked for some tea half an hour since and nobody's taken it yet."

A little shiver passed through me, a thrill that Max's tea was taken to him while everyone else, all the plebs, had to queue for theirs.

"Actually," I said, casually, "I'm with Mr

Cooper. Max, I mean. I could take it over to him if you like."

"No need," the woman said briskly. "Gemma can do it. It's what she's paid for."

After not one hour but almost two of carpet-chewing boredom, during which time I drank enough tea to re-float the *Mary Rose*, the filming finished. Everyone began to drift away, in desultory fashion, and after another five minutes Max came striding purposefully over, wearing a look of slightly disgruntled regret.

"Angel, I'm so sorry. I've experienced some duff acting in my time, but I've never known anybody need twenty-two takes for just one sentence before. You must be bored rigid."

"I'm fine," I lied. "So who's the airhead, then? Ginger?" The thought cheered me up slightly, but Max shook his head.

"No, she was fine. A vacuous creature called Tamara. I kid you not, the shampoo bottle learnt its lines quicker than her. And it had more presence."

Those of us who were joining the pub crawl piled in to a selection of muddy four-wheel drives. I was slightly piqued to discover that Max had left the Jag at home, and even more piqued when Ginger crammed herself next to Max and Brian in the back of one, leaving me to sit in the front with the driver. We headed out on the A3, southwards into the depths of the countryside. It was a perfect evening for a country drive, but spoilt for me by the heavily Kiwi-accented giggles and gushings coming from the back.

"Ow, really, Max." The way she said it sounded like Mex. "I never knew thet, Mex."

We pulled up in front of everyone's idea of the perfect Brit country pub, all thatched roof and pretty white-painted exterior. Several lilac trees were in full gloriously-scented bloom in the front garden. There were even roses growing round the front door. It was exactly the kind of place I'd envisaged Max taking me on a balmy summer's evening, and here we were sharing it with a film crew and a pile of rowdy Australian actors.

"Pimm's all round?" Max suggested, catching my eye and winking.

"Sod thet. I'm heving a pint of the ember nectar," Ginger declared. "All that stending round waiting for Tem to remimber her lines has made me dry as hill."

"So, Fiona," Brian shouted to me inside, over the Friday-evening hubbub. "What did you make of location filming, then? Not exactly glamorous, is it?"

"Oh, it was fine," I lied again. "Really interesting." I could practically feel my nose growing, like Pinocchio's, with all the fibs.

We all took our drinks outside to the garden, drenched in the evening sun. Couples sat under parasols at the benches, their hands entwined, and mums and dads tucked into fragrant plates of pasta and fondly watched their young children playing happily amongst the lilacs. There was a stream gurgling at the end of the garden where the lawn sloped down to some trees, and two little girls in matching gingham summer dresses were feeding a gaggle of noisy ducks, throwing bread to them with delighted giggles and entreaties to their parents to watch them. It was a perfect, idyllic early summer scene.

I found myself wedged on to a bench between Ginger and a girl a bit older than me with lank mousy hair, while Max stood miles away with his pint of real ale, surrounded by back-slapping men all roaring with laughter. They looked as if they'd been playing rugby and won, rather than filming.

"So what's your name?" I asked Ginger, more out of politeness than anything else.

"Cassandra," she said, taking a huge swig from her lager. "Sandra to my mates."

"I'm Lisa," the mousy girl said. She wore serious-looking horn-rimmed specs and a soulful expression, like a labrador waiting for its walk. "Don't you think Max Cooper is just the divinest man you've ever seen?" And she drained her glass of wine to its dregs.

Cassandra and I exchanged glances. "Another one of those?" she asked Lisa.

When she returned with it, Lisa spent the next three weeks or so telling us how she'd been in love with Max since starting to work as an office junior for him a year ago. She got through two more glasses of wine, while Max himself steered noticeably clear of our table.

"I'm never going to get a look-in," Lisa slurred drunkenly. "Not while he's got that cow Melanie protecting him."

"Who's Melanie?" I enquired. I'd had no idea all this had been going on while Max was at work. It was like another world.

"His PA. She won't even let anyone speak to him without an appointment."

"So what do you do, Fiona?" Cassandra asked me.

"Actually, it's Flora. Look, I'm just going to – er – you know. Powder my nose."

It was no good – I couldn't stand it any more, listening to Lisa dribbling on about my boyfriend and pretending to be enjoying myself. I gestured vaguely towards the pub entrance and clambered inelegantly over the bench. Perhaps I'd disappear for a while; nothing too dramatic, just shut myself in the loo for a bit until Max started to wonder where I was.

It was cool inside the Ladies, which were a cut above the usual pub lavs, with bowls of pot pourri, boxes of Kleenex and bottles of hand lotion dotted strategically around. I went into one of the cubicles and locked the door, glad to be away from Lisa and her drunken ramblings.

Then the main door slammed shut and I heard two women come in, laughing uproariously.

"That's a good one," said one, with an Australian accent. "Six inches, eh. I'll have to tell Sandra. She'll love it."

"D'you think she needs rescuing?" said the other. "Only she's been stuck with Luscious Lisa all evening, the poor love. She looks bored rigid."

"Who's Luscious Lisa?"

"Plain girl from the office. Madly in unrequited love with Max, and tells anyone who'll listen after a couple of drinks. As if he'd look twice at her."

The Aussie giggled. "Now now, Mel! Don't be a bitch! Although I have to say, he is rather gorgeous."

"Isn't he just."

They both laughed again, and there was silence, punctuated with the small noises of make-up being reapplied and hair being fluffed up. I flushed the loo, and was just about to unlock the cubicle and go out when the British voice spoke again.

"Did you clock who was sitting next to Sandra?"

"Yeah, I think so – young girl, dark hair? What about her?"

"That's Max's girlfriend."

My hand froze on the latch. I felt wrong-footed, and horribly guilty, as if I'd been caught doing something forbidden.

"You're joking!" A gasp of disbelief, followed by an amused snort. "Jesus! She only looks about fifteen!"

That'll teach me to come straight from school, with no make-up.

"She's seventeen."

"No! Shit! I'd never have put Max down as a cradle-snatcher. I thought he had more sophistication."

"You know Brian, the sound guy? He bumped into the pair of them a while ago in Monty's. It's a jazz club in town. He said she was all dolled up to the nines – full raver's kit – and that Max's eyes were out on stalks."

"Yeah, but – seventeen." She whistled, but not out of admiration. "How old is he? He must be thirty if he's a day."

"Next month. We call them Lolita and Humbert Humbert in the office."

There was a second or two of scandalized silence, then both women began to laugh again. But it wasn't the laughter of before, of sharing an entertaining joke. They were sniggering, unpleasantly, knowingly, and it made me clench my fists in anger, tears of injustice prickling behind my eyes. What did they know about me? How dare they judge our relationship?

The door slammed again, and there was silence. They had gone. I sat down on the loo seat, shaking with anger and a deep sense of unfairness and other, less readily identifiable emotions. Eventually, realizing I could hardly stay there all night even if that's what I felt like doing, I unlocked the door and went slowly out. Lisa was standing in front of the mirror, peering at herself and wiping smeared mascara from under her eyes. I hadn't heard her come in. We both jumped at the sight of each other.

"Oh, Flora," she said, turning towards me and putting her specs back on. All the drunken slurring of before had gone, totally. She sounded stone-cold sober. "I didn't realize who you were. I'm so sorry."

I frowned. "What for?"

"For going on like that. About fancying Max." Oddly, her revelations hadn't especially bothered me, or at least not in the way she was apologizing for. I guess I just hadn't seen her as competition.

"Oh, that," I said, wearily. "It's OK, it doesn't matter."

She turned back to the mirror and spoke to my reflection.

"Are you sure? Only you look a bit stressed."

"I'm fine. Look, when you came in here, was anyone coming out?"

"Only Cruella De Vil."

"Who?"

"Mel. Melanie – Max's PA. Oh, and wossername, that Aussie model who couldn't act her way out of a paper bag. Tamara. Why d'you ask?"

Because they're a pair of bitches, I thought to myself; *oh, and did you know they all call you Luscious Lisa in the office? Luscious Lisa and Lolita – we make a good pair.*

"I just wondered, that's all."

Max was waiting for me outside the Ladies, clutching his pint glass and a refill for me. Lisa turned an unflattering shade of beetroot at the sight of him and scuttled off, back out to the garden.

"There you are," Max said. He peered anxiously at me. "Cassandra said she thought you'd come in here, ages ago. I was wondering where you'd got to. You look rather stressed – are you OK?"

I would be, I felt like snarling, if everyone would just stop telling me that I look stressed.

"I'm fine."

"I'm sorry for having abandoned you like that, but I couldn't get away."

"Vital post-shoot business?" I enquired, sarcastically, but he didn't seem to notice.

"Not really. Just chatting. Flesh-pressing – you know how it is. Anyway, I'm so sorry I've been neglecting you. I'll make it up to you, I promise." He offered me my replenished glass. "Another drink?"

I brushed it aside, moodily. "No thanks. And when did you start drinking beer? I thought you were a gin-and-tonic man."

He looked startled, as if I'd accused him of something shameful. "I like a pint occasionally. Are you sure you're OK?"

I sighed. It was hardly his fault his catty PA had been gossiping about us in the Ladies.

"Well, to be honest, I'm not feeling that great."

He was instantly full of concern, looking around for someone to drive us back to pick up his car, but I deflected him.

"I think I just want to go home."

"Sure, no problem. I'll get Mel to call us a cab

straight back to the flat – I'll collect the Jag in the morning."

But I'd had enough of the evening, of the day.

"No, Max. I mean home. Not the flat – I want to go home."

chapter fourteen

If my being home before nine o'clock on a Friday evening was unusual, my family's response to me walking in through the front door was totally unheard of. After weeks of appearing distinctly uncomfortable if we happened to be in the same room together (if not actively avoiding each other altogether), they actually seemed pleased to see me.

Mum emerged from the sitting room as I came in, with her hands full of supper things and a slightly startled expression on her face.

"Hello, love," she greeted me. "We thought we heard the door. You're home early."

For once. I mentally finished the sentence for her. It didn't seem worth the hassle to say it out loud though. Besides, strange though it felt, I was glad to be home.

"Is everything all right?" She regarded me more closely. "You seem a bit—"

"Stressed?" *Here we go again. . .*

"No, actually, I was going to say subdued."

"I'm fine," I lied. I followed her into the kitchen, where she laid down the tray of dirty dishes.

"We were just about to watch a video with Hattie. That new Josh Hairnet thingy she's been going on about. Why don't you join us?"

"Hartnett," I corrected her, a thousand pretexts why I couldn't watch the video with them thronging my brain. "It's Josh Hartnett. You're getting as bad as Gran."

"Oh God, don't say that." She smiled at me, and all of a sudden all the excuses dissolved away, and I couldn't think of any good reason for not going and sitting with them, my parents and my little sister, and having a family Friday night videofest with a gallon of Coke and a bucket-load of popcorn on the side, just like we used to. In the olden days, before they started getting on my case about the inappropriateness of my clothes, the loudness of my music, and the unsuitability of my boyfriends.

It wasn't exactly like before, as Hugh was off out on the piss with his rabble-y mates. But it was still cool, a blast from the past, with Hat and me chilled out on opposite ends of the sofa with the popcorn between us, Mum tucking into the Quality Street, and Dad with his daring half-pint mug of Newcastle Brown making derogatory comments about all the guys.

"He looks like a real jessie," was his observation on the delicious Josh.

"Ooh, Dad," Hattie squealed.

"You've upset her now," I told him. "She wants to marry him when she grows up, don't you Hattie?"

"No I don't!" she objected, going red. "Shut up, Flora!"

"Just as well really, or you'd be Harriet Hartnett. Now that *would* be tragic."

When the film was finished, Hattie eventually hauled herself off upstairs to bed and Mum went to put the kettle on for bedtime drinks. I'd forgotten how set in routine my family liked things to be. Nothing wrong with routine, though. In its place.

"That was nice," Dad said to me, pressing the remote to rewind the video.

"What, the movie? I thought you said he was a jessie," I teased him.

"Nah, the film was rubbish. I meant having you at home with us to watch it. Makes a nice change."

"Well, you know, I wasn't doing anything else, and I thought it would be, um. . ." I mumbled, feeling suddenly and inexplicably shy. "Nice," I finished, lamely.

"Well, it was," Dad said. He bent to retrieve the video from the slot. "Very nice."

I don't know what made me say what I did next. Feeling all gooey and soft round the edges from having spent a rare evening in the bosom of my family, probably. That's what Ruby would have said, at any rate, although you'd have thought I'd have known better, knowing what my father is like. Knowing how unreasonable and intransigent he can be under that bluff I'm-such-a-family-man exterior.

"I've been thinking," I began, carefully. Which was a lie, for a start. The idea had only just occurred to me. "How about if I invited Max round for a meal – say, Sunday lunch next week?"

Dad straightened up from the video, dangerously slowly. Our eyes met, and his held mine for a long moment.

"I don't think so," he said, at last. His voice sounded perfectly normal, but his nostrils were flared and his mouth pinched into a thin tight line.

Of course, me being me, I had to push it.

"But you could get to know him a bit better," I protested. "I'm sure if you—"

Dad held up a hand, a silencing hand that brooked no argument. "I already know him. And I don't like what I know. Now there's an end to it."

And he left the room, pushing the video into my hand as he did so.

Bloody great, I fumed inwardly, all the way upstairs and into my bedroom. *So that's it, is it –*

I'm not even allowed to mention his name any more, am I? I stomped around in my room for a bit, then strode out and into Hattie's without knocking. I needed another female opinion: it was no use asking Mum, not on this one, and Hattie had already proved herself on my side. Besides, what choice did I have?

She jumped up from her bed when I entered as if she'd been shot, and a whole pile of papers slid down off her lap on to the floor.

"God!" she complained. "Don't I get any privacy round here?"

I flapped a hand at her. "Never mind all that. You come in my room uninvited often enough. Listen, I want to ask you something."

"Go and ring one of your poxy friends if you want advice," she grumbled, crawling around and retrieving the papers. "I'm busy."

"I thought you were supposed to be going to bed." I bent to pick up a stray one that had floated over towards the door, but she leapt to her feet and snatched it from me.

"That's private!" she snapped.

"OK, OK! Don't get your knickers in a twist!" I craned my head to look at whatever it was, intrigued. To my enormous surprise, it was a photo of me. It had obviously been scanned and then printed off on the computer. "What on earth is that?"

245

"It's a picture," she replied, sulkily.

"Yeah, of me!"

"So? There's no law against it, is there?"

"Harriet." I put on my best impression of Mum being stern. "What are you doing with a picture of me?"

She scowled. "You'll only tell."

"No I won't."

"You so will. You're such a dobber."

"I won't. I promise." To tell the truth, I was getting worried. Why on earth should she think I'd tell on her having a contraband picture of me? It was unusual, certainly, but hardly something Mum and Dad were likely to throw a moody about. "Where did you get it?"

"You gave it to me."

"No I didn't!"

"Yeah, you did. Ages ago."

Something stirred at the back of my brain, some memory of a school project she'd been doing, family pictures to send to a penfriend.

"Oh, that's right. I remember now." I looked at her; her shuffling feet, her scarlet, ill-at-ease face, her fidgeting manner. The thought balloon suspended over her head that said, I AM A LIAR; she is so lousy at hiding the truth. "But it wasn't for a project at all, was it? There probably isn't even a penfriend. So what did you want it for?"

She mumbled something I couldn't hear.

"Sorry?"

"I said, I wanted to pretend it was me."

"What?" I laughed in disbelief. "I didn't know you were such a fan!"

"Don't be stupid," she said, witheringly.

"So why. . ." There was a resounding clunk as the penny dropped. "This wouldn't have anything to do with chatrooms, would it?"

She went even more scarlet. "Might do."

"Oh come on, Hattie. Don't give me that. If you wanted your little pals to see what you look like, why on earth didn't you just send them one of yourself?"

"Because if I did, he was never going to believe I was eighteen, was he!" she burst out.

"Who?" I was beginning to have a nasty feeling about all of this.

"Gary."

It seemed important to stay calm. "Gary who? Look, Hattie, I don't want to spoil your fun, but you know what they say about getting too friendly with people you meet in chatrooms. You don't know anything about this Gary."

"Yes I do! He's twenty, he's a student and he lives in London." *So there.* She didn't say it, but she may as well have done.

"So he says. Hat –" I manoeuvred her over to the bed and sat her down. Time for a sister-to-sister chat. "You know people can be who they want on the Net. They can say anything they feel like. You can't take anything at face value."

"I can with him. We tell each other the truth," she insisted stoutly.

"What, like you're Britney, you look like me and you're eighteen?" It just slipped out, I couldn't help it, but she took grave offence.

"I don't care what you say!" She leapt to her feet. "He is not a perv! We're just friends, OK?"

"OK, OK!" I looked at the photo of me again. "Why did you print it off? Why didn't you just e-mail it to him?"

"He wanted me to send it."

"He gave you his address?" Another nasty thought entered my mind. "You haven't given him yours, have you?" She just shrugged. I was horrified. "Hattie, are you stupid or what? Don't you read those magazines of yours, or watch the TV? Don't you know that sickos go into these places to pick up victims? This Gary is probably about fifty."

"You can talk!" Her eyes blazed at me from beneath her untidy fringe. "You know all about dirty old men, don't you – you and your precious Max!"

I don't know why it wounded me so much, but it did. It was only what Hugh had said about him, after all. But she'd been an unlikely ally, my little sister; the only one of my family who'd said she could see why I was with him, and it had meant a lot.

I took a deep breath. "Please, Hat. Promise me you won't do anything stupid."

"Like what?" she scoffed, enjoying the feeling of the rare power she wielded over me.

"Like arranging to meet him."

She didn't answer, just marched to her door and held it open.

"Just bog off, will you. I want to go to bed."

Even though that evening ended up the way it did, with Dad and me back to square one over Max and Hattie and me falling out, it did make me start asking myself certain questions. Such as why, when I distinctly remembered Max telling me he wanted to introduce me to his friends, to show me off to them, he never did so – although if that evening in the pub after the shoot was anything to go by, perhaps it was just as well. Such as why, having satisfied his conscience by telling Mum and Dad about our relationship, he then seemed quite content to drop me off on the doorstep after every date without any further suggestion that he might at some stage come in, to try and persuade them round to our way of thinking. Although there was probably no point, as I'd told him how frosty things had become at home in general, and I didn't see the sense of creating hassle.

Well, there you go. Those two "althoughs" say it all, don't they? I asked myself those questions, but didn't get round to asking Max. Instead I made excuses for him; for why I hadn't met his friends or his sister yet, for why he dropped me off at home but never came in. It was the way our relationship had developed, and I was too wrapped up in the joy of it all to let any minor disquiet rain on my parade. Because in every other way, things seemed perfect – *he* was perfect, Max, or as near to perfect as I could have wished for. The perfect gentleman, and the perfect boyfriend. Being with him had opened up all kinds of possibilities that could never have existed with someone of my own age. I don't just mean things he could afford that no one of my age ever could, but also his level of expectation and experience. Although things didn't always work out the way we either intended or envisaged.

Take his university reunion, for example.

"Did I tell you I'm going to Cambridge next weekend?" he just happened to mention, a couple of weeks after what I'd begun to call The Great Filming Experience. (Moral: never turn up uninvited when Max is working. You might not like what you see.)

"For work?"

"No, it's a college reunion."

I immediately felt peeved. God knows why – he quite often had to work at weekends and that never bothered me, it was just the way it was. But a reunion was different. I think it was the thought of him off somewhere enjoying himself without me, to be honest. It was why I said what I did next.

"Can I come?"

"What, to Cambridge?" He looked a bit doubtful. "Well . . . I'm not sure."

"Why not? Because all your posh Oxbridge chums will look down their noses at me? Or because they'll look down on you for having dumped Marina and hooked up with someone my age?" I flashed at him, wondering as I did so why I felt so defensive.

He looked at me for a long, cool moment.

"My chums, as you call them, aren't in the slightest bit posh. And it's only you who keeps going on about your age. For someone who professes not to care about the age gap, you don't seem to lose any opportunity in bringing it up."

I was instantly repentant, and rushed over to where he was sitting on the sofa.

"Sorry Max. Sorry sorry sorry." I threw my arms around him. "It's just that I still can't believe we're together. I have to pinch myself. I still don't understand what someone like you sees in someone like me."

"It's what I ask myself the whole time. Only the other way round, of course." He hugged me back affectionately. "Do you really want to come?"

"Yes." I'd barely thought about it. My question had been more of a reflex than a genuine wanting to go too, but now I'd asked it, I liked the idea. I liked it a lot. "It'd be fun, just you and me, a whole weekend together."

"What about your parents?"

"Oh, I don't think they'd want to go."

"Ha ha. You know what I mean." He looked serious. As well he might. For all the time we'd had together, I'd never spent a whole night with him before. I'd always gone back home. Not because Mum and Dad wanted me to – it just wouldn't have been advisable. I didn't want to rub their noses in it, I wasn't that keen on proving my point. Besides, where was the sense in attracting even more hassle? "Would you tell them where you were going?"

"You're *joking*! Dad would be round your place with a carving knife to shred your bits. No, I'll find some excuse. I'll tell them I'm going somewhere with Nat and Ruby, or something."

"Are you sure? Wouldn't it be better to be honest?"

"Oh, yeah. Course it would," I said

sarcastically. "Look, Max, you can come round and tell Dad we're going off together for the weekend if you want, but I'm not going to. My way is best. Trust me."

He took a bit of persuading – he kept saying he didn't want to deceive them – but after a while he capitulated, as I knew he would. He just couldn't resist the thought of having a whole weekend together, rather than the snatched few hours in his flat that had become the norm. Not that there was anything wrong with his flat – but it wasn't the same as the luxury of unhurried time, of two nights together in a nice hotel.

The plan was that we'd drive up to Cambridge on the Friday evening, and come back on the Sunday. There was apparently a whole programme of events planned for the reunion weekend, including a cricket match for Old Boys versus Current Boys, or whatever the terminology is, but Max said he didn't especially want to go to all that, just to the dinner on the Saturday night. Thoughts of that post-shoot evening in the pub filled my mind, images of Max surrounded by adoring (not to mention slobbering) females, all with long ginger hair and Australian accents. But I got a grip, and maturely told him that I'd love to go to the dinner with him and meet all his old university cronies; and so it was fixed.

I told Mum and Dad that I was going with Nat to her aunt's in Southsea. Or rather I told Mum. Dad never seemed to stand still long enough these days for me to tell him anything. It was a complete fabrication, of course; Nat didn't even have an aunt in Southsea, although she did say she'd cover for me if necessary.

Hugh didn't buy it at all. "*Southsea?*" he said, raising a disbelieving eyebrow. "What the hell do you want to go there for?"

"Rock festival," I invented wildly, thinking as I did so how much easier it would be if I could just tell him the truth. In the old days I might have been able to. Not now, though. Like the parents, he would just give me grief.

"Oh yeah. Sure," he said, sardonically.

"Haven't you heard of the Southsea Rock Festival? There's some good bands on. Nat's, er, cousin is playing in one." I dug myself ever-deeper into the hole, wondering why I couldn't just leave it. It would have been so easy for Hugh to check up on what I was saying, and then my cover would have been blown wide open. Luckily for me, he didn't seem to care that much.

"So presumably Max is going too." He put inverted commas round the name, distastefully, as if he could hardly bring himself to say it.

"He doesn't like rock. He's more into jazz."

254

That, at least, wasn't a lie. And I hadn't exactly said he wasn't going to be with me, had I? Oh God, the straws we clutch at.

It was a brilliant weekend. Better than I could ever have hoped for. The sun shone continuously, and Max was the best company: funny and witty and affectionate. He'd booked us in to a gorgeous hotel just outside the city, all sweeping staircases, open fireplaces and opulent drapes. Our room had a four-poster bed and the hugest, most luxurious bathroom I've ever seen, bursting at the seams with freebie upmarket lotions and potions and fluffy towelling bathrobes. There was an enormous basket of fresh fruit waiting for us on our arrival, and a bottle of champagne on ice.

"Bloody hell," I said, when we walked in. "Is this the bridal suite or something?" And then felt instantly stupid, for showing up my lack of sophistication and experience.

Max just laughed. "You deserve the best," he told me. "We all like treats occasionally, don't we?"

On the Saturday we drove out to the seaside, somewhere miles away on the Suffolk coast with huge skies and miles of empty pebbly beaches, and I felt as if we'd been transported into a Constable painting as we walked hand in hand along the shore. We went to a little country pub for an enormous lunch, and afterwards I told him about Hattie and the chatrooms. And Gary.

"Tell your parents," he said, decisively.

"Do you think I should? Only she'll hate me."

"Definitely. They need to know. And she won't hate you, even if she thinks she does at the time. Pippa says she gets that kind of thing all the time from Barney. I know your sister's older, but it's the same principle."

"Hat said I should know all about dirty old men," I told him.

"That must have been upsetting for you." Then he stopped walking, and caught hold of my arm. "It doesn't matter what other people say about us. You know it doesn't. Especially not cross little sisters. We knew we were going to get stick."

"Have you been getting it too?"

"A bit."

"From Melanie?"

"Melanie?" He looked uncertain, as if unsure who Melanie was. "Oh, Mel. No. Not her. Just generally. It's why I haven't told many people about us."

"Are you ashamed of me?" I had to ask him. "Is that why you haven't introduced me to your friends?"

"Ashamed?" His aghast expression told me

all I needed to know. "Of course not. Of course I'm not ashamed of you. But I don't want small-minded people to spoil what we've got." He caught hold of my hands, drew me towards him. "Look, let's go on holiday this summer. Let's go sailing together – that Aegean thing – I'll ring Pippa tonight and get it sorted. I love you. You must know that by now. I don't care how old you are – I've never met anyone like you, who makes me feel the way you do. You've changed my life."

He hugged me, and then kissed me, and as I kissed him back I thought, *Do I love him too?* For the first time, I wondered what love was, exactly. I fancied him, certainly. Just looking at him still had the power to make my toes curl. I loved being with him, he made me feel wanted and special and attractive, and a million and one things nobody had ever made me feel before. Maybe that was what he meant, too. Was that love? I took the coward's way out.

"I love you too," I told him.

In the event we missed the reunion dinner, as we got lost driving back to the hotel and arrived too late to get changed. Max didn't seem to mind. We nevertheless got dressed up in our finery – he'd bought me a dress especially, long and black and elegant, the kind of thing I'd never normally wear – and ate at the hotel instead. It was a wonderfully leisurely meal, and afterwards we went back up to our room where Max had asked room service to deliver another bottle of champagne.

"I could get used to this," I told him, pouring two foaming glasses and turning round to offer him one. "It's so—"

I stopped dead in my tracks. Max had a small leather-covered box in his hand. He held it out to me, smiling, and for one dreadful, awful heart-stopping moment I thought he was going to propose.

"Open it," he said instead. "I was going to give them to you last night, when we arrived, but I forgot."

Forgot? Them? That didn't sound like an engagement ring. Trembling slightly, I put my champagne glass down and opened the box.

Inside, nestling amongst the ruby-red velvet, was a pair of sparkling diamond earrings. I had no need to ask if they were real diamonds. Max just isn't a cubic zirconia kind of guy. I had never in my life seen anything so exquisite, so expensive, and so utterly not me. I just don't really do diamonds, not that I'd ever had the chance before. Big dangly stuff from the local market is much more my style than dainty little studs, however expensive. It seemed churlish to say so, though, not to mention ungrateful in the extreme.

"They're beautiful," I told him, and put them in my ears, and he looked so pleased I knew I'd done the right thing.

On Sunday morning we did Cambridge, all the touristy things, and after another gut-bustingly vast pub lunch we drove back. As the car purred along the M11 I felt pretty much like purring too, replete as I was with good food, invigorated from all yesterday's fresh air, and totally loved-up.

Then my mobile rang, and the whole thing was spoilt.

It was Nat. She was gabbling, near-hysterical, and it took me ages to calm her down enough to discover what she was trying to tell me.

"They know," I made out, at last. "Your Mum and Dad – they know you haven't been with me this weekend. They've figured out you're with Max. I had to ring and warn you. Oh God, Flora – what are you going to do?"

chapter fifteen

All of which put a bit of a damper on our lovely weekend, to say the least – for the rest of the way back all I could think of was what on earth were my parents going to say. Part of me, the sensible there's-no-need-for-a-scene part, told me that Nat had overreacted, and that in all probability they wouldn't do anything. What, after all, could they do? Send me to my room? They knew Max and I were an item, even if they didn't approve. And surely us spending a weekend together was only moving the relationship one step further on.

However, the other, instinctive and altogether larger part of me wasn't at all reassured, and that's the part that won. I switched off my mobile so they couldn't ring me themselves, and spent the remainder of the journey with my stomach churning in babyishly fearful anticipation, huddled both literally and metaphorically on the edge of my seat.

Max did his best to help. He even offered to come in with me, to "face the music" as he put it when we got back, but it was no use. I couldn't shake off the feeling that I'd been somehow *naughty*, and now I was going to be soundly told off. Resentment added itself to the mass of other feelings fermenting away inside me – why did my parents still have this power over me, why was I feeling so ridiculously chastened? This time yesterday I'd been in a top hotel with my lover. He'd bought me diamond earrings, for God's sake!

I wouldn't let Max come in with me; I told him it was something I had to do by myself, although in reality I knew that just the sight of him was liable to send Dad into a frenzy, but he insisted on waiting outside in the car. In case I needed him, he said. Nervousness made me giggle when he said it, visions of Dad chasing me down the path with a shotgun and me leaping into the Jag, the getaway car, and roaring off down the road with Max. Not that the thought was funny in the slightest.

They were all in when I got home – Mum and Dad, Hugh and Hattie. The entire family, gathered in the kitchen as if waiting disapprovingly for my arrival. Bloody typical, I thought gloomily. We're never *all* home together on a Sunday afternoon any more – why today, of all days?

"And where do you think you've been, young lady?" my father greeted me, as I walked in.

"And no rubbish about rock festivals, please. We've seen through that one."

"If you know where I've been," I countered, "why are you asking me?"

Not the best response. Dad erupted as if I'd lit his fuse. He was incandescent with rage, roaring about oversexed middle-aged divorcees and flashy gits with more money than morals having debauched his daughter, all but cannoning off the walls in his outrage. It was scary, I have to admit. Nobody else could get a word in edgeways. Eventually, Mum managed to manoeuvre him, still bellowing, out of the kitchen.

"Welcome to the House of Fun," I muttered under my breath.

"So it's true then," Hugh said, repressively. "You have been away with him."

Since when had my brother appointed himself Keeper of Moral Standards? "I don't think that's any of your business."

"It is my business when it's all he's been going on about for the past twenty-four hours." He pulled a sour face. "What did you have to tell him all that crap about bloody Southsea for?"

Mum came back in at that point, looking decidedly dischuffed, and Hugh beat a hasty retreat, throwing me the kind of look you might give a pool of vomit.

"It's the lies, Flora," Mum said. "That's what we find hard to cope with."

I'd had enough of being treated as if I'd committed some heinous crime. "For God's sake! You all know Max and me are together – what's so wrong about us going away together?"

"Because you lied about it. Why didn't you tell us the truth?"

"Isn't it obvious? Because I knew the kind of response I'd get! So how did you find out?"

"We saw Natalie in town yesterday, glued together at the lips with some boy. Hattie seemed to think it was that lad you were keen on a while ago. Anyway, it was pretty obvious you weren't in the picture, so your father rang Natalie last night and spoke to her mother. She told him that Nat was out with her boyfriend, and there was no aunt in Southsea. Then Hattie discovered you'd gone to Cambridge with – " She took a deep breath, obviously barely able to bring herself to say his name. "With Max."

My head reeling with all this information (Nat's boyfriend? Lad I was keen on? The only lad I'd been keen on recently was Danny; surely it wasn't *him* Nat had been with?), all I could think of to say was "How did Hattie know that?"

"I found it in your diary." Hattie sounded triumphant and self-satisfied, in equal measure. "Cambridge with M, it said."

"You went in my room?" I turned to her, furious. "You looked in my *diary*?"

"We didn't know where you were." Mum raised her voice too, to match mine. "You clearly weren't where you said you'd be, you'd constructed these elaborate lies to cover up, your mobile seemed permanently switched off – we were desperate. We were *worried about you*!" she shouted, and I was shocked. Mum never shouted. Never.

"My phone's out of credit," I said, defensively. "That's why it was switched off."

"It doesn't cost you anything to receive calls, does it? Had it not occurred to you we might need to contact you in an emergency?" Her eyes glittered dangerously in her angry white face. It didn't do to prolong situations when she was in this kind of mood.

"OK," I muttered. "I'm sorry, all right?"

"Sorry's not good enough. Your father's been on the verge of calling the police, reporting you missing."

I was seething at Hattie, for being such a little sneak. For one tempting moment, I considered spilling the beans to Mum about her chatroom adventures with Gary-the-so-called-student. That would show her. But I pushed the thought away, reluctantly. Despite the fact Max had been so certain I should tell them, now really wasn't the time. It would only make me look small-minded; and anyway, the mood Mum was in, she probably wouldn't listen anyway. It wouldn't hurt to fire a couple of warning shots across Hattie's bows, though.

"There was no need for that: I wasn't missing. Anyway, the police would have wanted a *photo of me*," I said, looking pointedly at Hattie. "They might have put it on the *Internet*."

"What?" Mum said, looking baffled. "What are you talking about?"

Hattie's expression changed instantly, from nauseatingly smug to majorly worried. She shook her head vigorously behind Mum's back and made pleading cow eyes at me.

"Nothing," I said, "it's OK."

"Will you leave us alone, please, Harriet?" Mum pushed a weary hand through her already dishevelled hair. "There's things I need to discuss with Flora."

Uh-oh. Harriet. She must be taking this seriously, then. She'd be calling me Florence next.

Hattie scarpered, and I went over to the kettle, checked its water level and plugged it in.

"Fancy a coffee?" I didn't really want one, it was just something to do with my hands, to avoid having to look Mum in the eye. I just wasn't in the mood for a face-off, but I knew I wasn't going to be let off that easily.

"No, I don't. Stop fiddling around and come and sit down." Her sternest voice. I didn't sit down, but decided attack was the best form of defence.

"What is Dad's problem with Max?" I turned round from the kettle.

"Well, if you don't know by now. . ."

"I know he doesn't like him being older than me. I don't mean that. What's all that bollocks about more money than morals? Max can't help earning a lot."

"It's more than just about what he earns."

"What then? I thought he used to like Max, once upon a time. In the old days, when they worked together." I suddenly had a vivid mental picture of Mum arranging the flowers Max had sent the day after their house-warming do. "You were singing his praises yourself not so long ago, saying how thoughtful he was." Mum opened her mouth as if to say something, then thought better of it and pressed her lips together instead. I was baffled. "What? What's the big mystery?"

"There's no mystery. You'd like that, wouldn't you? It would make him even more attractive, I daresay, a touch of enigma."

"No it wouldn't. Look, Mum – come on. Be reasonable. All we've done is fall for each other – I don't understand what all the fuss is about."

"Well, that's plain." She looked at me,

weighing up whether or not to tell me. Then she shrugged. "Make no mistake – the bottom line is, your father thinks he's too old for you. But he never quite trusted him, even back in the old days, as you call them, because of Max's money – call it your father's working-class roots showing, but he's never really been able to believe that men who don't have to work for a living aren't somehow shifty and feckless."

I didn't have a clue what she was talking about. "Don't have to work? What d'you mean? Max has got a fab job – you know he has!"

"You don't honestly think he's able to live the way he does solely on a TV producer's salary?" She gave a short laugh. "Then you're even more naïve than I gave you credit for. I take it that means he hasn't told you about the independent income?" I shook my head, wordlessly. "His father died suddenly when Max was at university, and left him and his sister a tidy sum. His mother had been dead for years, and his father was well-off. Have you heard of Cooper's Crisps? Well, that was Max's father. He owned the business."

"So was he, like, a millionaire?" *I've just been away for the weekend with a millionaire's son. . .*

"I hardly think so. Not a millionaire – not from a crisp factory. Max never went into details with us, but it's always been obvious that he's worth a fair amount. It always stuck in your Dad's craw a bit, all that privilege – private education, and then not just any old university, but Cambridge. And then he went to work at our provincial little local rag. It made Dad feel patronized, as if Max was slumming it."

"He got over it, though. Didn't he? You told me. You said –" What *was* it she'd said, exactly? I couldn't remember now, only her fond tones as she'd arranged the lilies in her best vase. "I just thought you liked him." I said lamely.

"We did. Although to be truthful, I was always fonder of him than your father was. He'd worked damned hard to get where he was, and then along came young Max with his First from Cambridge and just kind of – leapfrogged over him." Her lips went thin again. "And now he's all grown up, and he's buggered off with his daughter," she finished, tartly.

"Well, I don't suppose he did it just to spite Dad!" I burst out. "Is that what he thinks? It sounds like jealousy to me, some kind of stupid old-fashioned class thing! I can't be doing with it."

"You can afford not to."

"What's that supposed to mean?"

"Only that you haven't had to struggle for anything. Your father's made certain of that, by the sweat of his brow, as he sees it."

"I never asked him to."

"Oh, Flora." She stood up, exasperated. "That is such a teenage thing to say. *I never asked him to*. You may as well say, I didn't ask to be born."

"Well, I didn't."

I didn't see her point, just as she didn't see mine, and we glared at each other like two territorial cats on a wall. Mum moved away first. She re-boiled the kettle and made two mugs of tea, placing the teabags in the cups and measuring out the water and milk with such controlled care that I could tell she was still angry. When she had finished she handed one to me.

"I wanted coffee."

"Suit yourself." She snatched it away again, with such force it spilled on the floor, and tipped it fiercely out into the sink before I could change my mind. *Now who's being childish*, I wanted to say, but didn't dare. I looked at the spilt tea on the cushioned vinyl, its spreading brownness spoiling the blue and turquoise pattern. Mum had been so thrilled when it had been laid – ridiculously, disproportionately enchanted. Our old house had had ancient terracotta tiles, pitted and stained and guaranteed to destroy anything remotely breakable that was dropped on them. So many glasses and plates and cups had met their fate on that floor, I could virtually measure my life by them.

"Mum." I took a deep breath, as if I were about to launch myself off a high diving board. "I'm sorry if you and Dad don't like me being with Max. Honestly. But the age gap really doesn't matter, not to us. And we care about each other." *He told me he loved me, yesterday. He gave me diamond earrings.* I'd taken them from my ears as I'd walked up the garden path and hidden them in my pocket, guiltily, as if I'd come by them by nefarious means. Mum's eagle eyes would have spotted them in an instant; she'd have immediately cottoned on to their significance.

"I'm afraid Dad doesn't see it like that. The way he sees it, Max is preventing you from being with someone your own age. It's like he's hijacked your youth, that's what he told me the other day."

"Hijacked my youth!" I scoffed.

"Sneer all you like – it's how your father feels. He finds the age gap impossible to come to terms with."

"Are you saying he'd approve of Max if he was the same age as me – even with all his nasty horrid money?"

"I don't know if he'd ever actually approve," she said, ignoring my sarcasm. "But I know for a fact he wouldn't be as strongly anti as he is now." She took a careful sip of tea. "I think if I were you I'd be wondering why Max hasn't told you about his money."

"Maybe because it doesn't matter."

"Of course it matters. You can't tell me you'd feel the same way about him if he lived down Station Terrace, drove a Ford Cortina and was on the dole. You wouldn't have looked twice at him then." I started to protest, but she held up a quelling hand. "Don't look so shocked, Flora. It's not heresy, it's human nature. Believe it or not, I don't think your father is reacting in a very helpful or constructive way either. I keep telling him that the way he's behaving is having the opposite reaction to the one he wants, it's actually driving you towards Max instead of away from him. But he can't help it. He can't bear the thought of you being with him. And now he knows Max has taken you off on a dirty weekend, he's never going to forgive him."

I'd been right about Nat and Danny. The next day she came up to me at school, looking contrite. She's got A-levels in hangdog, has Nat – it drives me round the bend.

"Flora," she began, "I am *so* sorry."

"What for, exactly?" I enquired, sweetly.

"For landing you in it with your parents. I haven't a clue how they found out."

"Maybe it was something to do with seeing you in town playing tonsil tennis with a *certain someone*," I said, my voice laden with meaning.

The way Nat's face flamed proved that my suspicions were correct.

"Oh my God," she whispered. "I never thought. . ." She trailed off, mortified.

"You never thought what? That you'd be spotted? Or that I'd find out you were seeing Danny? Or just that, as per usual, you didn't think at all?" I wanted to shake her, to slap her silly pretty face. Not only because her thoughtlessness had got me into trouble with my parents, but because she hadn't told me about her and Danny.

She twisted her lips. "I've said I'm sorry."

"So how long has it been going on, then?"

"Ummm. . . Can't remember, exactly. A couple of weeks, maybe." I knew she was lying. Nat's the type to minutely catalogue every moment of a relationship, to celebrate weekiversaries.

"A couple of *weeks*?" People were beginning to stare, to nudge each other and snigger in that oh-so-sympathetic way they have when they witness a public row, but I didn't care. I was far too wound up. "And you never told me? Bloody hell, Nat – what kind of a friend are you?"

"That is way harsh, Flora – I've been a bloody

good friend to you. Which is more than I can say about you lately!"

"What's that supposed to mean?"

"I cover up for you, I listen to you dribbling on about your elderly boyfriend for hours on end, and what thanks do I get? Nothing! And then I'm expected to apologize for going out with the lad you ditched ages ago! You ask me, you're just a – a dog in the manger who's forgotten what friends are supposed to be for!"

She looked at me furiously, her big baby-blue eyes filled with tears that hovered perilously on her lower lashes. I couldn't bear to look at her. I clenched my fists, turned on my heel and marched off.

Ruby tackled me about it at lunchtime.

"You've really upset Nat, you know," she told me, mildly.

"Oh, have I. *I've* upset *her*. How completely tragic."

"You know she's got a History exam this afternoon. She's really worried she's going to screw it up."

"And the reason that's my problem is. . .?"

"You did lay it on a bit thick, you know. I overheard."

"She gave back as good as she got. Anyway, if you overheard, you'll know what it was all about."

Ruby shrugged, as if it didn't matter. "You know Nat. She could do ditzy for a living. You should have spelled it out to her, that she was to stay incommunicado until you were back."

"It's not just that." Didn't Ruby understand anything? I gestured, helplessly. "Did you know she's seeing Danny?"

"Oh, that. She's been seeing him for weeks."

"You *knew*? And you didn't tell me?"

"Not my place to tell."

"So why didn't *she* tell me?"

"Didn't want to upset you. She knew you'd be like this about it." She peered shrewdly at me. "For someone who professed to hate him, you're getting your knickers in a mighty twist about it, I must say."

"No I'm not!" *Yes I am*. I tried to stay calm, in control. "I just think she's making a big mistake, that's all. He's bad news. He'll chew her up and spit her out, just like he did with me. Just like he *tried* to do," I amended.

"Then she's got to find that out for herself, hasn't she. Look, Flora, you know she's fancied him for, like, ever. You and he never really got off the ground, and it all came to a sticky end months ago. *And* you're with Max now. Give the girl a break, can't you?"

It kept going round and round in my mind – Nat's irresponsible daftness in wafting oh-so-visibly round town when she was supposed to be miles away with me, and her going out with Danny behind my back, after what he'd done to me. Surely anybody in their right mind would feel the same sense of having been let-down? Surely I had a right to be annoyed with her? But I just kept hearing Nat's hurt angry voice: *you're just a dog in the manger who's forgotten what friends are supposed to be for.*

If Mum had thought her revelations about Max's inherited money were somehow going to put me off him, she couldn't have been more wrong. I had this feeling she'd anticipated me being annoyed that he'd hidden things from me, and us falling out about it. I also had a sneaking suspicion that she'd thought her comments about Dad never forgiving him would somehow make me choose between them, and come down in favour of Dad. I could just see it from her viewpoint: *sow a few seeds of doubt in her mind about just how open and honest Max has been with her, then imply her father is never going to get off her case about him. That'll make her start to think twice about continuing a relationship with him.*

Well, it didn't. To be honest, I didn't care where Max got his dosh from. Well, obviously I cared to some extent, I mean, if he'd been a bank robber or a drugs baron then Mum might have had a point, but the way things were it seemed pretty clear to me that she'd just been trying to mix it. And how could I ask him? What could I say that wouldn't sound accusing or, worse, gold-digging? Mum tells me you've got a massive inheritance? Is it true you're independently wealthy? I couldn't think of a single way of phrasing it that wouldn't sound wrong, wouldn't come out as if his money was suddenly the most important thing about him.

So in the end I decided against asking him about it. I was clear in my own mind that he hadn't intended to deceive me, whatever Mum's intended implication. And if she'd been attempting to prompt me into finishing with Max because of how Dad was going to be about him ever after – well, that was just ludicrous. Being on the receiving end of my father's disapproval and reprobation was hardly new.

But that didn't mean I wanted to put myself in his firing line any longer. All in all, home just didn't feel like home any more; I didn't want to be there any more than was absolutely necessary. So I took a few essentials to the flat – toothbrush, toiletries, spare set of clothes; nothing major, nothing that implied I was intending anything other than the odd stopover – so that I could stay on occasions without having to plan ahead. The first time I stayed overnight my heart was in my mouth when I went back home, certain there was going to be a replay of the return-from-Cambridge scene. But there wasn't. Nothing was said at all; it was almost as if Mum and Dad had washed their hands of me.

To Ruby's evident delight, her persistence with Tom Sheldon had obviously paid off, as he'd had a change of heart and asked her for a date. I couldn't see the attraction myself, this after all was the guy who'd humiliated her at Kaz's party by turning her down and then getting off with the birthday girl, but hey, what business was it of mine. Feeling slightly guilty about the way I'd neglected her of late, I asked her if she wanted to bring him round for supper one Saturday. She accepted at once, telling me how impressed Tom was going to be with my swanky boyfriend's swanky flat. Not that I minded; I enjoyed showing him off myself. Then it occurred to me that it might be an idea if I asked Max – perhaps just having two people turn up for supper out of the blue might be taking him for granted just a tad.

"Don't you want your friend Nat to come too?" was his only comment. "It's always been Rubanat before – I thought you three were joined at the hip."

I didn't want to admit that we'd barely

spoken for days. "Er – no. She's seeing Danny."

"Who's Danny?"

I gazed incredulously at him. How could he have forgotten? "Danny Oldfield – you know. Tosspot."

"Oh, you mean Poem Man? Yeah, I can see you wouldn't necessarily want him along. Although come to think of it, if it hadn't been for him, we wouldn't have bumped into each other that day, would we? I'd quite like to shake him by the hand and thank him."

He was joking. I think – I never got the chance to find out, because there was no way I was going to invite Nat along, with or without Danny. After the way we'd fallen out, I just couldn't be that two-faced. So it was just the four of us – Max and me, Ruby and Tom.

Well, what can I tell you about that evening? Disaster just about sums it up. The first shock was discovering that Max can't cook. Luckily, I found it out before our guests arrived rather than during the meal. Now that *would* have been embarrassing.

"What are we going to have on Saturday night?" I asked him, a few days beforehand.

He looked blank. "How d'you mean?"

"When Ruby and Tom come. What are we going to have for supper?"

"No idea. Surprise me."

Now it was my turn to look blank. "Me surprise you? But it's your flat!"

"Granted. But I don't cook in it."

"You mean, because they're my friends, I've got to do the cooking? You meanie!"

"I don't mean that at all. Calm down. I just don't do cooking. I can't – I'm rubbish at it."

I couldn't believe he'd got to the age he had without being able to cook, and told him so. Quite heatedly, as it happens. I'd had this enchanting vision for months of us *entertaining* in his flat, me floating around with the drinks and nibbles, him looking tasty in a pinny whisking up a light-as-air soufflé and charming the pants off a succession of increasingly elegant guests. Ho hum. So much for fantasy.

"I never told you I could cook. It's not a problem, we can just go out."

"But I don't want to go out. I want to entertain our guests here."

He gave me a funny look. "OK then. You do the cooking."

Not much liking the corner I'd painted myself into, I had to agree or face looking petty.

"Right. I will. I'll do my famous spaghetti Bolognese."

It's not really famous, but it's one of only two things I can be sure of not ruining, the other being scrambled eggs, and I didn't think I could really offer that to Ruby and her new man. She'd think I was taking the piss.

So spaghetti Bolognese it was. Actually, I was quite pleased with my efforts. I'd defrosted some prawns I'd found in Max's freezer for a starter, mixed with chunks of tinned ruby grapefruit and set on some salad leaves. The Bolognese sauce had been considerably enlivened by a mugful of red wine, and I'd bought fresh strawberries for pudding. The table was laid with an apparently brand-new damask cloth I'd discovered, still in its wrapper, at the bottom of one of the kitchen drawers, along with some decent glasses that usually lived on top of the dresser.

Freshly showered, Max drifted into the kitchen, drawn by the smells of cooking.

"Mmm. . ." he said, dipping in a spoon and tasting. "That's good." Then he spotted the wine bottle, open on the counter. "God, you didn't put that in, did you?"

"Yeah. What's wrong?"

"Only that it's over twenty quid a bottle. Claret's not usually used as cooking wine."

"Don't be a party pooper. Anyway, you can afford it."

"We may as well drink the rest, as it's open." He poured out two glasses, and offered one to me. "What time are they due?"

"Nearly an hour ago. I'm starving – if they don't get here soon I'm going to make a start without them."

At that moment, the doorbell went. When they came in, it was obvious why they were late – Tom had been drinking. Not that he was falling down drunk, just acting like a moron. Tom Sheldon is one of those lads who considers himself an authority on everything, and terribly witty to boot, and the drink he'd consumed just served to accentuate the fact that he was neither of those things. He's also got this really annoying habit of quoting huge chunks of film and TV scripts, as if it means something to the other person. It's what passes as conversation with him. He started quoting Monty Python as soon as he entered the flat.

"Your father was a hamster and your mother smelt of elderberries," he said, ignoring Max's outstretched hand, and Ruby fell about laughing, the daft cow, as if he'd said something original and hilarious.

"Er, quite," said Max, looking nonplussed. "Glass of wine?"

"No thanks mate, never touch the stuff. Got any beer?"

I glared at Ruby but she didn't take the hint. It set the tone for the rest of the evening, Tom being Michael Palin and John Cleese to the accompaniment of Ruby's hysterical laughter, while the two of us tried our best to ignore him. The food was OK – not that he noticed – but Max actually fell asleep at one point. I kicked him under the table, hard, and asked Ruby to give me a hand in the kitchen.

"Can't you shut him up?" I hissed at her, clattering dishes around pointlessly.

"What? Why? I think he's really funny."

"No he's not. He's just immature and stupid. His material's not even contemporary."

"*Fetchez la vache*," Tom said, roaring with laughter, his voice floating in from the dining table.

"Monty Python is classic comedy."

"Oh is it. That's what *Tom* says, is it?" I slammed some cups and saucers around.

"At least he's making an effort. Which is more than I can say for Max."

"He's had a busy week. He was working today, he didn't get in till nearly eight."

"He was bloody *snoring* just now."

"Oh, he so was not!"

"Yes he was. He probably didn't even want us round in the first place. We're probably too immature for him, too."

"You're not. It's Tom. I don't know what you see in him, he's a total prat."

"Cheers, Flora. Say what you're thinking, why don't you?"

I didn't know why I was falling out with Ruby when it was Tom I was pissed off with, for monopolizing the evening in such a boring way.

"I didn't mean that," I said, humbly.

"Yes you did. You've never liked him. That's when you've been bothered to give him the benefit of any opinion at all."

"What d'you mean?"

"You didn't even know I liked him, did you? Not until Nat told you. You're so bound up with Mr Perfect, you don't take any notice of what's going on around you any more." Somewhere in the background the telephone rang, and I heard Max answer it. "How would you like it if I told you the guy you were nuts about was stupid and immature? No wonder Nat says she doesn't want anything to do with you any more – I'm beginning to think she's got a point!"

But I never got the chance to reply, because just at that moment Max came into the kitchen.

"It's your mother on the phone," he told me.

"What? Why's she ringing me here?"

"Your mobile's switched off, apparently. Flora, sweetheart, I think you ought to come and speak with her."

His tone was gentle, solicitous, and that alone should have told me something was wrong. But

283

I was still angry with Tom, and with Ruby for defending him. I marched through and snatched up the phone.

"Hello?"

"Flora. I'm sorry for disturbing you. Max said you had friends round."

It never occurred to me how odd it was, for Mum to be apologizing for disturbing our little supper party as if we were a proper established couple and she had no right to invade our Saturday evening privacy. I was too annoyed, too peeved, too irritated and altogether too bound up in myself, just as Ruby had accused me. I just wanted to get rid of her, and then get shot of Ruby and Tom, so Max and I could have the rest of the evening, what was left of it, alone together.

"So what's the matter?" I demanded, gracelessly.

"It's Grandpa. He's had a heart attack."

chapter sixteen

Grandpa had been born and bred in a little mining village in County Durham. According to family legend, all the men in his family had been miners; it was pretty much the only work in the village, to go down the pit and lump it. I remember him telling me and Hugh about it when we were little, and us listening to him, wide-eyed at his knee, like a Werther's Originals commercial.

"But what if you didn't want to?" I recall asking him. The thought of going down into a mine at the age of fourteen and that being the rest of your life was, well, unthinkable. Although I quite liked the idea of the pit ponies. That's what I'd have been if I'd been born then, and male, I decided. The pony boy. (In my defence, I was young. And it was my Serious Pony Phase. Come on – we all have one.)

"There was no want, pet," Grandpa told me. "It's what we did."

"Did people get killed?" No pony crap for Hugh – he was in his Buckets-of-Blood Phase, something he's only recently grown out of. He wanted all the gory details.

"Oh aye, they did that. There was a big flood in the early twenties, just before I was born. My Uncle Frank died in that. He was a hero in our house, Uncle Frank. Then there was a fall in thirty-seven. Two of my mates perished in that. Len Cozens and Harry Dobbs. We were at school together as nippers, Len and Harry and me. Always in trouble. Got caught scrumping apples at the schoolmaster's house, we got such a caning." His faded-denim eyes took on a faraway look, like a sailor scanning the waves for landfall. "They were only seventeen. Well, we all were. But I was still alive, and they were dead. Sacrificed their lives to the Great God Coal." He gave an abrupt, bitter laugh. "That was life, back then. Harsh for all. Short and harsh, for some. The unlucky ones."

The pit was closed in the early sixties, and Grandpa found himself unemployed, along with all the other men of the village. Having worked hard all his life, tough demanding work, men's work, he was suddenly at home all day, getting under Gran's feet. With six children to support (the youngest being Dad), he had to do something to put bread on the table; so he borrowed a bucket and a ladder and went round cleaning people's windows, all the accumulated dust and grime blown down from the pit over the years. Then he borrowed a bicycle and went further afield, and then he started offering handyman services as well, odd jobs like mending fences and fixing washers on taps and cutting down trees that had outgrown their gardens, and before long he found himself in his forties with a whole new job he'd forged for himself. Not a career. This was an age, he informed us solemnly, before such airy-fairy ideas as careers and job satisfaction. If you were lucky enough to have a job you stuck at it for life; unemployment was shameful, a disgrace, something that brought dishonour on not just you but your whole family.

He even bought a van in time, a Morris Something-Long-Defunct that he had painted burgundy red, with his name in gold letters on the side. George Wilcox. Handyman Services. Then, in time, the lettering was changed to George Wilcox & Son, the son being Dad's eldest brother, my Uncle Jack. All of Dad's three brothers went into something similar when they left school, tradesmen of some kind, one a plumber, the other a mechanic, and his two sisters worked in local shops until they were married and then left to have their families. All my aunts and uncles on Dad's side still live up in County Durham, within eight or so kilometres of where they'd grown up cheek-by-jowl in their dark poky little terrace house that Dad always insisted was nevertheless filled with love and happiness. You know the kind of thing: We Might Have Slept Ten To A Bed But We Never Stopped Laughing, Oh Aye, It Was A Laugh A Minute.

Dad was the odd one out, by all accounts, the clever one who got in to the grammar school, a sixteen-kilometre bus ride away. (At least we were spared I Had To Walk There In My Bare Feet Because We Couldn't Afford Boots.) He didn't go on to university – a bit of a mystery, that one, given the reported inevitable excellence of his school grades – but instead got a traineeship at the local newspaper as a junior reporter. And the rest, as they say, is history. From Grandpa's humble beginnings to our life of unalloyed luxury that you see before you now.

Dad always talks about the love that had surrounded him when he was growing up, and I don't doubt it; but the relationship between him and Grandpa was always very different from the one he has with Hugh, which is jokey, affectionate and, given that Hugh is half a head taller than Dad and built like the miner Grandpa used to be, surprisingly physical. By contrast, the most physical contact I've ever seen between Dad and Grandpa is them shaking hands when greeting each other. He always deferred to Grandpa, even when they were visiting us, and treated him with a kind of distant respect. Love undeniably existed between them – they were father and son, after all – but you could hardly call their relationship demonstrative. Which made Dad's reaction to Grandpa's death all the more unexpected.

Oh yes. He died. When I got home, that awful evening – Max piling me into the car and driving the short distance in record time – Dad was sitting grey-faced at the kitchen table clutching a tumbler, a quarter-empty bottle of Bell's in front of him. I'd never known him drink whisky before, never. Mum was standing by the sink, her arms round Hattie who was wailing like a banshee.

"What are you all doing?" I cried, gesticulating wildly. Max had come in behind me, for the first time since telling them the news that we were a couple. "Dad! Why are you drinking? You've got to drive up to Durham to see Grandpa!"

"No I haven't," he said grimly. He slopped out another two fingers of Scotch and poured it down his throat without appearing to swallow. "I haven't got to drive anywhere, because he's dead."

For an instant time seemed to stop, the moment suspended for ever with dreadful clarity; Dad at the kitchen table with the whisky bottle, Hattie entwined with Mum, and Max bobbing around somewhere in the background. I could hear the gentle ticking of the long-case clock in the hallway, and the soft whoompf as the boiler turned itself on. Normal, everyday sounds, punctuated suddenly by someone shouting. Me. I couldn't seem to stop, it was the shock I suppose.

"He can't be! Mum didn't say he was dead. A heart attack, she said! He can't be dead! It was just a heart attack! You said so!" I turned to her, appealing, accusing.

"Darling." She moved towards me, Hattie still clinging to her like a lamb hassling a ewe for milk. "The phone went just after I spoke to you, it was Gran again. Telling us that –" She gave a sharp inward breath through her nose, as if assailed by a sudden twinge of pain. "Telling us."

I'd never really believed before that people's legs gave way after a shock, but that's what happened. My knees just buckled outwards, and I found myself clutching at the corner of the counter. Max instantly picked up a stool and came towards me, offering it to me, but I brushed him aside, impatiently.

"It was just a heart attack," I whimpered, pathetically. "Mum said so. She said so."

Dad pushed the bottle and glass aside and slumped forwards on to the table, laying his head on his folded arms. He looked as if he had fallen asleep.

"What's the matter with Dad?"

"What do you think?" Hattie wailed. "Grandpa's dead, that's what's the matter!"

"All right, Hattie, love," Mum murmured, soothingly.

"Can I do anything?" Max stepped forward, his features carefully arranged into an expression of polite regret. He looked as if he'd rather be anywhere but there. I suddenly found myself fervently wishing that he would just go away, and then felt a terrible stab of guilt. How could I think such a thing? He was only trying to help.

"Thank you, Max," Mum said, in a low voice, "but I don't think there's anything you can do. Maybe it would be best if you were to go."

At that moment his mobile burst shrilly into life, the tinny bright tones sounding ridiculously inappropriate under the circumstances. He scrambled to switch it off, embarrassed at being responsible for something so mundane having interrupted our family grief.

"For God's sake!" I yelled, heaven knows why. It was hardly his fault someone was ringing him.

"Sorry," he muttered. He bent to gave me an apologetic peck on the cheek, and then slipped quietly out of the room. I barely noticed him going, and it was only later that I realized Dad hadn't acknowledged his presence. Maybe he hadn't even noticed he was there.

Later still, Mum asked me if I knew where Hugh was.

"At a party, I think. Oh my God." The reason she was asking me sank in. "He doesn't know, does he?"

She shook her head, her lips pressed together. "His phone's switched off. As per usual. You kids, we buy you mobiles and then we can never contact you on them when we need to."

I let the K-word and the implied criticism of me pass. "I don't suppose he'll be late. He's got another exam on Monday, he's going to want to get up and revise tomorrow."

"Yes. He's a good lad. Studies hard."

Unlike you, Flora. "I study hard too," I objected.

"Jesus Christ!" Dad exploded, suddenly. "Can you not give it a rest?"

"What?" I didn't have a clue what he meant.

"This continual going on the defensive. You read blame into every comment we make. Your mother was only saying. . ." He sighed. "Ah, what's the point. I canna be arsed."

Mum winced at that slightly. She hates it when he swears. Offends her nicely-brought-up sensibilities, I daresay.

*

The funeral was to be in ten days' time, on the Tuesday. The plan was, Dad would go up on the train at the weekend to help the family with "the arrangements", whatever they might be, and we were to follow by car on the Monday. I overheard Dad on the phone to Uncle Jack, tersely discussing it all. I asked Mum why he sounded so irate.

"He offered to go up before, but they told him there was no need. He feels like they're shutting him out."

"Why doesn't he just go, if he feels like that? They can hardly stop him."

"It's not as simple as that. He wanted to go up to be with Gran, but she says Jack and Beryl are taking care of everything, and she's perfectly OK. She's also got it into her head that he can't afford to take all that time off work."

"Well, she has got a point. You know how he's always going on about how busy he is."

"His father's just died – I hardly think the paper's going to quibble about a week off under the circumstances."

Back to square one. "So what's stopping him?"

She looked at me over the top of her specs in that don't-mess-with-me-I'm-a-teacher way she does so well. "Are you telling me you really don't know?"

"Yup."

"You've never picked up on the family tensions?"

The only family tensions I was currently aware of were our own. "Nope."

"It's complicated. Basically, I suppose Dad thinks the rest of the family feel he looks down on them because he's done well for himself."

I snorted derisively. "You mean that old working class versus middle class thing again, like with Max only the other way round? Oh, do us a favour! You don't really think that, do you?"

"I'm not saying it's what I think. It's how Dad feels, that's all."

It seemed to me like Dad had a bloody great chip on his shoulder, and I said so. "Anyway, why's he so bothered? It's not as if they were especially close, is it?"

"Of course they are," she said, quietly. "That's why he cares about it so much."

"No, I mean with Grandpa. They never had a particularly close relationship, did they."

She gazed at me as if she'd never really seen me properly before. "He idolized your grandfather. Can't you see how devastated he is?"

"OK, OK," I said, grumpily. It felt as if I was being chastised for being insensitive. "How was I supposed to know? They never showed it."

*

I couldn't cope with the idea of going to the funeral. The drive up, sitting in the back of the car with Hattie (Hugh was bound to insist on going in the front) who'd barely stopped sobbing since the news. The inevitable whole family-in-mourning thing once we got there, the embarrassed discomfort of not knowing whether to speak of Grandpa or not, the horrible possibility of witnessing the public grief of Gran or Uncle Jack or Aunt Maureen and not knowing how to respond. It was all too much.

But most of all, I couldn't bear the thought of the funeral itself, of Grandpa being lowered in his wooden box into the cold Durham clay – that vibrant, vital, so alive man dead and rotting alone in the ground, his bones gnawed by maggots. Burial has always seemed to me a spectacularly barbaric way of disposing of the dead, especially for those left behind – how can they not be consumed with images of their loved ones' decomposition? I'd had a recurring nightmare about it when I was small, a dream of being buried alive in the ground and nobody noticing I was in fact not dead at all, which I'm sure must have been deeply symbolic. I've always considered cremation much the better option – clean and quick, and a nice pot of ashes afterwards to scatter in a favourite place or even keep on top of the telly so your relative can watch *Coronation Street* and *Blind Date* in perpetuity. But Grandpa favoured burial; with typical gritty practicality he'd bought the plot years before, for himself and Gran. He'd even paid for the headstone, apparently. His forward planning was somehow touching, but it was no use. I just couldn't face the thought of being there to witness his final departure. So I told them I didn't want to go.

Man. Armageddon is probably the right word to describe the fallout. Dad didn't explode with fury this time, instead he looked at me with chilly distaste, his face an icy impassive mask. It was worse than all his customary shouting, much worse. I knew where I was with him losing his temper, I'd grown up with him being like that, I knew the pattern. This glacial control was a totally unknown quantity: I didn't know where it could lead.

"I should have guessed," he said. "I might have known you'd have preferred to cosy up with your boyfriend than pay your last respects to your grandfather."

I tried to explain, that it was nothing to do with Max, that it was about me, my feelings, my wimpishness if you like, but he wouldn't listen.

"I don't know you any more," he cut across me, coldly. "You're no daughter of mine."

"Oh, thanks a lot! Don't you think you're being a tad melodramatic?"

"Do you want to know what I think, Flora? I think you've turned into an uncaring, selfish little bitch. That's what I think."

I was shocked. He'd never said anything to me like that before. He wasn't what you might call a stranger to swearing, but he'd never called me names before.

"I'm not uncaring – I loved him too!" I bellowed, tears of horror and dismay springing to my eyes. "You don't have the monopoly on love, you know!"

"You wouldn't know love if you tripped over it in the street."

"And whose fault is that? You brought me up. Great example you've been. Let's yell at the kids the moment they do something we disagree with – that'll show them how much we care!"

He regarded me for a moment, utterly without emotion. "So why don't you just go," he said, at last.

"What?"

"You heard. If you don't like it here, why don't you get out. You're hardly ever here in any case. May as well make it permanent."

"Right, then. Fine. I will!"

I'd never have suggested leaving myself, but now he'd said it, it seemed the right thing to do.

Not just the right thing – the only thing. How could I carry on living there after what he'd said to me?

"He didn't mean it," Mum said. She sounded calm but her expression was flat and blank "He's just upset about Grandpa. He didn't really mean you should move out."

"I'm upset too. He didn't even stop to consider that, did he?"

"You're *both* upset. Come on, Flora – you know what he's like. It'll sort itself out in a day or two. You've got your exams to think about, you can't just go charging off like this."

Something else he didn't care about.

"Can't I." *Just watch me, then.*

She sighed, not a resigned sigh but a frustrated, exasperated one. "You're so alike, you and he."

Alike? Pah! Bollocks we are! "No we're not, we're totally different."

"Both stubborn as hell, both so black and white about things."

I'm not stubborn. I could hear the contradiction for myself, didn't even bother saying it. Carried on flinging things into the bag instead, the huge rucksack Hugh had used on his Duke of Edinburgh expeditions.

"Will you stop doing that and pay me some

attention." It was a command, not an invitation. I stopped, mid-fling, and looked at her in surprise. "Why?"

"Why?" The blankness on her face disappeared as a whole range of emotions slid across it, one by one. It was fascinating, but scary as well: I had the feeling that, with that one unthinking word – WHY – I'd opened a can of worms, a whole Pandora's Box of reprisal, all aimed at me. But the worse thing was, I knew I deserved it. "*Why?* Well, let's see now – how about because I'm your mother, and deserve a bit of respect? How about because I'm utterly fed up of you acting as if you're the selfish little hub around which the universe revolves? How about because I think it's high time you stopped being so damned self-absorbed, and started thinking of other people's feelings for a change? How about all that, for starters?"

I flinched, and dropped my eyes from the withering beam of her gaze. "OK," I muttered, uncomfortably. "You've made your point."

"Have I, Florence? I wonder."

Florence. *What Grandpa always called me.* . . I felt suddenly exhausted, and sat down on the edge of the bed. "You have. I'm sorry, OK?"

"But not sorry enough to come to the funeral."

The funeral. I felt myself being backed into a corner. "I don't know. . ."

"Well I do," she said crisply. "I've decided. You're coming." I started to speak, but she held up a silencing hand. "No arguments. If you think I'm going to stand by and watch you let your father down like this, you've got another think coming. You can come along out of respect for your family, if nothing else. Now I suggest you get on with your packing, if you're so intent on moving out."

I stared at her, dumbfounded. "I thought you didn't want me to go rushing off? My exams, you said – I've got my exams to think about!"

She shrugged and turned away, and I felt tears prick behind my eyes, childish tears of dismay that the situation I now found myself in was wholly of my own making. "I've changed my mind. I think you're right – I think you and your father need a bit of space between you right now. Living on top of each other will only add fuel to the fire. Your exams are hardly going to suffer if you're away from home for a few days."

"OK. Fine. If that's what you want." Righteous indignation replaced the dismay. I pulled the rucksack's drawstring tight and fastened the webbing straps. "Anyway, I have to go. I can't stay here after what Dad said to me."

She turned, and her expression softened slightly. "Where are you going to stay? Max's, I suppose?"

Where else did she think I was going – to London, to sleep rough at Embankment station? Wasn't that where all the drop-outs went?

I nodded, curtly. "You can get hold of me there, if you need to. If you want to."

"Of course I'll need to get hold of you – we'll have to talk about the arrangements for going up to Durham." I noticed she didn't say she wanted to, though.

Max was very understanding and sympathetic, making space in the wardrobe for my clothes, clearing his toiletries from the bathroom shelf. I had the distinct feeling he was pleased I'd gone to stay with him, even though the circumstances behind it weren't exactly what you'd call ideal. I kept apologizing to him as I unpacked – sorry to land on you like this, sorry to be a nuisance, sorry my father is such a bloody idiot, sorry my life is such a *fucking* mess. . .

"Don't keep saying sorry." He took the pile of T-shirts from my hands, gently, laid them on top of the chest of drawers and put his hands on my shoulders. "You're not being a nuisance. I'm glad I can help out."

"It won't be for long."

"It can be for as long as you like. Although I'm sure you're right – Roger will come round eventually. He's not an unreasonable man. It'll just be the shock of his father dying so suddenly." He looked thoughtful, wistful even, and I remembered how Mum had told me that he'd lost his own parents, years ago. He never spoke about it, but it must have been horribly traumatic. I couldn't begin to imagine it. "Don't answer this if you don't want to, but why did you tell them you weren't going to the funeral?"

I shrugged. "Durham's a long way, I get carsick. Anyway, I've never looked good in black, it's not my colour."

"Why do you do that?"

"What?"

"That I-don't-give-a-shit thing? It doesn't fool me. I know you're upset about losing your Grandad."

"He's Grandpa, not Grandad. And he was turned eighty. It was a shock, he'd always been so fit, but it wasn't exactly like he'd been snatched away in his prime."

"Even so. Don't be too hard on your dad."

I took the T-shirts back, turned away from him, busied myself with putting them in a drawer.

"I'm not sure I want him to come round, as you put it. Not after what he said to me. He was so –" Tears welled up in my eyes when I remembered what he'd called me, stupid self-pitying tears. I dashed at them, angrily. I didn't want Max to see me like this – feeling sorry for myself, wounded. Vulnerable. "He was so *distant*. It was as if he didn't recognize me. Or hated me."

"He doesn't hate you. Don't be daft. He's your father, how could he hate you."

"Well, Hugh certainly hates me. He called me a hard-nosed little cow. Mum virtually implied that having me around the place was going to make Dad even more upset, and Hat wouldn't even say goodbye when I went." Just about the only good thing was that Ruby and I had made up – she'd been really sweet to me since Grandpa died.

"Sisters, eh. What are they like." He stood in front of me, put his hands deliberately on my shoulders. "Nobody hates you, Flora. They're your family. You're all just coping in different ways. You've got out of your dad's hair for a bit, and you've agreed to go to the funeral. It'll all blow over, in time. I'm sure it will."

chapter seventeen

Max had been right about one thing – it did blow over, sort of. But not until after the funeral, and only then because I decided enough was enough, it was time to go back home. I couldn't bring myself to before then, couldn't stomach the thought of all the reproachful looks I'd be bound to get, of Dad's behaviour towards me, whatever that was going to be. So I stayed at Max's for the week.

"You've moved *in* with him?" Ruby said, in horror.

"Not in. Not permanently in. Just temporarily, until Dad gets a grip."

"A grip on what?"

"Life. Reality. I don't know, Rube. Stop going on about it, it's already doing my head in."

"What about the exams?"

"What about them? I'm still doing them. I've moved out of home for a bit, not run away to join the circus."

"You are still planning on going to Cambridge, are you?"

"What's that got to do with it?"

"Only that it doesn't seem that sensible to have fallen out with your parents to that extent. Not if you want them to support you through university. Unless Max is going to do that, of course. You know, *in loco parentis,* kind of thing."

I glared at her. "Don't you start. He's not my parent, he's my boyfriend, OK?"

Grandpa's funeral was just as bad as I'd been dreading. I went up by myself on the train, and when I went back home afterwards, Dad wouldn't speak to me. He'd been remote and aloof up in Durham, but this was different. He completely cut me dead, as if I didn't exist. It was both upsetting and deeply infuriating.

"Why's he *doing* this?" I yelled to Mum after two days of this treatment, frustrated beyond belief. "Who's the grown-up here? I thought it was only people my age who were supposed to behave like that, it's so *bloody* rude!"

"Give him time," Mum said. "It's still early days."

"Early days of what – terminal bad manners? I should have stayed at Max's."

"You'll have to make allowances for him. I know it's hard for you, but he's not well."

"Don't tell me he's going to be the next to pop his clogs," I muttered.

305

"Flora." She gave me a sharp, admonishing look, and I felt an immediate twinge of guilt. "How can you be so cruel? He's just buried his father – have some compassion."

"So if he's ill, how come he hasn't been to the doctor?"

"He has. While you were away." She spoke as if I'd been on holiday, popped away for a nice little break, not been virtually kicked out by my father and encouraged to go by her. "She says he's clinically depressed, it's not uncommon after a sudden bereavement. Just try not to provoke him, love, please. It's all I ask."

Hattie, apparently, was going up to London on the train for the weekend with some of her little friends. They were going to do the sights – the Tower, Madame Tussauds, the London Eye – before going to see *Cats*, and then hit Oxford Street for some serious shopping the next day. All my alarm bells rang when Mum let these plans slip one rare evening when I was home, Max having gone on a mate's stag night and not anticipating being back until the early hours, if then.

"Are you sure?" I asked Mum, suspiciously. London was where Gary-the-so-called-student lived. "Which friends is she going with? Where's the money coming from?"

Mum gave me an odd look; hardly surprising, really, as my concern for Hattie's doings is normally on a par with my interest in the Gross National Product of the Benelux countries – i.e., zilch. "Of course I'm sure. She's going with Amy and Jade and a couple of others – it's Amy's thirteenth birthday treat, you know her parents are rolling in it. I just hope Hattie's not expecting similar when it comes to her turn. There was a proper invitation for it, it's been stuck extremely visibly to the fridge for weeks. I do wonder sometimes whether you're actually part of this family any more." She never seemed to let an opportunity to have a dig at me slip by these days.

I investigated the invitation, which to my admittedly inexpert eye looked to be a home-made Word job. If Hattie was capable of scanning photos of me and pretending they were her whilst getting up to God-knows-what other kinds of duplicity, she was certainly up to knocking this kind of thing out on our PC as a cover for other less wholesome activities.

I tackled her about it that very evening, waving the invite under her nose like incriminating evidence.

"What?" she whined. "What is your *problem*? Don't even bother asking if you can come too, because the answer will be *no*, OK?" Now she was knocking on the door of thirteen she had acquired even more of an attitude problem than usual.

"If you really think I want to come too. . ." I began indignantly. Then I checked myself. What was the point? I cut to the chase. "Are you really going with Amy and Co, or are you meeting Gary?"

"Who?" Her face looked so blank she almost managed to convince me of her innocence with just that one word. But only almost. This was Hattie we're talking about – my sneaky, manipulative little sister.

"Don't give me that. Gary-the-so-called-student. Your pervy friend from the chatroom."

"Oh, him." She scowled. "Don't be stupid. I stopped visiting that chat ages ago. Why should I be meeting him?"

"Oh, dur." I pulled a face. "I wonder. Could it possibly be anything to do with the fact that the last time I heard, you were about to send him a pic of me and pretend it was you? And that you virtually admitted you'd given him your address? Oh yes, and that he just happens to live in London? Yeah, that'll be it."

"I already told you, I'm not meeting him. Get off my case, will you."

She went to move away, but I grabbed her arm. "Hattie," I said, urgently. "Hat. This is important. Please, just look me in the eye and promise me you really are going to London with Amy, and you're not meeting Gary."

To my enormous surprise, she did just that. All the strop fell away from her as her eyes met mine. "I really am going with Amy," she repeated, meekly. "I'm not meeting Gary. I promise." Then she pulled away, and the old feisty Hattie was back. "D'you believe me now?"

"I suppose. Have you really stopped communicating with him?"

"I said so, didn't I?" She gave a huge put-upon sigh. "God. You're getting worse than Mum."

"No I'm not! I could have really landed you in it if I'd wanted to – after you went sneaking in my diary when I was in Cambridge with Max. Just as well for you I'm not a dobber."

"Yeah." She had the grace to look slightly shamefaced. "I know. I was well relieved you didn't. That's when I stopped, if you want to know the truth."

"Well, I hope you're grateful. You could have been grounded for life over all that, if I hadn't kept my mouth shut." I couldn't resist rubbing it in.

"I know," she said humbly. "What can I say? You're such a warm, wonderful, utterly fab sister." Then she shot me a cheeky grin. "Not," she added.

*

It was Max's thirtieth birthday at the beginning of July but neither of us were in the mood for a celebration, me because of the ever-worsening atmosphere at home, and Max because – well, who knows why Max wasn't. He just said he didn't want any fuss and why didn't we just go out for a meal somewhere. So that's what we did, only there was fuss because the next morning I was woken up early by the absolute pressing urge to throw up. Max found me with my head down the toilet bowl, groaning piteously.

"Flora! God, what's the matter?"

"I'm being sick, what does it look like?"

"Are you OK?"

"Of course I'm not bloody OK!"

"You're not pregnant, are you?"

"Pregnant?" It would have been quite comical if I hadn't been feeling so lousy. "Of course not. I probably just had too much to drink. Why on earth would you think that?"

"Well, you know. Morning sickness."

"What, at five a.m.?"

"Well, it is the morning."

"Don't be an idiot, Max. I'm hungover, not pregnant. Christ, that's all I'd need. That would really make my wonderful life complete." I sat back on my heels and tore off a piece of loo roll to wipe my mouth. "Actually, I feel better now. I wonder if it was that venison. I thought it tasted a bit iffy."

"Venison is supposed to taste iffy. That's the whole point of it, it's gamey."

"Gamey's not the same as iffy. This was definitely iffy."

"Do you want me to ring up in the morning and complain?"

"It is the morning. As you pointed out." I threw the paper down the toilet and flushed it. "No, don't worry. You didn't have much of a birthday as it is; I don't want to ruin it completely by making you accuse the restaurant of poisoning me. I'm fine now, honestly. I'm going back to bed."

"I've been thinking," Max said, later.

"Uh oh. Call Maximum Security – brain cell on the loose."

"Shut up, missy." He gave me a playful push. He seemed in a very good mood, considering the wash-out his birthday had been, and the fact his sleep had been disturbed by having to get up to mop my fevered brow. He gets very grumpy when his sleep is disturbed, as a rule. Something I'd discovered during those days of staying with him.

"OK then, Einstein. What have you been thinking?"

"It goes something like this. Your exams are over now."

"Ye-es."

"And you've officially left school for the summer."

"Ri-ight."

"And you've been having a pig-awful time at home."

"Mm-hm."

"So why not move in here properly?"

"Properly?"

"Yes. Or maybe just for the summer to begin with, and see how it goes."

I stared at him, aghast. I'd thought I could see where the conversation was going, thought he was going to say why don't we go away on holiday somewhere, or tell me that he'd booked somewhere as a surprise, produce some airline tickets even – but not this. It threw me completely.

Max laughed. "Don't look like that! It's nothing heavy – I'm not asking you to marry me!"

I wanted to say, but it is heavy, how can I possibly move in with you, I've got my A-levels next year, then I'm going to Cambridge. How on earth do you think I can come and live with you? But I couldn't. Even if I'd found the right words I couldn't have uttered them, I couldn't have brought myself to destroy the look of sheer pleasure on his face. It was as if he believed he was offering me something infinitely precious. Maybe he was, maybe it was just that I wasn't the right person for it to be offered to.

"Blimey." I was playing for time. Hoping it wasn't too obvious. "This is all very sudden."

"Not really. We've been together for months now. And it's the circumstances, isn't it? It's not exactly a bundle of laughs at home for you right now. I can see how much it's getting you down – you go round with a perpetual frown on your face."

"Sorry."

"It's not a criticism, just an observation. I want to see you smiling again. I want to make you happy."

"Oh Max." I really didn't want to have this conversation. I didn't like where it was heading; it felt like I was on a boat set adrift, sailing into dangerous uncharted waters. "You do make me happy."

"I know how it feels when your parents are set against what you're doing and decide to make your life uncomfortable if you persist in doing it. It's how my father was with me."

"Oh?"

"He didn't want me to go to university. He especially didn't want me to study music, which he considered a total waste of time. He wanted me to go into the family business instead, after A-levels."

"You mean the crisps?"

"That's right." If he was surprised I knew about it, he didn't show it. He must have thought he'd told me. "He said it was more befitting the boss's son, that I should start at the bottom and work my way up so that I'd have earned my inheritance when it came, instead of faffing around playing the piano. As he put it. He thought it self-indulgent. He came from what you might call humble beginnings, you see, I suppose you'd say he was a self-made man. Didn't have much time for education altogether, if truth be told, although he sent my sister and me to boarding school when our mother died. He thought university students were idle layabouts." He laughed, shortly. "I worked my socks off to get in to Cambridge, and all he could think of was that it was three years down the drain that could have been spent working for him."

I could scarcely believe the irony, that Max's privileged upbringing had always been such a bone of contention for Dad. That he had held it against him when all the time their backgrounds were more similar than either of them could have realized.

"I can't really see you working in a crisp factory."

"It's not just a crisp factory any more, it's a whole business enterprise. But you're right – I'm not cut out to be a businessman. Anyway, he thought he could bulldoze me into changing my mind, and then when he realized he couldn't he refused to speak to me all through my final two terms at school. That's why I understand how you're feeling right now."

"Ah. I see. You're offering me protection from Nightmare Father from Hell."

"Kind of." He smiled at me, leant across and took my hands in his. "No. It's all crap – I can't pretend I'm being altruistic. I've got a vested interest. You know how I feel about you. I think I fell in love with you at your parents' party, I told you I was just attracted to you but it was more than that, much more. I've never felt this way before about anybody. I think it was last night – this morning, I mean – that it all crystallized in my mind. When you were throwing up, and I asked you if you were pregnant. I know it was an idiotic thing to say, God only knows where it came from, but afterwards when you were asleep again I suddenly thought, I'm thirty years old, I've got this gorgeous girl: why on earth aren't I settling down with her?"

I couldn't think of anything to say that was adequate. I gave a shaky laugh. "Bloody hell. Are you saying you want to have my babies?"

(A faint memory came floating back, something he'd said about Marina, about how he'd wanted children but she hadn't. . .)

He laughed too. "No! Well, yes. Maybe. All in good time – who knows?" He hugged me close to him. I could feel the rough fabric of his shirt against my face, smell the clean washing-powder smell. He was always so wholesome and pristine, even when dressed like today in weekend-y casual clothes. It's what comes of sending your clothes to someone else to be washed and ironed, rather than having to grab a clean shirt off the ironing pile like Dad does, or even sometimes retrieving an already-worn one from the laundry basket.

"I can't tell you," Max went on, "what a breath of fresh air you are after all the others."

"Others?" I blinked. I felt overwhelmed by what he'd been saying, didn't know what he meant.

"All those – those *Venetias*, and *Portias*. After Marina, I mean. Whilst I was with her, some of them. All the bounty-hunters at university who'd got wind of the fact that I was now Cooper's Crisps, and were only interested in what I could buy them. I was heartily sick of women who saw me as a meal-ticket for life, but you didn't even know, did you? You just wanted me for myself."

For your body, actually. . . I gave myself a shake. "Max. I'm only seventeen. I—"

"Sssh." He placed a tender forefinger against my lips. "I know. I'm going too fast. I'm rushing you. Don't panic, you'll still be able to do everything you've planned. A-levels, university, whatever. Just that I want to be there while you do it. That's all I'm saying. I want to share the rest of my life with you."

The rest of his life. How long was that going to be? Ten years? Thirty – fifty? Could I see myself with him fifty years down the line? I didn't know what I might be doing in fifty days' time – fifty hours, fifty minutes – let alone fifty years. My head spun, I felt dizzy with the enormity of what he was saying, the implications of it all.

"At least think about it," he was saying. "Hmm? You don't have to make a decision yet. But just think about it. Promise me you'll think about it."

I can't think about it, I don't want to think about it, it's too much to think about. . .

I opened my mouth. "All right," I croaked. "I'll think about it."

"I thought he was too good to be true," Ruby declared. "Looking like that, and all that wonga to boot. I knew there had to be a catch."

"So why's him wanting me to move in with him a catch?"

"Do you want to move in with him?"

"No."

"There you go, then. That's the catch. Under that suave exterior he's probably insanely jealous. He probably wants to keep you under lock and key and monitor your every movement."

"I don't think so – I think I'd know by now if he was jealous." She always did have a vivid imagination. "But seriously. He says he wants to spend the rest of his life with me."

Ruby sucked on her teeth and shook her head. "Sounds dodgy to me. You're too young to say that kind of thing to – I'd run a mile if any guy said it to me."

I grinned at her. "Hey, be honest – what guy's ever going to say it to you!"

She ignored me. "You've got plans for your life. If you move in with him, before you know where you are he'll be trying to run it for you."

"That's what I'm worried about." I sighed. "Why is life so complicated, Rube? All I've ever wanted is someone who'll treat me as if I'm special. Someone to – to *adore* me."

"Adoration ain't all it's cracked up to be."

"Tell me about it."

"Life's a bitch, babe. So what you gonna do?"

"I don't know."

"I think you do." She regarded me gravely. "If you're going to be fair, that is. I think you know exactly what you have to do."

The following weekend I still hadn't told Max that I wasn't going to be moving in with him. Although he hadn't pressed me for my decision, either. Part of me hoped that he would just forget about it and never mention it again, but deep down I knew I had to tell him whether he referred to it again or not. Just pretending he'd never mentioned it wouldn't be fair, just as Ruby had said.

We were in the flat late on Saturday night, watching TV and finishing off a bottle of wine. Or at least, I was – Max was practically falling asleep, his eyelids doing that strange down-and-up thing they do when people are struggling to stay awake, his head drooping on to his chest and then snapping upright again. I was just about to suggest he give up and go to bed when the doorbell rang.

That woke him up; he came to with a start, frowning and looking at his watch.

"Who on earth's that?"

The bell rang again, insistently, as if somebody was leaning against it.

"Why don't you answer it and see?" I said. I stood up, picked up the wine bottle and glasses and headed for the kitchen. The sound of angry male voices made me turn back again. Or rather, the sound of one calm but insistent male voice – Max's – and one angry one. My father's.

"Dad?" I went towards him, still holding the bottle and glasses. "What are you doing here? What's the matter?" A small thrill of alarm went through me. "Has something happened? Is it Mum?"

"Nothing's happened. I just wanted to come and see the *pad*, that's all." He put scornful inverted commas around the word. "The *love-nest*." He swayed slightly, and put a hand on the door-jamb to steady himself.

"What are you talking about?" I peered at him suspiciously. "Have you been drinking?"

"Yes. I have. And so, apparently," he indicated the bottle with his head, "have you. You do know she's under-age, don't you?" he said, turning to Max. "I could have you for that. If I felt so inclined."

"Don't be ridiculous, Roger. Come in off the doorstep, and we'll make you some coffee."

"O-ho!" Dad crowed, triumphantly. "Mustn't stand on the doorstep, must we. Mustn't let the neighbours hear our little tiff. Oh no. That would never do. Mustn't let them find out you've

320

been *screwing* my *seventeen-year-old daughter*!"

He looked pleased with himself, as if he'd said something clever. It was horrible. I'd never seen him in this state before; it was like having him turn into one of Hugh's mates before my eyes.

"Dad!" I hissed at him. "For God's sake, come in! You're making a complete prat of yourself!"

Between us, Max and I managed to get him inside and into the sitting room, where he stood glaring at us.

"You want to know why I've come?" he said to Max. "You really want to know?"

"I expect you're going to tell me," Max replied, coolly. "Although it might have been better if you'd come sober, rather than in this state."

"Bollocks to that!" Dad bellowed, and took a threatening step forwards. I was terrified that he was going to hit Max, take a swing at him, although he was so pissed he'd probably have missed. I wondered how much he'd had. It was hard to tell. Not a great deal, knowing Dad. He never could hold his drink.

"Flora," Max said, "why don't you put the kettle on for some coffee?"

"I don't want bleeding *coffee*!" Angry spittle flecked his lips.

"Fine. You don't have to drink yours. So what do you want?"

"I want an exclam— an explanation."

"An explanation for what?"

"Ah man. Don't play games with me. I'm warning you."

"Roger." Max tilted his head slightly to one side, assessing him. "Don't threaten me in my own flat. Just tell me why you're here."

"All right. OK. Fair enough." Dad wiped his mouth, with the back of his hand. "I want to know what you think you're doing with her."

"With Flora?"

"Of course with Flora!" he roared, waving his arms like a windmill. "Who d'you think I meant, Princess sodding Anne? I want to know what your intentions are. There. Isn't that what people like you say? What are your intentions towards my daughter? Because to tell you the truth, man, I think you're a cad and a bounder." His little speech over, he stood and swayed as if he was on board a ship in a force nine gale.

I put the bottle and glasses down, hurried over to him. "Sit down, Dad," I urged him. "Come on. Sit down. Let me ring Mum to come and collect you."

He stared at me. There was a terrible look in his eyes, a hunted, haunted look, as if he was drowning.

"Aye," he said. "All right. You do that, pet. You ring her."

322

"Look, Roger –" Max hesitated. "What you asked me. It was a fair question, and it deserves an answer. I just want you to know that I care a great deal about Flora, and I'd never do anything to hurt her. I promise you that."

Dad looked at him for a few long moments. Then he subsided on to the sofa, his head in his hands. "Give me my daughter back," he muttered. "Please, Max. It's all I ask. Just give me my daughter back."

chapter eighteen

Dad's Pissed Moonlight Visit. It was the stuff of family legend, the kind of thing that gets brought out and recounted for years after the actual event, so that in time the edges get smoothed and the impact lessened. It becomes romanticized, made humorous even – *that Roger Wilcox! What is he like?* Maybe, in time, even I might be able to laugh about it, about the night my father turned up roaring drunk and fighting mad on my thirty-year-old lover's doorstep, and begged him to give me back.

At the moment, though, it wasn't even slightly funny. I was left wondering how on earth it had come to this; wondering just when the whole amazing, dizzying adventure had turned into a nightmare, and at what point I had chosen Max over my family. We'd always been close, as families go – not in a sickly, sentimental, Little-House-on-the-Prairie kind of way, but in a normal, natural, falling-out-occasionally-but-generally-pretty-solid fashion. But now look at us – Mum and Hugh were barely talking to me, and as for Dad – well. I absolutely didn't recognize the person he'd become, the person who'd cut me dead since returning home after the funeral, who'd come staggering in to Max's flat. He was a stranger. I daresay that's exactly how he was feeling about me. OK, Hattie was behaving pretty much as normal towards me again, but I suspected that it was only out of gratitude because I hadn't landed her in trouble.

And then there were my friends. Ruby and Nat were my best mates, but it was scary to realize how close I'd come to losing their friendship. It was fortunate for me that Rube says what she thinks at the time and gets it over with, so didn't appear to bear any grudges for how I'd neglected her and taken her for granted; but I had some serious bridge-building to do with Nat, who Rube told me afterwards had been ditched by Danny (now there's a surprise) the same day as Dad's Pissed Moonlight Visit. There must have been something weird in the air that night.

Ruby always reckoned that I was lucky Mum and Dad had never done the heavy parent stuff over Max. They never banned you from seeing him, she pointed out. They never grounded you – they never told you that you couldn't have him. But I wasn't so sure. Perhaps I needed them to: perhaps if they had done the heavy parent stuff I wouldn't have got in so deep. They trusted me to work it out for myself, and look what a pig's ear I made of it. I deceived my family, I used my friends as alibis, and I fell out with all of them. I chose Max: if I hadn't actually loved him I'd certainly loved being with him, and how he made me feel. That's what had made my choice so hard. But now I'd come to realize that I loved my family too, and suddenly knowing what I should do wasn't hard at all.

He didn't understand why I finished it, I could tell, although he said he did. It was all terribly civilized and enlightened and grown-up, with me saying my meticulously-rehearsed piece while Max listened politely, nodding in all the right places and being careful not to interrupt. Then when I got to the end he said, "It's because I came on too strong, isn't it?"

"How d'you mean?"

"It's all right, Flora. I do understand. I shouldn't have asked you to move in. It was too much too soon." He smiled at me, that wonderful smiley Max smile that always turned my insides to mush. "I just got carried away. I should have had more sense; I should have known it would frighten you off. I should have realized you wanted your independence, a clever ambitious young woman like you."

"That's a lot of should haves." I stirred my

coffee with painstaking care, and avoided meeting his eyes. We were at the new café in town, sitting outside at one of the trendy zinc tables in the bright summer sun. I'd thought it best to meet on neutral ground. "It's not your fault, Max. You only said how you felt."

"What if we were to forget about the moving in?" He went to take my hand, then thought better of it and let his own drop to the table. "How about if we were to just carry on like before?"

I looked at him; his beautiful face, his gorgeous brown eyes. How could I explain? How could I say that being adored only works if you adore back? How could I tell him that I didn't love him?

I shook my head.

"It wouldn't work," I said, softly. "I'm really sorry. I did care about you though. I really did." He pulled a rueful face. Pushed his chair back, stood up and looked down into my eyes.

"I know you did, Flora."

I couldn't bear it, couldn't bear seeing the hurt behind his smile and knowing I was the cause of it.

"See you around, maybe?" It seemed better than saying goodbye. Less final.

"Maybe." He laid a hand on my head, like a kindly uncle or a priest. "Have a lovely life. You deserve it."

He took a handful of money from his trouser pocket, extracted a five pound note and folded it carefully under the saucer of his undrunk coffee. Then he walked to where he'd parked his car beside the kerb outside the café, climbed in, and was gone with a roar of exhaust.